TOGETHER
They
FALL

The Cubes of Destiny
BOOK 1

MATTHEW J. CROUTCH

ARCHWAY
PUBLISHING

Archway Publishing books may be ordered through booksellers or by contacting:

Archway Publishing
1663 Liberty Drive
Bloomington, IN 47403
www.archwaypublishing.com
844-669-3957

Because of the dynamic nature of the Internet, any web addresses or links contained in this book may have changed since publication and may no longer be valid. The views expressed in this work are solely those of the author and do not necessarily reflect the views of the publisher, and the publisher hereby disclaims any responsibility for them.

Any people depicted in stock imagery provided by Getty Images are models, and such images are being used for illustrative purposes only. Certain stock imagery © Getty Images.

Interior Image Credit: EDGARDO D. GONZALES

ISBN: 978-1-6657-2325-1 (sc)
ISBN: 978-1-6657-2326-8 (hc)
ISBN: 978-1-6657-2427-2 (e)

Library of Congress Control Number: 2022909572

Print information available on the last page.

Archway Publishing rev. date: 06/07/2022

To my Mother, Eileen, my Grandmother, Roberta, and my Sister, Laura. I thank you for making my dream a reality.

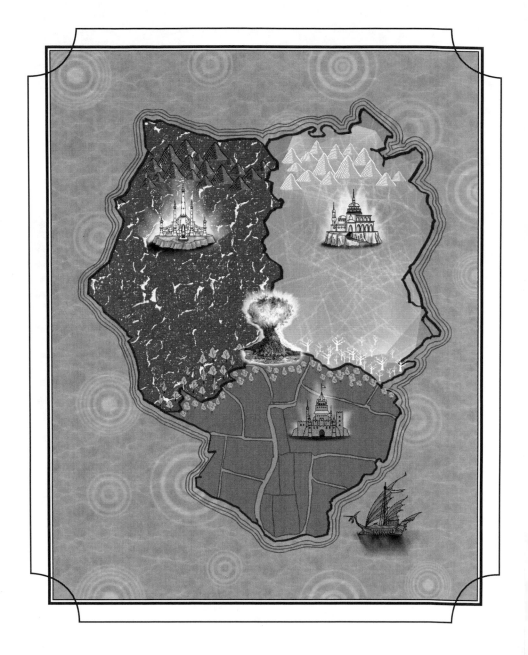

PROLOGUE

AVALIN USED TO be the most beautiful planet in the cosmos. Legend says the original God that ruled the world was killed and usurped by a Dark God. There's been chaos ever since. Eight heroes set out to defeat the Dark God, Val-Sharect. In doing so, they became Gods themselves and decided to split the world into eight land masses, each leading their chosen people onto different continents.

Our story begins on the Continent of Giana.

Far north of the capital city of Giana, on the lavish estate of the Queen's head advisor, the plague had begun to take its toll. The dimly lit master bedroom in the manor was filled with an atmosphere of loss and loneliness. Lord Lindar Mobious stared at his wife Elnora's lifeless body as it lay on their bed. He feared to turn around because he knew his daughter Tavia's corpse was behind him on a cot where she had lain, treated in the same room as her mother. With all the knowledge of magic he had, why could he have not prevented this? The death of his wife and daughter, lost to the plague, was the result of a slow search for a cure. The epidemic had swept through the land like a strong wind and had infected many elves, just like his family. He searched his mind for someone to direct his fury towards. Queen Merri should have heeded his warnings! She had not acted swiftly enough! All he wanted to do was to cradle his wife's head in his arms. He was shaking with rage at the loss of his loved ones. He shouldn't even be in the room, but if he died of the plague, at least they would be together again.

A sound behind Mobious alerted him that someone had entered the room. He turned to see an older elf, in a medical uniform. The Queen's royal doctor, Mobious quickly realized. He looked over at him with a mournful, yet angry face. He had almost forgotten that he had summoned the doctor, tasked with finding a cure.

"You called, Lord Mobious?" the doctor asked in a calm, professional manner belying his inner fears. It did not pay to cross Lindar Mobious.

"Greetings, doctor." Mobious turned to face the doctor. "I do believe that you told me that you had a cure for this plague, yet here my wife and daughter lie dead before me, because they have not been given said cure. Care to explain?" Mobious' voice was cold and restrained.

"I tried my best, sir." The doctor shifted uncomfortably where he stood. "Based on their symptoms, I was sure your wife and daughter had two more weeks before the plague would take them. If I had known they were on death's door, I would have pushed my colleagues harder to complete the potion, but it's still being tested."

Mobious ran his fingers through his long pale blonde hair; a gesture of the restraint he was attempting to maintain. He advanced slowly towards the doctor. He placed the palms of his hands together, fingers touching beneath his chin. Mobious looked as if he were praying, but he was building energy for a spell. He could see the doctor's ghostly pale skin crawling with fear; their eyes locked. He knew the doctor suspected what was about to happen to him. However, the reality would be far worse.

"That is unacceptable, Doctor," Mobious said ominously. "Can you imagine the agony of losing your entire family? Watching them suffer, as they cling to life. Just to witness their last breath as you stand idly by, unable to intervene." He quickly removed his hands from beneath his chin and barked a command. A ball of red-hot energy flew from his hands to the doctor. The doctor barely had time to take a step back, so quick was the attack. As soon as the ball of energy hit the doctor, he fell to the floor screaming in agony. His flesh started to turn a bright red as his body temperature rose rapidly. Within seconds, the flesh began to peel away from his bones. As his bones became exposed to the energy, the doctor's screams ceased, and the bones charred and crumbled. This type of punishment was nothing Mobious hadn't done before. Failure begets death. The charred remains would be disposed of by a trusted servant. No one would dare ask him about the missing doctor; or the screams from this room.

It had been quite a while since he'd had the opportunity to exercise his powers to that extent. It felt good to feel the power again. What he saw before him was a reassurance that he was still master of Demonic Magic. Demonic Magic was forbidden, so he liked to keep people ignorant. Looking at the doctor's blackened and crumbling bones satisfied Mobious. He had recently returned from a long journey where he had learned this new spell, though some might refer to it as a curse instead. It works very well, he mused.

Mobious saw one of his servants appear in the doorway. A ragged-looking maid stood quietly at the door as she waited for Mobious to acknowledge her presence. She had seen the remains of the doctor lying on the floor but knew better than to say anything or look directly at Mobious. Any lack of obedience would be met by punishment, of that the servants could be sure.

"This is not a good time. I wish to be alone," said Mobious angrily.

The maid curtsied and handed him a note with a trembling hand. "I'm sorry, Master," she stuttered fearing her master would turn his rage towards her, "but the person who left this note said it was urgent."

Mobious snatched the note from the maid with a glare and dismissed the woman with a wave of his hand. The maid curtsied again and left the room quickly. Mobious knew that most of his servants meant him no harm or disrespect, but he had no patience tonight. This night the life he once knew had ended. The only two people in the world that he loved were gone. He was filled with anger and grief, as he wandered over to sit in a chair in the corner of the room. He couldn't bring himself to leave his family's side.

Looking down at the note, he noticed that the parchment was slightly different than what was commonly used in Terra. This suggested the note possibly came from another continent. Interesting, he thought.

The quality of the parchment suggested a noble class, but the grammar was definitely that of a commoner. A servant stealing the master's parchment. Disgusting behaviour, he thought as he sneered.

After quickly skimming the note and seeing words of interest, he thought he should read it more carefully.

"To Lindar Mobious Head Advisor to Queen Merri,

You got no idea who I am, but I know all about you and who you will become some day. By the time you has got this note, it will be shortly after the death of your wife and babe. I'm right grieved to you and whatever family you got left. I is writing to you cause I's also lost family but we found a solution to our problems but need your help. You have one year to obtain a thing called the Cube of Destiny. Once you gots it, my Master will learn you to reverse the sands of time and bring back your wife and babe. Don't tell anyone about this. They will not believe you or they will try to stop you. Burn this note.

A friend"

Mobious put down the note on the table and pondered what to do. Morning came, and Mobious was still deep in thought. This was too serious a topic to postpone for sleep. Sleep would likely bring nightmares of his loved ones anyway.

He had heard the legends of the Cube of Destiny but had not actually believed it existed. According to legend, the elves used to be a somewhat different race of beings that had fought against a great evil six thousand years ago with the help of seven other races. Once that great evil had been vanquished, each race had taken a piece of the Great Cube of Destiny to help their civilizations grow. With the Cube, one could see everything: the past and all possible futures. The part that interested Mobious the most, was the infinite power the Cube granted the user as well as the potential to reconnect the Cubes.

The Cube, if it indeed existed, should give Mobious the power to resurrect his wife and daughter and rule Giana as Emperor. The Queen would not be able to stop him. On the other hand, the note could be the ravings of a mad man. Still, how did he know of the deaths? It had been mere hours after when the letter arrived.

Moreover, what did he mean by knowing what Mobious would become? This person spoke as if he knew Time Magic. Such magic was considered forbidden and worse than Mobious' Demonic Magic. One simply did not mess with Time.

The possibility the Cube existed was too intriguing to ignore. If the man from the note turned out to be using him, Mobious would kill him in the most torturous way when the time came. There was only one option. He must find the Cube of Destiny. This would mean research, going through all the documents in the Capital's library.

His only obstacle would the Queen and her loyal Captain of Investigation, Ayleen. Anything Mobious did that might appear to threaten the Queen or the country, Ayleen would pick up on, and immediately try to stop him. She neither liked nor trusted Mobious and the feeling was mutual. He would have to find a way to distract Ayleen and punish the Queen for her failure to cure the plague.

He had recently read about a spell that might help him accomplish just that. The spell would cause mass chaos and probably numerous deaths. But that was a price he was more than willing to pay. He had to have that Cube.

I

CHAPTER

S THE CAPTAIN of investigation for the queen, running after people who broke the law was second nature to the elf known as Ayleen Ebella. While she wished that the man would stop, she also enjoyed the thrill of the hunt as the wind was blowing through her long sun-colored hair. The elf she had been chasing was known as the Mad Bear, or just Bear to the guards. He had a history of violent attacks on merchants, but nothing like this recent encounter. Usually, Bear would attack if he and the merchant didn't agree on a price. The only reason he isn't in jail is because he has wealthy friends who bail him out. However, this time Bear was yelling about some long-forgotten darkness that had come back to seek revenge. Then he stabbed one of the merchants and quickly ran off.

While she knew the streets of the capital city like the back of her hand, Ayleen had trouble navigating a small city like this. Thaldor was not like any town on the continent, as it was a hub for criminal activity. For years she and the queen tried to clean up the place with no success. Every time Ayleen or her team made any progress with this town, the criminal underworld would undo any improvements in a matter of weeks.

Bear was nothing more than your typical thug. His job in the underworld was to rough up merchants who didn't want to obey the crime lords of the city. Bear wasn't the sharpest tool in the shed, so if it wasn't for Bear's friends bailing him out, he would have a permanent residence in the castle's dungeon. Bear always started arguments due to his short temper and slow wit.

The merchants of Thaldor were used to paying the criminal organizations that secretly ruled the city. This was a sore spot with Ayleen, who felt that she had failed in protecting this city. All her life she had been devoted to upholding the law, but this city was the one problem for which she had never found a solution. The guilt she felt for not protecting the civilians of this city weighed heavily on her.

With bow in hand, Ayleen, while running after Bear, noticed blood was starting to pour out of the sleeve of his shirt. She had not shot him yet. It was curious as to why the man was bleeding and also why he ran as if he did not have an injury. For the amount of blood that he was losing, he should have been slowing down … a lot. If Bear had a final location he was trying to reach, the amount of blood he was losing would ensure that he would never reach his destination. Ayleen was glad that the man chose a path away from the eyes of the civilian population.

They entered an alleyway, and she was hot on his heels. After reaching the alley's midpoint, she decided now was the time to tackle him to the ground. While in pursuit, she prepared herself to grab the man's knees to drop him to the ground where she could easily make an arrest. As she sprang forward, confident she could make the takedown, the man somehow slid out of her grasp. After hitting the ground with a thump, she quickly jumped to her feet, swearing. She continued to chase Bear, who had a slight lead now.

Knowing that there was a chance that she could fail another tackle, she attempted to reason with the man. Obviously, he had to be suffering some kind of pain and wanted this to end as badly as Ayleen did. Suddenly, Bear turned and tackled Ayleen, trying to force her to the ground. However surprised she was, she had training to deal with this kind of situation. She dodged the man's attack and leaped onto his back, forcing him to the ground. Before she had a chance to tie his hands behind him, Bear threw her off and bolted. Her pursuit of Bear was revitalized but lasted just a minute before he stopped in a blind alley and turned to face her. Blocking his escape, she once again tried reasoning with him.

"Listen, I know you're not acting the way you usually do." Ayleen panted. "Please, Bear, I don't want to hurt you! I want to know what's going on and get you medical aid. You're bleeding badly!"

Bear gaped at Ayleen wordlessly. He grabbed a knife out of his pocket. She drew the string on her bow back, notching an arrow; she aimed at the man's chest. "I swear to Terra: if you charge at me with that knife, I'm going shoot you."

"You can't stop him, Ayleen." Bear gasped. "He is too powerful for any of us to oppose him," Bear said as he raised the knife to his throat.

Ayleen cried out as she tried to stop Bear from slitting his own throat, but unfortunately, she was too late. She couldn't believe Bear would kill himself! This was yet another failure in the town of Thaldor that would lie heavily on Ayleen's conscience.

Ayleen was shocked that the man would do this. She thought he was trying to get away. As she started her investigation of Bear's body, she noticed strange symbols carved deeply in his chest. Could this be why he was bleeding? She had seen these strange symbols before but only on dead bodies. In the past year, Ayleen and her investigative team had encountered twelve dead bodies with the same symbols that she found on Bear. This was obviously the work of a serial killer. But had Bear escaped only to kill himself? The fact that there were now thirteen victims in a year made Ayleen believe that the thirteen victims were some sort of sacrifice. If there was a fourteenth victim, this theory would be wrong. Thirteen is a magic number.

Three of her subordinates, a lieutenant and two privates, ran into the alley, too late. Ayleen had completely forgotten that she had called for help. Usually Ayleen would conduct an investigation by herself, but she had a feeling that if she were to catch Bear, she would need assistance. The lieutenant was a tall male elf with short brown hair who had been working with Ayleen for the past five years. The two privates, one male and one female, were new to the force, the female being the latest.

As Ayleen's lieutenant ran up to Bear's body, he apologized to his commanding officer. "Captain Ebella! Sorry we couldn't catch up to you sooner!"

She looked at her lieutenant and said, "That's all right. You're here now. Please help me investigate this body. Have the two privates scout the area so that we don't have any civilians watching us. We don't want any small children witnessing a corpse."

"Yes, ma'am," said the lieutenant as he headed over to the body, directing the others to the mouth of the alley to turn away any civilians who might approach. Luckily for Ayleen, there were no civilian spectators anywhere at this time.

"I don't get it. I tried to resolve this peacefully, and that usually works with Bear, but this was an odd situation," muttered Ayleen, as she stood up and checked herself for injuries. "Looking at the body, I found that Bear has the same symbols as the other twelve victims found over the past year."

The lieutenant looked at the body. "I can confirm that these are the same symbols as the other twelve victims. What is going on here, Captain? Thirteen victims?"

"I fear we may be dealing with a demonic cult or at least a user of demonic magic," Ayleen said as her face become pale.

Her lieutenant looked at her with concern. "The team has been calling the killer the Mad Wizard of Thaldor."

Ayleen stood up. "Have you forgotten the last thing they taught you before making you an investigator? We do not give killers monikers. But you may be right about it being a wizard. Thirteen is the number of ingredients needed for any spell to work. It could be as simple as thirteen tree branches, or it could be two of this and five of that, three of another item, and three of a final ingredient. However, the concept still works. With thirteen bodies, we could be dealing with demonic magic."

The lieutenant shook his head in disbelief and looked at her. "Captain, with all due respect, the demonic magic users would not risk being caught. Every time we have encountered a demonic cult, it has been hidden away from the public eye. There hasn't been any sign of them in years."

Ayleen gave him a scowl. "Lieutenant! The only school of magic that uses human sacrifices as an ingredient is demonic magic. Look at those runes carved into his chest! If we find a fourteenth victim, then I will gladly take my theory back. As for the plague, it has been eradicated for a year now! I doubt we will have any more plague victims today."

The lieutenant nodded. "Sorry, Captain, I apologize for the way my words came across. I merely wanted to offer a counterargument to your theory. However, after hearing your reasoning, it is a solid theory. Anyway, it would be best if you got to the Sacred Tree. The New Year's Eve celebration is starting tomorrow, and you still need to check the security detail and ensure a place of safety for the queen and princess, Captain. My officers and I can take care of the body."

She stretched and nodded to the lieutenant. "Keep me updated on what you find. I don't like the feeling of this at all. Not the day before New Year's. This isn't good. I'll find a local wizard and teleport my report to the queen." With that, she left the scene.

Thankfully Thaldor was close to where the celebration was to take place. After finding a wizard, Ayleen started the hour walk to the centre of the Tree. While walking there, she had many questions in the back of her mind. First off, if Bear's suicide was a sacrifice to cast a demonic spell, then what kind of spell was the caster planning? Second, who would be this powerful to go uncaught and frighten Bear into suicide? And finally, what was his or her end game?

The princess stormed through the hallways of the castle. She had just been told that she would not be allowed to attend tonight's New Year's Eve celebrations. Apparently, Captain Ebella told her mother that there was a threat against the Kingdom. This was insignificant! The princess needed to be at the celebration to spread her message to the people.

All the servants bowed as she went past. She imagined that they were all admiring her fair skin and sun-kissed hair; not to mention her regal presence. However, they were worried about her and afraid of her temper. Most of the servants were concerned about her questionable beliefs and the fact that she planned to act on them once she became queen.

She was a woman with a mission. What was important to her was the necessity to speak to her mother. Now. As she entered the throne room, her mother was finishing up with one of her advisors. The Princess patiently waited until the advisor left the room.

"Princess Dariusa, thank you for waiting. Was there something you wished to discuss?" The queen acknowledged her daughter formally.

"Yes, there is, Mother!" the princess stated boldly. "What is the idea of cancelling our appearance at the celebration tonight? We had all this planned out! The wizard providing the portal is here now! But now you refuse to let me go just because some captain told you there's a threat!" The princess' face was flushed with anger.

The Queen sighed and stood up, making sure she could look her daughter in the eye. "Dariusa, it's for your own protection. Our own protection. You can't expect us to go to a party when there is a threat in the closest town. This is very childish of you, but we know you will see it one day that our word is right."

"See it one day? I see it clearly now!" the princess snapped and went on a tirade. "You are afraid to go out of this castle! Ever since father died of the plague, you've been afraid! It's your fault he died! You didn't listen to Lindar Mobious when he warned you! You used to have more of a spine than this! So what if there's killer on the loose? We have guards! We have the best warriors in Giana on our side! There is no reason not to go to the party!"

The queen fired back. "Dariusa, I am not discussing this with you! Guards would be useless against a magical attack and Lindar is not available to go with us!" She continued more calmly, "It is my decision that we will stay in the castle and have our own celebration. We hope you understand that this is for your safety and we do not like this either."

"That's easy for you to say! You keep treating me like a child! I am not a child, I am thirty-two! An adult!" Dariusa yelled. "I, for one, see what you are trying to do! You do not want me to speak to the people! Please, mother, reconsider your decision! We do not need to be locked up in this castle out of fear! Once we do that, the people will view us as weak and disobey us!"

The queen returned to her throne. "Dariusa, we are not speaking of this again. Please, do not bring up your father anymore. The loss of him still weighs heavily on us; as do the deaths of all the other elves. We cannot change the past. We will stay in the castle tonight and hopefully next year we can attend the celebration."

"Next year! Mother, that is too late!" Dariusa clenched her fists in rage. "My subjects need their princess now more than ever! We are close to the return of Terra's avatar and they need my guidance!"

"Silence!" roared the Queen in a rare outburst of temper. "Princess Dariusa, we are done talking about this. The Priestesses guide the people on matters of Terra, not you! My decision is final. Please leave us."

The princess didn't have anything more to say. As she stormed back to her chambers, she realized how weak her mother really was. She wasn't a strong queen; she was a little girl afraid of making the wrong decision again. Dariusa needed to show everyone that Terra needed a strong leader. Soon she would be queen; maybe sooner than later. Her mother was unfit to rule anymore. Giana will have a new leader; a strong leader. A leader who is not afraid to go outside of her own castle. Dariusa started to make her plans.

The next day, at the New Year's Eve celebration, Ayleen arrived two and a half hours before it started as she had done every year since joining the Guard. This was to make sure all the safety precautions were met as per the Queen's request. She knew the safety of the people was the biggest priority. She knew that there would be many people, in the thousands, attending. Luckily for her, there were plenty of guards here to help her if anything were to happen.

The celebration itself was massive, as it was every year, with two hundred tents, shops, games and other activities. Ayleen was amazed that so many people from different walks of life came together every year for one day, for this celebration. This celebration was always held in the centre of the continent where the eldest tree stood alone in the middle of a large field. Five hectares of land were deliberately kept clear as all the major celebrations took place here. As with most years, people started setting up tents days before the celebration. There were several neighbouring towns, with Thaldor being the largest.

According to legend, the first elves were born from the blossoms of this tree. While this legend was a core part of the elf religion, most elves regarded it as just legend and not fact. Ayleen was one these elves who believed that this was just a legend. However, when she was younger, her mother told her the story, and Ayleen wondered what if it was true and what life would have been like for the first elves. She credited her natural curiosity and her admiration of her father with the start of her interest in investigation and eventually becoming the Captain of Investigation for the Queen.

She had received word from Queen Merri that due to yesterday's report, she and Princess Dariusa would not come to the celebration. They would have a private party at the castle where it would be safer. She wished that she could be at the palace where the Queen was so that she could protect her friend. Twenty years ago, when Ayleen was made Captain of Investigation, she met Queen Merri for the first time. The two of them had a private conversation about Ayleen's duties. Somehow this conversation, scheduled for ten minutes, turned into a two-hour visit. They'd been friends ever since.

The Queen's daughter, on the other hand, was a completely different story. Many elves did not like Princess Dariusa, and Ayleen was not an exception. The Princess came across as someone who was out for her own best interests; spoiled and temperamental. The only group of people that were fans of the Princess were noblemen who wanted to marry her to gain social power; to be the next Prince Consort.

There was another reason for her being here early which was to meet her informant, Tyran Dori, who was to come to the area one hour before the celebration started as Ayleen had requested. This thief-turned-spy was only working with her to stay out of prison for the latest crime he had committed. He had broken into a Duke's manor and was caught with his daughter. There were two reasons he was at the manor; the first reason was to rob the Duke while the second reason was to see the Duke's daughter. Ayleen couldn't tell if he was overconfident or just stupid for getting caught.

Ayleen and Tyran met privately in a tent set up for the celebration to discuss some developments. The tent was set up for the Guards as a post. Inside there were bows and arrows with other weapons in case any security problems arose.

"Tyran, do you have any information regarding the twelve victims because right now I have found another victim, and I'm worried about what could happen next if this victim was the last," Ayleen said in a frustrated tone.

Tyran started to scratch his head where his sandy-coloured hair lay cut short. "The only information I got from my contacts was that the victims who were seen alive acted like they were in a trance. They also said that the victims had weird symbols carved into their bodies. They all appeared to have committed suicide. All of them were from Thaldor. By the way, who was the recent victim, and why do you look like you have been in a street fight?"

With a heavy sigh, Ayleen looked at her informant. "Bear was the latest victim, but he wasn't found dead, though he did seem trance-like. He had the symbols carved in his body like the other victims. However, he attacked a merchant then ran off. When I caught up to him, we had a bit of a tussle, and then he slit his own throat in front of me."

"What! That doesn't sound like Bear at all," exclaimed Tyran in shock. "Bear wouldn't kill himself! He has too many friends to bail him out when he gets caught! Are you sure that was Bear?"

With a bit of anger in her voice, Ayleen looked directly into Tyran's eyes. "I know what I bloody saw, Tyran. And yes, I am just as shocked as you, but right now I'm more worried about the fact that we have thirteen bodies with symbols on them. In my book, I know that means that there is a major demonic spell being prepared and I don't know how to prevent that spell from being unleashed. So, I need you to go out into the underworld and try to get any information that could help me prevent someone from using demonic magic to attack the citizens. I've already warned the Queen not to come tonight."

"I understand, Captain. I will work my hardest to find out some information for you. I may be a thief, but I do not want any people to die," Tyran said as he started to get ready to leave the tent. "Before I leave, I have one question. You mentioned that these murders may be a preparation for a magic spell. Isn't there anyone you can consult on the matter?"

"There is this one person, but I prefer not to talk to him if I don't have to," Ayleen replied. "His name is Lindar Mobious, and he's the Queen's head magical advisor. He may be the most powerful wizard on the continent, but the man is so arrogant that it is nearly impossible for me to talk to him without starting an argument. Granted I sometimes provoke him unintentionally. It is better if we speak to each other as few times as possible."

"That is understandable. I've heard of him," Tyran stated as he headed to the exit of the tent. "It's time for me to go and mingle with the partygoers. I'll try to get you as much information as I can. As much as I enjoy working with you, I would love to regain my freedom as soon as possible."

Ayleen had one more thing to say before Tyran left and wanted to make sure he knew this information. "It's the biggest party of the year; that means people of all walks of life will be here, and that includes criminals. Make sure you talk to them and see what they know. Your freedom will come one day."

"Yeah, yeah, I know." Tyran continued to walk away.

For the rest of the day Tyran would not be able to enjoy the New Year's Eve celebration like everyone else; he would be talking to every criminal he could find. While he did not like Bear, he knew that Bear would never commit suicide; not willingly anyway. The very idea bothered Tyran. This was the work of a serial killer who knew magic, this much he knew for sure. He had a few ideas of who to talk to, however, he knew that most of them would not co-operate if they knew he was working for the captain. He only hoped that the underworld hadn't got word yet.

The party was in full swing, thousands of people wandered the tent city while musicians played, and entertainers put on a show. Ayleen wandered through the crowd to look at shops while keeping an eye on the people. While there were thousands of elves, it did not feel crowded. As per usual, there were men drinking in the alehouses that were set up around the grounds. Women were either talking amongst themselves or browsing the many shops that had been set up. Like every year the children congregated around the games and the snack stalls.

While she was making her rounds, she noticed a shop that sold jewelry. She wouldn't tell anyone this, but collecting jewelry was her guilty pleasure. She remembered her mother always having a new necklace every week. Ever since the death of her mother she had collected jewelry in her memory; which she often donated to charity events. Ayleen believed that the death of her mother was her fault. She had lost count of how many people told her it was an accident. No matter how many people told her this, her feelings of guilt had never changed.

Inside the shop, many types of jewelry were laid out on the tables. At the back of the shop was a middle-aged elf wearing a very fancy red outfit. There was something weird about the shopkeeper, but Ayleen could not figure out why she felt this way. She approached the shopkeeper to ask him a few questions, however the feeling she had did not go away. Looking at his face, Ayleen saw an elf, but her brain did not agree. Something about his features did not stay steadily elfish; however, she thought that this was her imagination.

Noticing that Ayleen was looking at him, the shop owner stepped out from behind his counter and moved towards Ayleen saying, "Can I help you with anything, Ma'am?"

Ayleen looked around and said, "What do you have in the way of necklaces? I've been looking for one to add to my collection."

The man in red went back to his supply and brought out a necklace. "I just got this in from the north. From what my supplier told me, this necklace is made from blood-gold and the stone in the centre was fished out of a lake near Mount Sanguis on the continent of Invictus. This is only ten gold, today only."

"Ten gold?" Ayleen couldn't believe that the shopkeeper was selling this so cheaply. Looking at the necklace, she knew it was worth at least a thousand gold, especially if the stone came from Invictus. She knew it was blood-gold, but for the amount of gold used for this necklace, a small shop keeper could not afford to buy it. What was the shop keeper trying to do? Even if he had stolen it, he still could not sell for that price. Ayleen held the necklace for a minute then something came over her that made her want to buy it. Maybe this merchant was an idiot or something. She didn't mind buying something at a reduced price if the merchant was not aware of the value of his goods. She paid the merchant and left the tent with the necklace, promptly putting it on.

As she left, the man in red smiled and said, "Good job, Ayleen. Now all I have to do is wait. One down and six more to go."

Ayleen continued her patrol of the grounds. Occasionally, she would examine the amulet she'd bought. If she only came away from the celebration with this amulet, then the day would be worth it. If the day went as well as her time in the shop, then she would have nothing to worry about. She had a feeling that today was going to be a great day, and nothing could go wrong.

For the next couple of hours, Tyran talked to every criminal he knew at the party and who was willing to talk to him. His journey led him to one of the many alehouses set up on the grounds. He knew that he had to go into this particular alehouse but was reluctant to enter because of who was running the place. As he entered, he noticed many criminals sitting together. Fortunately, he did not see the woman who was in charge. Quickly he sat down at a table to start a conversation with a few criminals he knew just in case this woman showed up.

"So, what's the word on the street, fellas?" Tyran asked casually as he looked to a tiny elf who had a hat on top of his small head. Tyran knew this elf very well. His name was Klep, also known as 'The Vanisher'.

"Tyran, my friend, you haven't been heard from in a while, and now you come to me as if you never disappeared. What do you want?" Klep growled in a direct and aggressive tone. His two associates sitting next to him were known only as "the twins." Tyran had had a beating from these two muscled giants a long time ago. Klep continued to talk. "From what I hear you are working with the authorities to downgrade your sentence. What did you do this time? Maybe it was one of your many girlfriends that finally had enough of you and turned you in."

Tyran let out a big sigh because he knew that Klep was half-right. None of this mattered now. The only thing on Tyran's mind was to get information about the serial killer. "Look, Klep, I don't have time for this. All I want is information, and yes, I am working for the authorities because there is a bloody serial killer that is targeting people like us and I would like to stay alive. Plus, the last victim was none other than Bear!"

"Well, that changes everything, Tyran," Klep drawled as he waved a hand to dismiss his two bodyguards. The two men left the table without argument and headed for the bar. "People in the underground are calling the serial killer 'The Mad Wizard of Thaldor'. My boys had told me that the day before the some of the victims were found, they also went to an abandoned house after receiving an invitation. From there I can only guess that this wizard puts a mind control spell on his victims. For the next twenty-four hours they carve markings into their own skin, and then kill themselves."

Tyran was shocked. How did Klep know this much about the victims? Could Klep be involved in this somehow? And if he was, why was Klep telling Tyran all these details? "That's some grizzly details you have there, Klep. How in Terra's name do you know all of this?"

"You have always been an idiot, Tyran, and today is no different." Klep leaned forward in his chair to get his mouth closer to Tyran, so that didn't have to talk too loudly. "Look, it's bad for all of us if there is a serial killer loose. I may dispose of bodies for criminals but ninety-five percent of the time, those people did business with my employers, and they tried to screw them. However, a serial killer in my part of town is bad for business because it means that we don't have order in the criminal underworld. Tyran, you know that if we kill, it's only because the person deserved it. This serial killer preys on anyone he can get a hold of, and most of us in the underworld would like to keep some sort of order. That's why I took it upon myself to learn about this bastard and possibly put an end to him. But if the Queen and her Guard think that they can stop him faster, then more power to them."

Tyran knew that Klep was good at his job, when it came to disposing of bodies. He also trusted Klep enough to know that he was telling the truth. He stood up and started to leave the table. "Thank you, old friend; if we catch this bastard, I will be sure to let you know so that you can dispose of him."

Klep chuckled. "You're very welcome, Tyran. Before you go, I think a young lady is looking for you from behind the bar. You may want to deal with that before leaving." Tyran looked to where Klep was pointing to see the very woman he did not want to talk to.

It was now or never, and while Tyran did not want to talk to her, it was better to get it over with. He decided to sit down at the bar and waited for the woman to finish serving a customer before he started a conversation. "Hello, Izabael, is this going to be what I think it is because my answer is still the same."

"Tyran Dori, you have a lot of nerve denying my offer," Izabael said as she fluffed her blonde hair. "I'm offering the chance to sleep with as many women as you could possibly want. All you need to do is to scam them out of everything they have."

"I'm not that type of criminal. I did it once for you, and I felt so bad that I returned everything I stole." Tyran was furious at Izabael for asking him to do more of her dirty work. The only reason why Tyran had not punched this woman in the face yet, is because she is a woman and had a lot of "boyfriends".

Izabael started to chuckle at Tyran. She knew that Tyran was no pushover, but that was the most exciting part for her. "Fine! Do not do any more of my jobs. Zed won't be so easy to dismiss. You know he is very persuasive when it comes to jerks like you who don't toe the line."

Tyran had enough of Izabael's tirade. He decided to leave the bar without saying anything. No one stopped Tyran from walking away.

The New Year's Eve celebration would conclude with a prayer at midnight but for now there were food vendors, dancers and singers. Ayleen enjoyed herself while keeping an eye on the crowd as she was meant to do. Throughout the evening, the main conversation was about the Princess and how she would take over the kingdom from her mother, Queen Merri. Most elves were worried about the Princess' radical views on expanding the elven territory. The last war the elves were in was over two hundred years ago. People at the party knew if Princess Dariusa had her way, then the elves would most likely end up in another war.

There were, in fact, some supporters of Princess Dariusa at the celebration. Among the princess' supporters, there was a growing movement that Terra would come back to the planet to ensure a new age of peace. Not like the continent needed it. The elves hadn't been at war for as long as Ayleen could remember. The Princess wanted to conquer some of the territories of the continent to the north where the blood-gold mines were located. The biggest problem with conquering this area, was that the elves would have to battle the race called Humans and all reports said that their continent had been in so many civil wars that they could be considered masters of combat. Any attempt at conquest would be a losing battle. They're savages.

Closer to midnight, the people all started to dance near the Tree, circling the Tree as they went. The Tree was so large it would take fifty people to form an unbroken circle around it, fingertip to fingertip. It was thousands of years old. Ayleen was on the sidelines looking out for any threats within the crowd. For the next hour, everything went like clockwork. As she watched the dancers, she couldn't help but notice how many couples there were on the dance floor who looked like they were in love. At the age of ninety, she was almost half-way through her life and wondered if she had wasted too much time on her career and not enough in finding someone to spend her life with. She had always wanted a family of at least one child. However, she knew that she was too in love with her work to devote any time to a family right now.

Around ten minutes before midnight, people started to gather in the field where the sacred tree lived. Every year on this day the elves that gathered here prayed to the goddess, Terra for all aspects in their lives. For the past century, the midnight prayer was led by the High Druid, Jeldite. This year he had to be helped by his daughter, Karayna. This would be the last year that Jeldite would lead the prayer. This was due to his age and recently becoming blind. His daughter had to turn his body to face the crowd to prevent him from talking to the Tree.

"Father, father … the other way! You're looking at the Tree." whispered Karayna.

"Oh, sorry." The old man laughed it off, but the daughter was seen sighing in frustration.

"Elves, young and old, male and female, poor and rich, come and listen to our story," Jeldite began. "Six thousand years ago the goddess freed us from the great evil god, Val-Sharect. With our freedom, however, there is a price. Let us pray. Sacred Terra, this we vow: We will take care of the land that you risked your life to protect. We will not refuse to help any elf that is in need. We are all descendants of the elves that came from the blossoms of this sacred tree. We are all equal, no matter what life we choose to live or what we have done. We will love one another like you have loved us. Finally, don't let hatred divide us. Let us act as one. So mote it be."

With Jeldite concluding the prayer every elf in unison also said: "Let us act as one". While Ayleen did not believe in the first elf coming from a blossom, she was a very religious person as most elves were. She had only one prayer for the goddess to answer, which was help in breaking her current case. She knew that this was a long shot but prayed for help anyway. The goddess was not one to interfere with the interactions of mortals, but Ayleen thought that if Terra could ever intervene, this would be the best time.

The people started to dissipate after the prayer ended. There were a couple of light tremors; Ayleen knew that this wasn't a big deal. Earthquakes on this continent were an everyday occurrence. Most of them you never felt. As she thought about it, she realized that this would be a problem if there was a stronger one due to all the people gathered. She decided to look for one of her comrades to discuss what they should do in case there was a stronger one. She didn't think this was a big issue, but she wanted to make sure everyone would be safe.

Before she could find another member of the Guard, she heard the entire crowd gasp. She wondered what the crowd was looking at and she decided to look up herself. As she looked towards the stars, she noticed that there was a comet passing overhead. Comets were a sign of good fortune and with this Ayleen thought that she may not have to worry about the tremors. The comet's tail glowed in three colours. Ayleen could make out blue, red and purple. Then the realization struck: the comet was headed straight for the celebration!

The crowd started to panic when they too realized that the comet was heading towards them. Over the uproar from the crowd, Ayleen shouted directions to get the civilians to a safe distance. The problem was that the group was so large that her voice could only be heard by a fraction of the people. Other members of the Guard also tried to direct the crowd. This was like controlling a bunch of chickens with their heads cut off. Ayleen knew that she could not possibly save everyone as families scattered in different directions.

The crowd was nowhere near far enough from the field when the comet hit the sacred tree. The force of the impact destroyed the Tree and sent shards of wood flying through the air. Ayleen anticipated a shock wave that knocked everyone in the field off their feet by diving behind an overturned table. She looked towards where the comet landed only to see nothing but dust. She tried to squint her eyes to see if she could see any better. As she looked towards where the sacred tree had been, several beams of light started to flash, blinding her.

The estate of Lindar Mobious had been quiet for the past year. Mobious had been away often. The master of the house was spending this evening looking out a window towards the centre of the continent. This was the beginning of his plan to save his family. A year he had waited for this moment. A year he had been researching the Cube of Destiny. A year of preparing this distraction. After all this time he would finally see his plans come to fruition. He only had a few more minutes.

Mobious was standing in his study, the room where he spent most of his time. Around him were many open books detailing with everything from religious texts to books about myths and legends. Usually this room would have been neat and tidy; however, Mobious had no time to spend on putting the books back, nor did he want to. Shortly after receiving a cryptic note, he had met a fellow user of magic with knowledge of the Cube of Destiny.

As Mobious continued to ponder about the last year, he felt that his protégé was right behind him waiting for his master to acknowledge him. "I assume you have some news to report. Otherwise, it was a horrible idea to interrupt me at this moment."

Without Mobious turning to face him, the young man bowed and put some papers on the desk. "Master Mobious sir, thank you for trusting me with gathering this information, and you can be assured that this will go no further. Professor Kratin T'mass has completed the research that you asked him to do. According to him, there is a monastery to the west, an order of monks called the Order of the Cube. He is convinced that this Order is in possession of the Cube of Destiny."

"This is good news. I've been waiting for something like this for too long." Still not turning to face his personal assistant, Mobious started to smile. "Does my friend tell us how we contact one of these monks, so that we can gather more information?"

The young man shifted uncomfortably where he stood, knowing what Mobious could do to that monk if he ever found him. "Your friend talks about a Brother Isaac who goes back and forth from the Capital to his monastery. The Professor states in his research that Brother Isaac would be the easiest monk to get a hold of."

"Then I guess we have to invite him over for a discussion." Mobious smiled again as he watched the comet enter the atmosphere. "Soon, my love, you will be back by my side, and our daughter will continue to play in the garden like she used to."

A bright glow towards the centre of the continent confirmed contact. Mobious contemplated the next part of his plan. If anyone were to find out what he was up to, then the Queen would send Captain Ayleen Ebella after him. Not that this bothered him. He just needed to make plans for that possibility. He already had a meeting scheduled for tomorrow morning to provide insurance that his plan would go undetected. There was no such thing as being too prepared. But for now, all he wanted to do was to watch the chaos from a safe distance.

II

CHAPTER

S THE BLINDING light dissipated, Ayleen lowered her arms that were shielding her eyes only find her skin was no longer a pale white, but purple. What was going on? As she looked around, she remembered that she was at the south part of the grounds where the celebration had been taking place. She looked to the northeast and saw light-blue-skinned elves with white hair and they were standing on the edge of a snowy forest. Just to the northwest, it was the complete opposite; a burnt scene with glowing embers, and elves of orange skin and red hair looking at each other with panic in their eyes. Neither seemed to be affected by the apparent temperature change in their area. Families or buildings on the dividing lines were split by colour or element.

As she turned around, she noticed that the ground that she stood on matched the colour of her skin. To the south where she was facing, now lay nothing but black trees. She could see the wave of change continuing south across the fields towards the capital. Elves that were close by all had purple skin and raven hair. She pulled a few strands of her hair in front of her face to check if her own hair was black. Sure enough, it was. This must be what the sacrifices were for. But why? Around her, people started talking amongst themselves. Most of this conversation was of confusion and panic. While she wanted to calm everyone down, she couldn't think of a damn thing to say that would help in this situation.

Turning back around to where the sacred Tree was, Ayleen saw that the Tree once marking the middle of the continent was no longer there. Instead there was now a giant meteorite floating where the Tree had been. This giant rock was divided into three colours that matched the direction it faced. Ayleen had never seen anything like this before in her life. She had heard of elven wizards discovering remains of meteorites along the coast of the continent. But she had never seen any up close. She'd also never heard of any meteorite that floated above the ground after it crashed. She knew that she had to be ready for anything.

Everyone was in shock and at a loss for words. There were dead bodies everywhere, most ripped apart by the exploding tree. Suddenly a random person yelled out, "What in Terra's name is going on here!"

From among the crowd one of the druids, who now had blue skin and white hair, tried to calm the crowd. "My fellow elves, please calm down. This may be a test from Terra herself or could be just an illusion. Please be patient while the other druids and I quickly investigate what has happened to the land. The Priestesses will confer with Terra!"

Ayleen had to do something, but what? She had to gather more information and the druids would be the only people who had any idea of what was going on. Before she could move towards the druid, she heard a cry from the northeast. "I thought druids can predict what happens to the land and any environmental changes. Where was the warning for this?"

"Yeah, didn't Terra tell the Priestesses anything?" another cried out this time from the northwest.

Now Ayleen was angry; being the daughter of a druid herself, she couldn't stand the disrespect that the druids and priestesses were being shown. Moving through the crowd she stumbled across Tyran. He now had orange skin and red hair. At least now she knew what part of the field he was on when the meteor hit.

"What in Terra's name is going on, Captain?" Tyran asked her with both anger and worry in his voice. The poor man was vibrating, with so much fear and anger.

"I have no idea what is happening, Tyran!" Ayleen was starting to get annoyed with the whole situation. She didn't mean to snap at Tyran. "Sorry. Did not mean to yell at you. Take this ring and tell the guards around the celebration to start evacuating people. They will trust you if you have this ring."

Ayleen took her ring off the middle finger of her right hand and gave it to Tyran. He nodded. "All right I'll do this. Where should we evacuate to? Anywhere specific?"

"Just get them as far away from this area as possible," Ayleen said, shaking her head. "After we evacuate the people, tell one of the guards to find a wizard to send a message south to the palace. I want to make sure that the Queen and the Princess are safe."

"As you wish, Captain." Tyran started to run towards outskirts of the celebration, where Ayleen and he knew would be the easiest guards to contact. Panic had already ensued.

Just seconds after Tyran left, the meteorite started to pulse. Ayleen rushed to the area where the druids were congregating just thirty feet away from the meteorite. While everyone in the crowd was fleeing, the druids were so preoccupied with debating on what they should do and what was going on, they did not see that the meteorite was emitting flashes of light.

"Excuse me, don't you see that the giant rock is glowing again? Don't you think we should get out of here? I'm getting you to safety now!" Ayleen yelled at the druids to get their attention away from their conversation and towards the obviously present danger.

As the people fled, bolts of black light shot out of the meteorite. Ayleen noticed these bolts of darkness spreading across the field. She had learned in her studies when her mother was alive that demons used black bolts of shadow to transport themselves. Her training taught her to stay calm in all kinds of difficult situations, but she couldn't shake the fear gripping at her heart.

"Everyone, run!" cried Ayleen trying to get the crowd moving faster.

As the bolts of black light fell to the ground, thick black smoke appeared on the spot. This smoke morphed into creatures made of shadows. As tall as the tallest elf, the shadow creatures stood seven feet, menacing as they chased the elves across the fields. Ayleen grabbed her bow and shot at one of them. The arrow went right through the creature as if it were made of air. She didn't dare shoot another arrow for fear of hitting an elf. When the creatures made contact with any of the elves, the elf suffered cuts, bruises and many were dying from multiple assaults. Other elves died from being trampled by their fellow elves as they ran from the creatures in terror.

These creatures knew which of the elves were the easiest to target. If they were chasing one elf, and another close to them fell on the ground, the creatures would redirect their focus to the fallen elf. The weapons they used were like blades of darkness that appeared on command. The way they used these weapons was like nothing Ayleen had ever seen. She knew a few sword masters in her life but the way these creatures were handling their weapons, they could put those sword masters down like it was nothing. She didn't know if she could defend her people, but she had to try.

Ayleen had enough of this. She took both her short swords and charged at one of the creatures to see if she could slow it down since weapons seemed to pass through them. As she leaped towards the invader, she swung at it, in an attempt to cut off one or both of its arms. As she expected, the sword and her own body went through the shadow creature like nothing was there. While her body flew through the shadow creature, she felt so cold it was painful. Ayleen noticed that while her sword wasn't digging into anything, the shadow creature looked like it was in pain. Ayleen wondered if she had done any damage to it or had this creature been in pain before.

Ayleen didn't know what else to do. If none of her attacks were affecting the creature then how could she possibly win? She had one more idea to try out, but she felt afraid of doing it. The last time she used this magic spell to summon a guardian, someone close to her died by accident. It had been almost seventy-five years since she tried this spell, but the situation gave her no other option. As the creature charged towards her, she closed her eyes and tried to concentrate on an image of a wolf. She did not have much time to cast this spell before the creature knocked her on her back, breaking her concentration. The creature lifted his hand up to attack Ayleen when two daggers came at it from the side.

"Hey, freak, stay away from my friend!" Tyran said as he ran towards Ayleen after throwing his daggers at the creature, distracting it. Tyran grabbed Ayleen and hauled her to her feet. "I told the guards at the edge to help evacuate the party guests and I came back to help you. And here I find that you are fighting this monstrosity alone! What is it?"

The creature swung his massive sword, as Ayleen and Tyran tumbled away in the opposite direction of each other. As she rolled from the dive to a crouch, Ayleen readied herself for another swing at the creature. "These things came out of that bloody meteorite that destroyed the sacred tree, and they've been attacking the people ever since! Physical attacks don't seem to be working on them at all!"

"Then why are we still using our swords and daggers against this thing? Don't you know any magic?" yelled Tyran, as he and Ayleen continued to try to stab the creature with no success while dodging its attacks.

Ayleen was a little frustrated with Tyran at his question, but she knew that Tyran didn't know about her past, nor did he realize that Ayleen was trying to cast a spell before the creature broke her concentration. "I tried, Tyran, I only know one spell and when I tried to cast it this creature tried to cut me in half! If you can distract him, I may be able to try to cast the spell again. But then, no guarantees. I haven't used this spell since before you were born!"

"Right away, Captain. Hey ugly, your mother was a puff of smoke!" Tyran tried to get the creature's attention so that Ayleen could refocus on her spell. Closing her eyes again she focused on the image of a wolf. She imagined a wolf made of energy charging at the creature and then lunging at his throat, biting the creature's jugular vein. Unfortunately, the wolf did not materialize, and the spell was lost. Now Ayleen was terrified that she could not do anything to the creature and all the elves she tried to protect would die.

Tyran grabbed his spear, trying to hit the creature with no success. After a few trades of blows with the beast, it suddenly vanished. Ayleen looked around and saw the other shadow creatures start to disappear. Tyran yelled out a cry of relief. "Finally, we beat these things. Good job, Ayleen. What kind of spell was that? This feels like the time that we got into that bar fight over a misunderstanding."

"First off, you got your ass handed to you, Tyran! I had to help you out! Also, we were there for a recon mission," she retorted. She gathered her emotions and looked Tyran in the eye. "Second, I did not do anything. That creature evaporated on its own. This was a magical attack. The person who caused this couldn't concentrate long enough to keep this attack going indefinitely or they got tired. This is what those thirteen deaths were for." Ayleen swore under her breath.

Ayleen saw that Tyran looked confused. He shook his head in disbelief. "Why would anyone want to kill this many innocent people on the holiest day of the year?"

"I don't know, my friend," Ayleen said as she gathered up her equipment and surveyed the damage. There were over a thousand elves lying dead in the fields, men, women and children. She wanted to cry, but knew that it was not going to accomplish anything. "Gather your belongings. We are going back to the meteorite and we are going to look for clues in hopes of finding out who in Terra's name did this. And why."

Coming back to the site where the meteorite crashed, Ayleen saw the dead bodies of her fellow elves. She prayed that Terra would protect them in their afterlife. She didn't know if a death like this would grant the soul peace. The Guards had come to search the bodies for survivors. The place had been a field of celebration and worship just minutes ago. Now it was Giana's biggest graveyard. She felt sick standing in this area, but knew that clues to this disaster had to be here somewhere.

Looking at the meteorite, Ayleen noticed that there was a magical marking on the bottom of it, as it hovered over the crater. Magical markings were like a signature for powerful spells. Every wizard and sorcerer had their own magical signature. A magical signature was like a part of their persona. No wizard can choose what their magical signature will look like. Magical signatures can be similar to their parents', but until the wizard casts a powerful spell no one can tell what their signature may look like.

Ayleen had recognized this signature from one of her previous murder investigations. For months, people had been going missing, and turned up in a way that you could only describe as horrific. The signature in question had a skull of a wolf with its jaws wide open, and an orange eye in the mouth. Ayleen knew that this was connected to the murders, and now knew for sure that the murdered elves were sacrificed to prepare for this spell. However, why would anyone want to cause this much chaos? Demonic wizards had never done anything like this before, and they were few and far between. Furthermore, who had this amount of power to call down a meteorite from the sky?

It had been a late night for Ayleen. She wanted to go home and rest, but she knew there was a lot more work to be done. For the next two hours she interviewed everyone she could. The only two people left to interview were the elder druid and his daughter. She figured if anyone would know what was going on it would be the elder druid. Looking around the area where the tents were set up for the celebration, she found the two resting in one of the wine tasting tents. While Ayleen wanted to let the pair rest after the night they had, she had to do her job and gather any information she could.

"Excuse me. Sorry to bother you. I'm Captain Ebella, and I just have a few questions for both of you. I can wait until morning if you are too tired," Ayleen said approaching the father and daughter. Karayna was wide awake. She stood up and tried to fix her messy white hair so that she looked presentable, but she and Ayleen both knew that everyone here looked like they had been through a rough time, and no one cared what anyone looked like at this point.

"What can I help you with, Captain?" The blue elf stood up and rallied her father out of his sleep. The elder druid was now bald and had orange skin. Ayleen was taken aback by the difference between father and daughter. Just hours ago, the pair resembled each other like a father and daughter usually would. Obviously, they had moved to the north side of the Tree and been in different sections when the meteor struck.

"Karayna, why did you wake me up so early? After the running I did, surely you could let me sleep a bit longer," a groggy Jeldite complained

MATTHEW J. CROUTCH

to his daughter. After a minute of his daughter explaining the situation to him, Jeldite nodded. "Sorry, Captain, I didn't realize that we had company. These old eyes are not what they used to be. If it wasn't for my daughter here, I would probably walk into a tree by accident."

"That's all right, Elder." Ayleen knew that this was going to be a slow start to her interview given Jeldite's condition. "I was wondering if you know anything from your two centuries of nature magic studies that would help explain the event that transpired tonight."

Jeldite looked off in the distance with a concerned look on his face. "My daughter has filled me in on what happened tonight, and described the meteorite and creatures in detail. While I know nothing about the meteorite or where it came from, the creatures my daughter described sounded very familiar to me."

Ayleen's interest was now aroused. If she could get anything at all, it would be a big help. "Please tell me what you suspect, Elder."

"From my studies I believe that these creatures are from the army of the Dark God, Val-Sharect." Jeldite repositioned himself, so that he was more comfortable. "Thousands of years ago, the Dark God had enslaved the entire planet forcing the citizens to do his every whim. Terra was one of the eight heroes who rose up and freed the planet from his tyranny. However, while Terra and her companions had the support of most of the inhabitants of this planet, the Dark God had a loyal army. When the Dark God was defeated, and sent to a different plane of existence, Terra and the others banished the army to the other plane as well."

"If this army is in another plane of existence, then how can they appear in our world?" Ayleen was confused. She knew that the Elder Druid was telling the truth, but needed some more information to understand the situation.

"These monsters, as you describe them, were only partially in our world." Jeldite continued his tale. "What you saw was a projection from the other plane. They can hurt you, but you can't hurt them. Unless whoever summoned them continues their concentration, they will return to the other plane. It would take a lot of energy to maintain their existence here for more than a few minutes."

"Do you know how we can defend ourselves, Elder?" Ayleen wanted an answer to this question so desperately. She had to know how to kill these monsters to protect the citizens of Giana, should there be another attack.

Jeldite looked down at the floor in shame. "Through my years of research, I have never heard of them coming through to our side since they were banished. You ask me if there is any way that we can defend ourselves from these creatures? I'm sorry, Captain, but I don't know if there is any way we can. The High Priestess will know more."

Ayleen left the tent in search of the High Priestess. She contemplated the Elder Druid's words. While she knew about the Dark God, this was the first time she had heard about his army being exiled with him. She wasn't sure if the shadow creatures were the exiled army, or creatures created by Demonic Magic. She needed to speak to Ahna, to see if she could shed more light on this situation.

Unlike Ayleen, the thought of sleeping now was nowhere in Tyran's mind. He was angry. The fact that anyone could willingly summon so much chaos, and kill so many elves infuriated the man. Even though his reputation was that of a petty criminal, the idea of taking lives sickened him. He was a thief, not a killer. Even when he was working with organized crimes syndicates, he refused to do any of their elimination jobs. Those kinds of jobs were for people like his friend, Klep or Bear. Despite his rule against killing, if he found out who caused this disaster, he might break his own rule.

Tyran wandered the grounds of the celebration to see if there were any survivors that the guards had missed. Throughout the area, corpses littered the walkways between the torn tents. If he wasn't so focused on his rage and looking for survivors, he probably would have been throwing up. There had to be someone still alive. All he wanted was a single person alive, so that he could feel that he had helped someone. Tyran lost count of how long he had searched for someone when he heard a woman crying. Following the cry, he entered a partially collapsed tent without realizing it was the tent he had entered hours before. The same tent where Izabael worked.

There in front of Tyran, he saw Izabael crying over the body of a man. While all that he could see was the back of her head, which was full of black hair, he knew it was the same Izabael that had tried to bully him into a job earlier. Tyran felt conflicted. On the one hand, he wanted to help her because she was a fellow elf in need. On the other hand, this woman was the definition of evil in his mind. He was shocked that Izabael, who only cared about herself, was crying over this man.

"Hey, Izabael, do you need help?" Tyran decided to put his anger towards Izabael aside and help her if she wanted his assistance.

"Of all the people that could come to my rescue, scum like you dare to offer help." Izabael turned her purple face towards Tyran. "Or are you here to laugh at my misery like the sick person you are?"

Tyran took a step back. With Izabael now moved to one side, he could see that the body was that of her younger brother. "I am so sorry about your brother, Izabael. I just came to see if there was anything I could do to help you. But if you don't want my help, I will leave you two alone."

"Help? You are the kind of person who only takes care of himself!" Izabael yelled at him as she stood up. "You don't care about me! If you did, you would have taken the job I offered you! You're pathetic! Criminals are supposed to help other criminals; that is how we have done business for centuries, Tyran! I tried to give you a simple job and you refused it because your morals couldn't handle the consequences! And now you think you can come into my tent and offer help like nothing has happened. You are no more than a coward." She said this with a sneer.

"Izabael, I think it would be best if you calm down. I don't want to fight with you. I will leave if that is what you want." Tyran continued to back away. He had no idea what was going through Izabael's mind, but he knew that she wasn't thinking clearly.

"Look at me, Tyran." Izabael continued to yell at him while pulling out a knife from her sleeve. "My brother is dead. My skin is purple. I'm hideous! My business will crumble. Everything I have worked for is gone. Now you come in here and act like a hero? Well, I've had enough of your games. If I'm going to fall, I'm going to take you with me!"

Izabael leapt at Tyran with her knife. Instinctively Tyran drew his knife to defend himself. Tyran easily dodged her attack and plunged his knife into the left side of her abdomen. Seconds too late, Tyran realized that his aim was too good. As Izabael dropped to the floor, Tyran caught her head before it hit the ground. He gently lowered Izabael to the floor as he heard a chuckle escape her dying mouth.

"There is the Tyran I knew you could be. You are merciless as a criminal should be." Izabael muttered these last words as she died. Tyran stood up; he couldn't believe that he had taken an elf's life, even if it was in self-defence. All he wanted to do was to help Izabael. But now the person Tyran intended to help lay dead by his own hand. This would haunt him forever. Without thinking anymore about this situation, Tyran picked up his weapon and left the scene of yet another disaster.

The afternoon following the attack, Ayleen gathered together a group of nobles to discuss the events that occurred at the celebration. They were meeting at the Staff and Sword Inn, close by in Thaldor. She noticed that the Queen and Princess weren't at the meeting, although she had sent an invitation by wizard. Since the castle was located far South within the continent, they would have needed to take a wizard's portal to get here in time. Therefore, the discussion on the defense of the continent started without them.

Among the participants, three important figures stood out as being the most knowledgeable in the defense of Giana. The loudest speaker was General Bloodthorn, a blue-skinned elf of great military experience. Although he had never encountered a situation like last night, his intelligence for strategic planning was rivaled by no other. Throughout the first half of the meeting, he tried to recommend that the Queen enact the conscription law to bolster the army. Ayleen knew that the Queen must consider the conscription law, but it would be met with great criticism and much negativity from the citizens.

The second prominent figure in this discussion was Duke Edwin Morgwyn of Thaldor, who was trying to convince the council that this was a sign of the 'end times', and there was nothing they can do to stop it. The purple-skinned elf had been quoting religious texts non-stop, and the people of the council, even the druids and priestesses who were present, were becoming annoyed that he had nothing better to offer.

Ayleen had heard that the Duke was first in line to marry the Princess. From the few times she spoke with the Princess, she always brought religion into every conversation. The Princess was well-known for her religious rants. Ayleen figured that the Duke was spouting religion to impress the Princess, who wasn't even present.

The third person of importance was High Priestess Ahna Alturest. She stated her argument when the other two men stopped talking; her orange skin made her look angrier than she was. According to her view no one here had enough research to act on anything. She agreed that they needed to defend themselves against the invaders but knowing that their weapons had no effect on the creatures, more research had to be done. Ayleen and the High Priestess had never agreed on much in the past, but this time she agreed to everything the High Priestess had said. Perhaps their discussion earlier this morning had helped. Ahna was not able to provide any more help than Jeldite had already.

Ayleen noticed that there was a person missing that should be here, Lord Lindar Mobious. She wasn't surprised that the wizard was late. He acted like he could get away with anything, because he was the head advisor to the Queen. The unfortunate part was that the Queen allowed him to act this way. Throughout her years of service Ayleen had never seen the Queen reprimand Mobious. Despite this, his help in this situation would be welcome and she wasn't the only one here that felt this way.

"I can't believe that Lord Mobious would be late to this meeting. He can bloody teleport!" Said the Duke. "Ever since the Queen appointed Lord Mobious, he has done nothing but walk a fine line between being an advisor and taking advantage! And yet the Queen still keeps that snake of a man by her side."

The High Priestess nodded her head in agreement. "I agree with you, Duke Morgwyn, however, let's not forget that Lord Mobious is the kingdom's greatest expert on magic and we need him to give his expert opinion on the events that have transpired. Even though Lord Mobious was not physically there, we need his opinion so that we can accurately plan for another attack."

Ayleen continued to agree with the High Priestess on this matter.

She was willing to put aside her differences with Mobious, if it meant a solution to their predicament. Knowing Mobious, however, if he did come, he would probably belittle everyone in the meeting, like he always did. Just as Ayleen was about to adjourn the meeting which she felt was going nowhere, Mobious suddenly arrived.

With a flash of light, a portal opened with Mobious standing at the other end. As Ayleen expected, Mobious now had white hair and light blue skin, since his manor was in the Northeast of the continent. As he stepped through the portal it closed behind him, disappearing as if it had never been there. The room fell silent as Mobious entered. Half of the people attending this meeting feared Mobious, while the other half, including Ayleen, could not stand the man.

"Lord Mobious, it is so nice of you to join us", General Bloodthorn snarled, looking directly into Mobious' eyes. "Tell me why you are late, when we have thousands dead and a potential war looming on the horizon."

"My apologies, General Bloodthorn," Mobious said contritely and bowed. "The wave of change that washed over the continent caused chaos at my manor. There were things that required my attention. But now the situation has been taken care of, and I am here at this meeting to help any way I can."

"That's all right, Lord Mobious, you are here now." Ayleen said coldly, as she looked up at Mobious. "We were hoping you would provide your expertise on magic to explain what happened at the Celebration. I have gathered some theories, but I would like to hear your thoughts on the matter, since you are the kingdom's leading expert on magic."

Mobious took a moment to sit down and get comfortable before he answered Ayleen's question. "In my professional opinion, Captain Ebella, the tragedy that occurred was the result of another world trying to invade ours by magic, the kind of magic which we have yet to understand. If we really want to defend ourselves, then we must learn the location of this other world, go there and kill them all before they can kill us."

"That's ridiculous, Lord Mobious!" The High Priestess yelled at Mobious. Ayleen had never heard the High Priestess shout at anyone like that before. "We know nothing about this enemy and you dare suggest that we go to their world, and try to wipe out an entire race of people? Do you not realize how many elves would die going to an unknown world? Even the General here would agree that it is a bad idea."

Without waiting for the General to respond to the priestess, Mobious decided to defend his opinion. "High Priestess Ahna, do you really have that little faith in General Bloodthorn's ability? And of course, we need to study our enemy, but do we have time? Everyone here is acting like a coward, not doing what needs to be done. Give me two weeks and I will come back here with all the research we need on the creatures. By that time, you should have plenty of preparations, in order to go to war with these invaders."

"Lord Mobious, I appreciate your confidence in my ability," said General Bloodthorn. "But at this moment we have no idea how to defend ourselves from these creatures. We don't even know if they can be hurt at all. I agree with the High Priestess. Even if you had two weeks of research, I doubt that it would be enough time for us to plan a successful counterattack. We need to bolster our defenses. And you need to provide a way of harming them."

Mobious leaned back in his chair and said, "So you really are a coward, General. I am amazed that you would confirm what everyone suspected. What I find most interesting is the fact that Captain Ebella has remained silent and not shared her own opinion with us. Maybe it is because she is as much of a coward as the General."

"You take that back, Lord Mobious, or I swear to Terra I will run my sword right through you!" The furious General Bloodthorn raged as he stood up, and placed his hand on the hilt of his sword. "As for Captain Ebella, while I disagree with her methods, I can vouch that she is a fantastic leader of the Queen's Investigation Unit."

"Thank you, General Bloodthorn, for your confidence in me." Ayleen raised her hand in an attempt to calm the situation down. "However, this is not the time to be arguing amongst ourselves. We must find a solution to this problem. If the invaders attack us again, we have no way to defend ourselves. As much as I hate saying this, I think for Mobious to gather research is a fantastic idea. On the other hand, his idea of going to the world of these creatures and attacking them, is not plausible at this time.

I'm currently investigating whether the magic that brought them here originated on Giana."

Mobious stood up and nodded his head. "Captain Ebella, I apologize for implying that you were a coward. I have seen now that you are willing to compromise, unlike the General. I will return to my manor and gather any information that I can on defeating these monsters. But I seriously doubt anyone on Giana has the power to bring those creatures here once, let alone twice."

The General sat back down in silence. He knew that this was not the place to fight Mobious. The Count and High Priestess remained silent in agreement with Ayleen. Ayleen was confident that a plan was possible. She adjourned the meeting with the agreement that everyone here would reconvene in five days' time in the capital city. Before Mobious left, Ayleen needed to have one final conversation with him.

"Lord Mobious, before you go, can I have a moment of your time?" Ayleen called out to Mobious as he summoned a portal to his estate. "I wanted to ask; do you feel confident that you can find enough information, so that we can defeat these creatures?"

Mobious smiled at Ayleen. "Captain Ebella, I have been the head magical advisor to the Queen for decades now. I think one simple research project won't be that hard to do. It's my job to protect the kingdom from magical attacks. You can trust in me."

"One more question, Lord Mobious," Ayleen asked. "I noticed you weren't at the Celebration. Were you at the palace with the Queen and the Princess?"

Puzzled, Mobious looked at Ayleen. "I had a private gathering at my estate. The Celebration always brings back memories of my late wife and daughter and I don't feel like I'm ready to deal with those emotions. You said the Queen and Princess were not in attendance as well? I thought for sure they would be there."

"That is absolutely understandable," Ayleen said. "I'm just trying to establish where all the important people in the kingdom were at the time of the attack."

"You're just doing your job, Captain Ebella," Mobious said as he turned towards the waiting portal. "If anyone is going to solve this mystery it will be you. I just hope you will be pleased with the answers you will find."

"We may have our differences, Lord Mobious, but the Queen trusts you enough to listen to your advice and that's good enough for me. If you can provide information that will help us defeat these creatures, I'm willing to put aside our differences for benefit of the kingdom," Ayleen said as Mobious nodded his head and walked through the portal.

Ayleen had always been at odds with Mobious. While she wanted to trust him, something within herself just wouldn't let her. He was arrogant, self-centred and took care of himself first. She hoped this once, he could prove useful without being condescending. His better-than-everyone attitude really grated on her nerves.

As Mobious stepped through the portal back to his manor, he was still shocked to see his once green and beautiful estate covered in ice and snow. He had not expected the land to be affected. As he entered his library, he turned to look out a window where his daughter's playground was located. What was a place of joy, was now frozen over; like his heart.

The next morning, Mobious headed to his desk and sat down. Looking at the clock on the wall, he realized that his assistant was about to appear with a report. Within five minutes of Mobious sitting down his assistant came into the library and bowed.

"Master Mobious, I hope the meeting went well." Like Mobious, the assistant had blue skin and white hair now. "As you requested, Master, I contacted Brother Isaac and informed him that you need to ask him questions about the Order of the Cube. He has agreed to meet you the day after tomorrow. He should arrive mid-morning."

Mobious was pleased with this. One part of his plan was done; another part was in motion. The last part was to convince the council to send the entire army to the other realm leaving a clear path for usurping the Queen and proclaiming himself Emperor. He walked towards his assistant with his hands behind his back. "You did well, Kenei."

"Thank you, Master, for allowing me to assist you on this journey," Kenei said happily. "It will be a great day to see Mistress Mobious and Tavia again."

Mobious chuckled and moved closer to his assistant. "Yes, it will be a great day when I can finally embrace Elnora and Tavia again. Over this last year you have been so much help to me. Your loyalty deserves much praise and I have decided to reward your service. Hold out your hand."

Kenei held out his hand expecting money as a reward for his work. Mobious grabbed his hand and muttered some words that he could not understand. Seconds after Mobious let go, the assistant started to shake violently. Kenei's happy demeanour was replaced with a look of horror. As his life melted away, so did the flesh of his body, reducing him to a puddle on the floor.

"Sorry for the deception," Mobious said coldly to the puddle. "But I cannot have any loose ends now. My plan is so close to fruition. I can't afford to have Ayleen talking to you or anyone that could possibly expose me. While you were loyal, I never trusted you to keep your mouth shut. And Ayleen is too good at her job."

All that remained of Kenei were his clothes. Going back to his desk, Mobious sat down and smiling to himself he said, "Things are going better than I expected."

III

CHAPTER

S AYLEEN LEFT the meeting, she pondered over what Mobious had said. Why was Mobious so adamant about attacking the realm of the invaders? Ayleen knew that any plan the council came up with had to be decided on at the next meeting which was only five days away. She wondered if Mobious was lying to her. It wouldn't be the first time. This feeling was vague, as she had no evidence to distrust Mobious on this topic. While she didn't trust him in general, she felt she had to trust him regarding magic.

So deep in thought, Ayleen had forgotten that she had asked Tyran to bring a carriage to the door for the long journey to the castle. She looked at the horse and wondered if it also changed like the elves, or was it always black like the ground she stood on. Tyran greeted her with a single wave of his hand. Ayleen knew that Tyran was still upset about the attack. She couldn't blame him. There was not a single person on the continent that wouldn't still be upset. But he seemed more upset than she expected.

"How did the meeting go, Captain?" Tyran asked, as he helped Ayleen into the carriage.

"We haven't made a final decision, but I hope that we can decide on something next time we meet in five days," Ayleen said, as she repositioned herself to drive. "To be completely honest with you, there is a feeling in my gut that I shouldn't trust the Queen's head advisor."

Tyran lifted himself into the carriage before answering Ayleen. "What? Honest-as-the-day-is-long Mobious? I'm shocked."

"Clever, aren't we," she said dryly. "It's just something that doesn't seem right." She started to drive down the road heading south to the castle. "What I found odd is Lord Mobious didn't know that the Queen and the Princess were not at the Celebration. As head advisor to the Queen he should have known her plans. The head advisor is usually with the Queen for all important functions. Mind you, the Queen has let Mobious get away with all sorts of things."

"You are probably onto something, Ayleen," Tyran commented. "From what you told me about Lord Mobious, he is a powerful wizard and would be capable of calling down that meteorite."

Ayleen turned her head in shock and puzzlement. "Do you seriously think that Lord Mobious could do this?"

"It makes sense if you think about it," Tyran answered. "Lord Mobious is the most powerful magic user on the continent. If he wasn't the one that summoned the meteorite, he would have sensed the person that did; or at least where the spell originated."

"I fear that you may be right, Tyran," Ayleen admitted with a bit of worry in her voice. "The problem is, any investigation surrounding Mobious would have to be done without the Queen's knowledge. The Queen trusts him implicitly, and would not tolerate any investigation without some proof first."

"I can help with that! I'm good at infiltrating places when I am not preoccupied." Anger started to seep into Tyran's voice as he added, "However, Ayleen, if Mobious is responsible for the attack, you better arrest him before I have a chance to kill him."

"Kill him? Are you serious?" Ayleen semi-shouted at Tyran. "Over the few years we have worked together, I have never once heard you say that you were going to kill someone. What is going on, Tyran? I don't like seeing you this angry."

"Let's just say something happened after the meteorite hit and leave it at that." That was the final thing said for a while. Ayleen knew that there might be more, but she didn't want to push him into telling her. Whatever Tyran was hiding, that was his business and Ayleen did not want to pry.

The pair continued south along the road towards the castle. This used to be a beautiful trip with fields of flowers along the side of the road but now it was all blackened. Ayleen used to play in the fields as a child. She couldn't imagine children playing in these fields anymore, and the thought of that brought tears to her eyes. She wondered what the castle would look like now. Would there be vines still surrounding the castle as she remembered, or would it just be a monument of stones.

The two wound up at the palace two days later. As they arrived, they saw that the formerly green vines that covered the castle were now black. The once lush gardens that surrounded the castle were black and purple. Ayleen remembered that the castle was once the most beautiful place in the whole continent, but now looked like something out of a nightmare.

As the carriage stopped, a servant of the Queen came out to greet them. Like Ayleen, the servant had purple skin and raven hair. Ayleen knew that just a few days ago he would have been pale-skinned and probably had blonde or brown hair. Ayleen wondered what happened to the Queen; if she had changed or was she still the same? If an elf was the same as before the meteorite hit, would they fear the elves who had changed? Or would they feel like they were better than the changed elves?

"Captain, do you mind if I leave you here? There is something that I need to do," Tyran asked Ayleen as she got down from the carriage. Ayleen only responded to him with a nod. Tyran left to go park the carriage in the carriage house a far distance away from the castle.

"Captain Ebella, the Queen and the Princess have been waiting for you." The servant bowed as Ayleen turned towards him. "My apologies, Captain, the way into the castle may be a little slower than usual."

Ayleen was very puzzled with this information. "What do you mean the way into the castle may be slower?"

"There is a massive group of elves in the entry hall," the servant said, as the pair walked towards the entrance. "People are in a panic. They want answers and believe that the Queen can provide them. However, there is a good number of people that are angry with the Queen and believe she is not doing enough to ease the situation. They fear she will take too long to act as with the plague."

Ayleen wasn't surprised by this at all. She figured that there would be a period of protests. She just hoped that none of these would get violent. As Ayleen and the servant entered the castle, she saw the large group of people that the servant had been talking about. The group was separated into the blue-and-orange-skinned elves and the purpled formed another group.

As Ayleen saw this, she decided to stop the servant and assess the situation. She sensed anger from both groups but didn't know where the anger was directed. She knew that if she tried to press through the crowd, she would only escalate the tension and potentially cause an incident. It wasn't long before she found out why the crowd was gathered here.

"Why hasn't the Queen done anything about the invaders yet?" a voice from the orange and blue side yelled out. "Why haven't we heard a word from the Queen since the disaster?!"

"What is there to be upset about? This is a blessing from Terra." This time the voice came from the side of the purple elves. "If you can't accept this, then you people shouldn't live in Terra's city. The Queen will be out anytime. I'm sure of it. We just need patience."

"Patience! Our crops are dead! We will starve!" another voice from the blue-and-orange side yelled out. "And why should we have to leave our homes, just because we don't believe that this is Terra's will? What kind of messed up logic is that?"

Ayleen could feel the tension rising between the two groups. She had no idea how to calm the crowd by herself. When she thought the two groups were about to erupt into violence, the Queen appeared at the top of the stairs. Queen Merri had purple skin and long black hair like Ayleen had speculated. She was accompanied by her daughter, Princess Dariusa, who looked the same as her mother.

"Our beloved subjects, please be calm," The Queen said, addressing the crowd. "It is clear that all of you are angry at the situation, but rest assured we are doing everything in our power to find a solution to this problem. We ask that you return to your homes until we find a way to deal with the situation. Our Captain of Investigation, and Magical Advisor are already working hard to find a solution."

With those words the group of blue-and-orange-skinned elves started to leave the castle. The purple-skinned elves stayed in the hall looking up at the Princess. The Princess descended the stairs towards the crowd of purple-skinned elves. The Queen noticed that this part of the crowd was the same group of people that the Princess usually spoke to on matters of religion.

The Queen stopped the Princess with a touch to her arm. "Daughter, we do not agree with your meddling in Terra's affairs," the Queen said, but the Princess continued down the stairs. "However, we realize that we can't stop your behaviour and wish that you err on the side of caution."

"Your concern is not needed, Mother." The Princess paused and turned around to speak to the Queen. "I'm just providing a service that these people so desperately need, and that are not being provided by the Elder Druid and High Priestess."

With that, their conversation ended as the Princess headed towards the group of purple-skinned elves. The Queen turned her gaze towards Ayleen and beckoned her to come up to her side. Ayleen followed this order with no question or hesitation. The servant that was with Ayleen followed a short distance behind her. When Ayleen reached the Queen, she bowed along with the servant.

"Greetings, Captain Ebella." The Queen greeted Ayleen formally. "We assume you have another report for us."

"Yes, I do, my Queen," Ayleen said. "May I suggest that we reconvene in a private room, so I can freely discuss my findings without prying ears?"

"We will be happy oblige your request, Captain. Follow me," the Queen said as she led the way into the castle and to her private study.

As they moved down the hallway, Ayleen noticed that the interior hadn't changed much since the last time she was here. The only change was the elves in the castle had the same skin and hair colour that she had;

whereas before they were all pale-skinned and blonde. The demeanour of the elves in the castle was as if the meteorite had never hit. They all continued to do their jobs as usual. She knew that these workers must be emotionally affected by the changes, but respected them for not letting it interfere with their duties.

As Ayleen followed the Queen, she spotted one of the Queen's advisors approaching. He met at the door to the Queen's study. Bowing to the Queen as she arrived. The Queen nodded her head in acknowledgement. "Is there something you need from us?"

"Sorry, Your Majesty, I did not mean to interrupt you." The advisor put his hands behind his back. "I came to inform you that there are multiple protests around the capital city. A few of them have resulted in violence."

"Has the military been informed of these violent protests?" the Queen asked the advisor.

"No, Your Majesty, I came here for your signature on an order for military assistance." The advisor gave the Queen a piece of parchment for her to sign. He continued to speak as the Queen read the order. "As you see, Your Majesty, I have written it up a standing order in case of riots."

Ayleen could see that the Queen had crossed out a line of the document. She could guess which line it would be. She couldn't believe that these protesters would become violent. In all her years in the service of the Queen, she had never seen the Queen's subjects turn to violence in such a mass. If Ayleen was alone in her room she would probably take out her frustrations and sadness with tears, but since she was with the Queen, she would contain herself.

The Queen handed the order back to the advisor after she had signed it. "We have crossed out the option of lethal force. We do not want any citizens of our kingdom to be killed while the army enforces the law. We have seen so much death the last few days that we do not want to risk any more innocent lives."

The advisor bowed again after taking the order. "Yes, Your Majesty, I completely understand. I apologize for putting that option in the order in the first place."

"No need to apologize." the Queen said to the advisor. "You are dismissed."

With the Queen's final words, the advisor turned and left in the direction of the army barracks. Ayleen hoped that no one would get hurt in the following hours, but she knew that it was unlikely. The Queen opened the door to her study and invited Ayleen in.

As the pair entered the study, the Queen shut the door behind them, then offered Ayleen a seat as she sat down herself. The room itself was filled with books along the walls. There was a portion of the books Ayleen couldn't read as they were written in ancient elfish. She knew that the Queen would be able to read these books since the royal family, druids, and priestesses are trained to read the language. She remembered one or two lessons that her mother gave her, but could not recall any of the language now.

"What do you have to report, Captain Ebella?" The Queen ask Ayleen as she poured two drinks and offered one to Ayleen.

Ayleen took the drink before answering. "As you know there was an incident at this year's Celebration. As an eye witness to the incident, I can confirm that a meteorite hit the sacred Tree destroying it and causing changes to three areas of the continent. We were then attacked by creatures from another realm whom our weapons were useless against. There were casualties, Your Majesty; however, if the invaders had stayed longer, there would have been more. This was in my first report. Since then, there was a meeting you were unable to attend in Thaldor. The Arch Druid and High Priestess found similarities between these attackers and the Shadow Army of Val-Sharect. Lord Mobious wants to send the entire army through a portal to their realm and attempt to destroy them. General Bloodthorn and I doubt this is a good idea."

The queen creased her brow and with a sigh said, "This is most troubling. There was no way to stop them?"

Ayleen lowered her head. "I'm afraid not, Your Majesty. I tried, but all our weapons never made contact with these creatures. Moreover, I believe this attack was deliberate and done by magic."

"Ayleen, my dearest friend." The Queen broke from her normal royal mannerisms and place her hand on Ayleen's. "Failure is the only way we learn. You know that. I do not blame you for any deaths, but I am curious, however, to know how you came to the conclusion that this was a deliberate magic attack."

"After the attack ended, I found a magical signature on the underneath side of the meteorite as it hovered over the crater." Ayleen put down her drink and took a book out of her backpack. "The magical signature was very close to the same signature that a dozen missing persons had on their bodies when found. The thirteenth died the day before which is why I sent you a warning, Merri." Having been friends for years, they often called each other by their given names when alone. "I believe those dead elves were sacrificed to prepare this spell. The signature in question was that of a wolf skull with its jaws open and a single eyeball in its mouth."

The Queen looked at Ayleen, puzzled for few seconds. "Ayleen, that is impossible. The magical signature you described is that of Lord Lindar Mobious. I hope you are not accusing my head advisor of mass murder."

"No, I am not, Merri. I had no idea what his signature looked like." Ayleen knew she had to play this carefully. If she had any hope of looking into Mobious, then she would have to convince the Queen she had good intentions. "I only plan on looking into Lord Mobious to eliminate him as a suspect in my investigation."

"We certainly hope so," the Queen said getting up from her seat and ushering Ayleen to the door. Her demeanour changed back to her royal speech. "Captain Ebella, while we are grateful for your service to Giana and Terra herself, we hope that you will be careful with your investigation."

Ayleen stood up and headed towards the door which was now opened by the Queen. "I can assure you, Your Majesty, that I will do everything in my power to find the guilty party and present enough evidence to satisfy any doubts you may have."

The Queen nodded and dismissed Ayleen. As Ayleen left the study, the advisor quickly approached the doorway, obviously out of breath. The advisor bowed when he saw the Queen. The Queen acknowledged the advisor again. "Yes, you may speak."

"The Princess requests your presence in her chambers, Your Majesty," the winded advisor said as he tried to catch his breath.

"Tell her we will be there in ten minutes," the Queen said as the advisor bowed again and ran off to tell the Princess. What could her daughter want at this time? This was not the time for any of her religious nonsense.

Across the capital city Tyran sat in the Grand Temple of Terra. Tyran himself wondered what the heck he was doing here. While he was a firm believer in Terra, setting foot in a temple made him feel uncomfortable, to say the least. Last time he was in a temple he scammed a priestess out of donation money; yet another part of his past he regretted. He just sat there in the middle of the giant temple alone. He expected there to be more people in the building seeking answers for what had happened the night before.

After about fifteen minutes of Tyran sitting there alone, he saw a blue-skinned elf come sit beside him. He looked over to see who had joined him. Tyran had to stare at the elf for a few seconds before realizing it was Klep. He was the last person he thought he would ever see in a place of worship. Tyran decided to start a conversation to figure out why Klep was here. "I doubt you are here to ask for forgiveness from Terra, so why did you come here and why do you choose to sit beside me?"

"I had to clean up your mess, Tyran," Klep said not turning to face Tyran. "Got to say you did a good job killing Izabael. If I wasn't on her payroll, I probably would have taken her out myself. Her business has been devaluating everything in the underworld. Tell me something, Tyran, taking out your first employer?"

"Are you out of your bloody mind, Klep?" Tyran clenched his fist while turning his whole body to the man next to him. "The only reason I killed her was self-defence! She charged at me with a damn knife, for Terra's sake! I was there offering help if she wanted it. When I got to her tent she was talking as if it was my fault for the disaster."

"That's pathetic, Tyran," Klep said without turning to face Tyran. "I know you told Izabael to take a hike. She probably threatened you and you came back to teach her a lesson like she deserved. How about you grow up and take responsibility for your actions and rejoin the underworld as a hired killer. You are obviously good at it. Couldn't find anything in the tent that would implicate you."

Tyran could barely hold in his anger but he knew that a temple wasn't the right place to deal with Klep. "I did not mean to kill her, you understand that? You're damn lucky we are in a temple, otherwise I would beat some sense into your small head."

"There you go, Tyran, you're already speaking like a hired killer," Klep said as he stood up from the bench. He headed towards the aisle and turned around. "I like you, Tyran. You say you didn't intend to kill her, but I know you did. You did me a favour, removing her, I'm going to make you an offer. I have a wide network of friends who will do whatever I ask them. If you need any sort of favour just call on us."

As Klep exited the temple, Tyran slouched on the bench. He couldn't believe what had just happened. I'm not a killer! He thought. I never wanted to be. And yet, Klep believed that he was a cold-blooded killer which meant he could call on a favour from one of the most connected criminals on the continent. He was so deep in thought that he didn't realize that a priestess had sat down beside him.

"Excuse me, sir, I couldn't help but overhear your conversation and wondered if you were all right," the priestess said in a soft voice. Tyran turned to look at her to see an elf that looked similar to Ayleen, but he knew it was a different person.

"Sorry you had to listen to that. You won't tell the authorities, will you? It really was self-defence. I'm not a killer," Tyran said morosely.

"Anything you say in this temple stays between you, me and the goddess." the priestess said calmly. "I feel so much conflict within you. Is there anything I can do to help?"

"I'm just so confused," Tyran said with a sigh. "Ever since the meteorite hit the sacred tree one thing has led to another and I did something I regret; I don't know how I can atone for it."

The priestess took a deep breath. "The first thing to do is to accept what you have done wrong, which you have already done. Next you should ask Terra for guidance and forgiveness. Lastly, you must forgive yourself and remember the lessons you have learned."

"Thank you, priestess," Tyran said as he stood up. "Your words have brought me a little bit of comfort, but I know there is more to do. If you would excuse me, there is a person I need to meet up with. She is probably wondering where I am."

The priestess nodded. Tyran knew what he had to do next. He would help Ayleen in her investigation, and bring down whoever caused all this terror. In his mind, this was the best way for Tyran to redeem himself. Izabael's death would not be in vain. If he could help it, no more people would die.

Back at the castle the Queen entered her daughter's chambers. She expected that the conversation she was about to have with her daughter would be mostly religious ranting. Throughout her daughter's chambers hung paintings of Terra as artists had interpreted from religious text. Most elves had one or two of these paintings in their house. Princess Dariusa had twelve in her bedchambers. Dariusa sat in the corner of her sitting room. She greeted her mother by standing up and bowing and then offering her mother a seat beside her.

"Greetings, Dariusa, my advisor said that you wished to speak with me," Queen Merri said as she sat down beside the Princess. "Like I said earlier before, Dariusa, I don't appreciate you pretending to be a priestess of Terra and I would once again ask you to stop this foolishness."

"Mother, you know well enough that I cannot do that," Dariusa replied. "But that is not why I called you to meet me. As you are aware, the blue-and-orange-skinned elves are fighting with purple-skinned elves, like us. I know it's not my place to make policies, but I will ask that you consider making a law for segregation. This will ensure the safety of all three variations. At least until tensions die down."

"Dariusa, you know I can't do that. That will divide the continent more than it already is," the Queen responded, shocked that her daughter would ask this of her. "The only reason why the blue-and-orange-skinned elves distrust the purple-skinned elves is that the purple-skinned elves are accusing them of being heretics. Yet they've done nothing wrong! Furthermore, high-ranking members of society, who have purple skin now, are preaching that they are the chosen people of Terra. A sentiment that I don't appreciate my daughter spreading. According to Captain

Ebella, skin colour was decided by where you were standing on the continent when the meteorite struck."

"Mother, there is a good reason why we are telling the purple-skinned elves that they are Terra's chosen," Dariusa retorted as she stood up. "First of all, the Grand Temple of Terra is in this capital city. The same temple where Terra made her last speech to the elves before she ascended to the realm of the gods. Second, the palace itself is in the purple zone. This is the place where our religious texts recorded that Terra and our ancestors were to build the palace. She said that the location of our palace would be crucial in the last major battle of the eight realms. Lastly, why would Terra turn all of the elves to a different colour if it's not to teach us something or prepare us for an event?"

The Queen sighed. She knew that there would be no way to change her daughter's mind. "Darling, your points are moot. The High Priestess herself is orange! My dear, we aren't sure if the changes were a gift from Terra or part of the attack by the creatures of the other realm. I know you think you have the continent's best interest at heart, but segregation would only bring more chaos. At this moment we need unity more than ever. I have General Bloodthorn preparing for an attack on the other realm, Captain Ebella investigating the source of the magic, and Advisor Mobious researching options. If we separate the people now there would be no certainty of everyone joining together in the battle against the shadow creatures."

"If you are worried about not having enough manpower for our army, then shouldn't you enact the conscription law?" The Princess questioned her mother. "If that won't work, then wait until after the defeat of these creatures to segregate the people. All I'm saying, Mother, is the longer we have these three variations together there will be violence on the streets. For every civilian's safety we need to be separated. Ever since the meteorite hit and people were changed, it seems they are feeling that with their differences, they can no longer get along."

Queen Merri stood up preparing to leave. She was furious that her daughter would even suggest this. "I understand how you feel, Dariusa, but I have to disagree with segregation. We will not talk about this again, in private or in public. When you are Queen you can decide to change the law however you see fit but I hope that until then, I can change your mind and prove that together we are stronger. It has only been days. People need time to adjust."

Queen Merri headed to the door to exit the Princess' chambers. Dariusa was determined to say one final word. "Thank you for hearing me out, Mother. It sounds like I have more work to do to convince you that my suggestion is the right way. I hope in the coming days that you see what I have seen in the last three days. You are too passive sometimes."

Without reply to her daughter, the Queen left the Princess' chambers. On the other side of the door tears began rolling down her cheeks. There were many questions on her mind where she did not have answers. Why was her daughter suggesting that the elves be segregated? Why were the purple elves so angry at the other elves? Was she too passive? When did she fail as a mother?

Tyran's return to the castle was different than he expected. When he arrived at the front gates of the palace, he told the guard his name and that he was working for Captain Ayleen Ebella. What he expected was the guards to ask him to wait for Ayleen to come out and clear him to enter. Instead one of the guards escorted him inside the palace to a private room where Ayleen was sitting at a table looking over some notes. As Tyran entered the room the guard closed the door behind him.

"Well, that was easier than I expected," Tyran chirped happily as he pulled out a chair and sat at the table.

"I asked the guards to bring you here as soon as you presented yourself at the gate," Ayleen said as she put away her notes. "I think you were onto something when we were in the carriage. I found out from the Queen that Lord Lindar Mobious' magical signature is the same signature that I found on the thirteen bodies and on the meteorite. Unfortunately, the Queen doesn't believe that Mobious had anything to do with the attack and the murders. She told me I need to bring solid evidence against Mobious before proceeding any further."

"At least you got a start, Ayleen, which is better than what you had a couple hours ago," Tyran said leaning back in his chair. "As for getting more information from Mobious, I may be able to get the information you need depending on if I can convince my friend to help me."

Ayleen was obviously intrigued at this. She had no idea what Tyran was talking about or who this friend was. But she needed every resource that she could get and if Tyran had a way to get what she needed from Mobious, then more power to him. She had a few questions before she could approve of this action. "How in Terra's name did you convince anyone to give you a favour this big? And, who gave you this opportunity?"

"You would know him as the "Vanisher"." Tyran smirked. "And the reason he owes me this favour is that he believes I did something that I actually didn't do. Before you ask, no, I am not talking about what he believes I did. So please don't ask."

Ayleen didn't know whether to be angry or excited. She had been after the "Vanisher" for years and would do anything to see him behind bars but an opportunity like this might never present itself again. Ayleen looked directly into Tyran's eyes to make sure he was telling the truth. "You know the "Vanisher", Tyran? And you never told me? You know I have been after that bastard for years. If this was any other situation, I would arrest you here and now for withholding information, but we don't have time to worry about him. Are you sure you can trust him?"

"I think we can trust him for this one thing," Tyran replied to Ayleen. "If it makes you happy, after we use his favour, I will give you everything I know about the "Vanisher". Right now, I will do anything to help you bring Mobious to justice even if it means killing him myself."

Ayleen had no idea what had caused Tyran to speak of killing anyone; it was not the Tyran she knew. But she had an idea in her head that would require Tyran to be in the same building as Mobious. "Can you ask the "Vanisher" to get you into Mobious' estate as one of his servants or caretakers? If you do this, you must promise me that you won't attempt to kill him until I have enough evidence on him. We need Mobious alive for as long as possible. If he winds up dead, then the Queen will never believe a word I say again."

"All right, I won't kill him, yet!" Tyran said as he stood up. "You need to promise me, Ayleen, that Mobious will receive punishment to the full extent of the law for what has done. And once I get that information you had better come as quickly as you can because I have little patience with the man who has massacred thousands of elves."

Ayleen nodded and leaned over to the side of her chair to grab a stone from her backpack, then she passed the stone to Tyran. "This stone here is a communication stone. It is magically enhanced with a spell so that we can communicate. Unfortunately, there is only one charge of magic. That means we can only use this method of communication once and then the stone becomes a regular rock. Once I have word that you have gathered significant evidence against Mobious, I will come to his estate as quickly as I can."

Tyran put it in his pocket. They said good-bye to each other. Tyran opened the door to the room and left. Ayleen sat alone in the room wondering if she had done the right thing or if she had just approved her downfall. She'd never seen Tyran so angry and willing to kill. And Mobious was a formidable enemy.

Lindar Mobious sat in the great hall of his manor reading a book. The sun was beginning to set and soon he would retire to his bedchamber. As he read his book his butler came and stood beside the chair waiting for his master to acknowledge him. Mobious put a bookmark in the book and placed it on the table. Mobious was frustrated by his butler. He had given the butler specific instructions not to bother him unless it was very important.

"What do you want?" Mobious fumed. "I told you that I was not to be disturbed by anyone during my nightly reading period."

The butler did not show any reaction to these words. "I'm sorry, Master, but you have a guest that refused to leave when I told him you were busy. He said that he was a representative of a mutual friend."

Mobious leaned over to look at the man behind his butler. While he didn't know the man's face, he knew that this man was working for the mysterious person that had told him about the Cube of Destiny. Mobious was in a little bit of shock. He thought that the mysterious person would only communicate with him via letters. He had no idea that he would actually see a real person representing his new mysterious friend. The man sat across from Mobious once Mobious had greeted him. The man himself was an elf with orange skin and red hair. The elf wore clothing that denoted nobility.

"I see that my master may have chosen the wrong form for me," the man said. Mobious was confused as to what he meant by 'the wrong form'. Before he could speak up, the man continued, "Lord Mobious, I'm here on my master's behalf to remind you that you have ten days to fulfill your end of the contract. If you require an extension, please ask me for it now as this offer will not be given again. Failure is not acceptable."

"Tell your master that I should have the Cube of Destiny within ten days." Mobious replied calmly even though inside he was a mix of confusion and rage. "I don't know if your master knows this, but it is considered rude to barge into someone's house and threaten them. Also, I'm confused as to what you meant by your master "picked" your form."

"My apologies. I'm a magical illusion sent by my master to communicate with you," the illusion said pointing his finger at Mobious. At that moment Mobious realized he was paralyzed. "As for my threat, my master can do whatever he wants. If he wanted you dead, he could send a spell through me to kill you. So, before you decide to try to counter any magic, please be aware that your life can be taken away from you at any second without any effort. Since I am an illusion, you cannot harm me for I do not exist."

Mobious was furious at this but there was nothing he could do. He realized that the illusion had not paralyzed his mouth, so he could still speak. "I told you that your master will have the Cube of Destiny in ten days. I have already invited a monk from the Order of the Cube to my estate. Once I gain his trust, I will take the Cube from the Order and deliver it to your master as our deal states."

"So, you don't need an extension," the illusion said as he stood up. "Lord Mobious, I hope you do realize that my Master will kill you if you do not fulfill your end of the bargain. As for the extension, it is now off the table due to your assurance you will have the Cube in less than ten days. I promise you if you fail, your death will not be a quick one. It will last over one hundred years. My Master has the ability to manipulate time and he has no problem using it against people who fail him."

As the final words came out of the man's mouth his body began to dissipate. Mobious now realized that he was no longer under the spell and could move his body again. He still could not believe what he had encountered. He had never known any sorcerer or wizard to use this kind of magic. He knew time magic was powerful and that was why it was taboo. But he had no idea time magic could do what he had just experienced. If he was to keep the Cube of Destiny for himself, he would need a better plan. He would confer with his own master on how to counteract Time magic.

IV

CHAPTER

TYRAN MADE HIS way to the least desirable section of the capital city. Through people he knew, he learned the location of the very person he needed to see. The only one that could help him. As he turned the final corner, he could hear the place before even seeing it.

The idea of stepping foot into Madam Charlottine's brothel made Tyran very uncomfortable. Unfortunately, he knew that this would be the best place to find Klep at this hour. He did not have an issue with ladies making money this way, but did they have to come on so strong? He always felt inadequate around them. As he entered the lobby of the establishment, he noticed that it was less busy than usual. This didn't surprise him. Most elves would be still trying to deal with the events that had happened recently. He went up to the counter where a purple-skinned elven woman was working.

"Hello, madam, I'm looking for Klep Ramloran." Tyran tried to sound casual as he put his hands on the desk. The woman looked up and smiled at him. He knew that even though he asked a direct question, she was going to try to sell him something that he wasn't looking for. His palms began to sweat.

"Well, honey, most fellas come in here looking for a girl," she said as she fluttered her eyelashes at him. "Are you sure there isn't something else you want instead? I can have one of my girls escort you to a private room. Or maybe two girls?"

"I'm sorry, ma'am, I do not have time for such pleasures." Tyran wondered what colour his skin flushed now that it was orange. He just wanted to get out of there as soon as possible. "All I need is directions to the room where Mr. Ramloran is visiting."

"Sorry, honey, I can't do that," the woman at the desk replied. She slipped around the desk to get closer to Tyran. She put her hand on Tyran's chest and started to massage it. "What I can do, is offer my services. If you don't like any of the girls that you see here, I'm also available for your pleasure."

Tyran didn't have time for her sales pitch. He took hold of her wrist and stared at the woman. "I want Klep Ramloran now! I don't have time for this. Would you please direct me to where he is? Thank you!" Tyran pushed her back. He was getting angry now.

"He is in room 104. Down the hall, second door on the right." The woman gulped as Tyran walked down the hall. She looked to the other women in the lobby for some comfort, but they all shrugged as if to say what can you do.

It took Tyran just a minute to reach room 104. From outside the room, Tyran could tell that Klep was with someone. Tyran pounded on the door until he heard Klep bark, "Who's there!"

Tyran announced himself and Klep opened the door enough that Tyran could see all Klep was wearing was a towel. He told Klep he needed to talk to him now. Klep had a confused look and wanted to know why. "What in Terra's name are you doing here?"

"I came for that favour," Tyran stated, wanting to leave as soon as he could. "I know you are busy, but this can't wait. Don't you dare say that I have to wait; otherwise, I will spread the word that Klep is a liar. You know how much that will destroy your reputation in the underworld."

Klep made a sour face but nodded as he opened the door wider, turned his back to Tyran and sat on the bed. Tyran walked to a table in the corner of the room and sat down. Then poured himself a glass of wine that was on the table. His hand shook slightly. He saw Klep wrap a sheet around the woman that was in the bed and escorted her out of the room. She was not impressed until Klep gave her several silver coins for her services. After he closed the door, he grabbed a robe that was hanging behind the door. Tyran was glad that he didn't have to talk to Klep while he was only wearing a towel.

"What was so damn important you had to bust in here like that, Tyran?" Klep snarled as he sat down across from Tyran. "When I said I owed you a favour, I thought you would take more time to think it over."

"I need to get into an extraordinary place," Tyran said. "I need to be able to get into Lord Mobious' estate. Before you ask, I already know my cover story. I am going to be one of his new servants. All I need from you is the means of making it happen."

Tyran had never seen Klep's jaw drop so much in his life. Klep stared for a minute then replied, "Are you out of your bloody mind? You're talking about infiltrating the estate of the head magical advisor of the Queen! Do you not know how much security he has? If you got past his security, he is the most powerful magic user on the continent, maybe the world at this moment. He'd sniff you out in a minute!"

Tyran took a sip of his wine. Then stared at Klep. He wasn't going to budge from this idea. Tyran put his cup down and stared directly into Klep's eyes. "I thought you owed me a favour and here I am. Now you're telling me, you won't keep your end of the bargain? What kind of business are you running, Klep?"

"All right, all right, all right!" Klep relented as he put his hands up. "Give me three days. I can get you into the estate if I am still good with my contact there. To be honest, that guy hasn't talked to me in three years, so I am beginning to worry that bridge has been burned. He is still working at the estate, I assure you."

"I don't have three days!" Tyran raised his voice. "I need to be in that estate in less than twenty-four hours, preferably less than twelve hours, if you can accomplish that. This is the only way we can catch 'The Mad Wizard of Thaldor'. If you can't get me in that estate today, I will find someone who can. I just came to you because I know you keep your word."

"Fine. I might be able to get you there in twelve hours." Klep cautiously replied. "This is going to cost me a lot more than I thought. I need to hire a wizard to summon a portal to Mobious' estate. And did I hear you right? Are you implying that Lord Mobious is 'The Mad Wizard of Thaldor'? In that case, if you can take him down, then I will owe you another favour."

In his head, Tyran was smiling at Klep's willingness to cooperate. He knew there were two reasons why Klep changed his attitude. The first reason was that he was nowhere near his two bodyguards and he believed Tyran was a killer. Being naked, he would be unable to defend himself very well. The other reason was Tyran caught Klep not only cheating on his wife but cheating on his mistress also. He needed to stay on Tyran's good side. Dropping the name of the Mad Wizard didn't hurt either.

"So, are we good? I can meet you in a few hours to teleport to Mobious' estate." Tyran added, "I just don't want to have to tell Kasara or Lilly what I saw here. To be completely honest with you, Klep, it takes a lot of courage to hire a girl here when your own mistress owns the brothel down the street."

Klep nervously chuckled. "Now, now, Tyran, there is no need to tell my wife or my mistress that I cheated on both of them. Give me six hours; I'll meet you at the usual drop site to teleport you. Just please don't tell either of them that I was here. Please."

Tyran finished off his wine and stood up. "Thank you for your time, Klep. I'm so glad we can come to an agreement. You're such a wonderful elf."

As Tyran left Klep's room, Klep buried his head in his hands. He knew that Tyran had enough information to blackmail him into doing anything. It was his own damn fault. How could he be so stupid to think that no one would ever find him in this place? He had to make sure that his wife never found out. It didn't pay to make that woman angry. Lilly might forgive him providing he gave her the right present. Kasara … she'd kill him. No doubt.

It was Ayleen's last sleep before heading back to Thaldor for the next meeting and she fell into a deep sleep that plunged her into a repeating dream. She remembered every detail of the field where she and her mother trained in druid craft. She could see the tall trees surrounding the area and the cabin just inside the woods where she and her mother lived. She could smell the scent of all the plants surrounding her. She remembered every single name of each type of animal that she saw wandering the forest as her mother began to teach her. She looked up at her mother as soon as she heard her name being called

"All right, Ayleen, today is the day you summon your first animal guardian," her mother said as Ayleen saw the wind blowing through her blonde hair. "Every druid must learn how to summon their animal guardian that can protect them against magical attacks. It is also the best way to communicate with the planet. The animal you summon is a spirit who will guide and protect you as well as help you talk to the spirit of the planet."

Ayleen's heart sank. She remembered what memory this dream was based on and couldn't wake herself up to avoid experiencing that terrible day again. She could only watch as her younger self responded to her mother, not knowing the tragedy that was coming. "But mother, I am a little afraid. What if I summon something like a bee or a snake?"

"Don't worry about that. I'm here if anything goes wrong. I promise," Ayleen's mother said as she knelt down and put her hand on the ten-year-old Ayleen's shoulder. "We're in a field where you can practice your magic to your heart's content. There is literally no one here that you can harm, and I will not let any creature harm you."

Ayleen wanted to scream to the younger version of herself but knew that her screams would fall on deaf ears. She saw her younger self reach out a hand in front of her and mutter some words. A flash of light appeared and disappeared. When the flash was gone, a butterfly was hovering in front of her. The young Ayleen was so happy that she had summoned her first animal spirit. She cheered and turned to her mother. "I did it! I can't believe that I actually summoned a creature."

"Very good, Ayleen. Now let's try something bigger," Ayleen's mother said as she knelt beside her daughter. "How about you summon a wolf.

You always wanted a dog, and we could never get one. But with a magical wolf, you can summon it at any time to protect you or play with you."

Not the wolf, anything but the wolf. Ayleen did not want to watch what was going to happen next. The younger Ayleen once again held out her hand and muttered some more words. Unfortunately, this time, nothing happened. The young Ayleen looked confused and looked towards her mother for help. "Why didn't that work, Mommy?"

"Ayleen, you need to focus on the anatomy of the wolf," said her mother. "Remember all the pictures your father and I showed you of the different animals in the forest. Just remember what the picture of the wolf looked like. Picture the skeleton of a wolf, then picture the muscles and finally the fur. I know if you work hard at this, you will make a great druid someday."

"Do you mean like this, Mother?" the young Ayleen asked as she held out her hand again. In the middle of the field, the legs of a wolf started to appear slowly.

"Very well done, my daughter. Now try to imagine the whole wolf, not just the legs." Her mother encouraged her. "You're almost there. You're getting so close, Ayleen. I am so proud of you. All you need now is a little focus."

She tried again, this time to make a full wolf, but something was going wrong. Ayleen saw her younger self summoning a dark creature. "Ayleen, stop! Don't do that! Stop! You're opening a portal to another realm!" her mother screamed.

Ayleen watched as the creature her younger self had summoned started to charge at her younger self. Her mother stepped in front of the young girl only to be attacked by the shadow creature. Ayleen watched her mother being mauled to death in the exact same way she remembered it happening all those years ago. By the time the creature had dissipated, her mother lay dead in front of the younger Ayleen. As the dream ended Ayleen realized that the creature that she had summoned all those years ago was very much like the shadow creatures that attacked them on the New Year's Eve celebration!

"I'm sorry, Mother!" Ayleen yelled as she woke up and sat up in bed. Sweat covered her entire body. It took a few moments to calm down. It always did. She thought she was done with these nightmares. She hadn't had this nightmare in over a year. She moved her legs off to the side of the bed. Ayleen sat there reminding herself that it was only a dream. Part of her was angry at herself. She vowed never to let that event ever get to her again. However, there she was, having a panic attack over a memory that happened eighty years ago.

Ayleen stood up and headed to her desk. Before she sat down, she lit a candle to illuminate the room. She assumed that it was very early in the morning since she couldn't see any signs of the sun rising. On her desk lay her notebook, her mother's journal and the amulet that she bought at the New Year's Eve celebration. She picked up the amulet hoping to figure out why exactly she had bought this thing. As she held it in her hand, she thought about selling it to get some of her money back, but there was a feeling deep within her soul that she couldn't part with it at all. It was probably just a random thought in her head.

Putting the amulet on, she turned her attention to her mother's journal. This was the only thing left that she had of her parents. After her father died in the line of duty, her mother used the journal as a record of her life, raising Ayleen as a single mother. Ayleen's mother only started the journal to cope with her husband's death. Ayleen couldn't remember if her mother had a journal before her father died. She started to read her mother's journal as she did every time she had that nightmare.

5919 of the Third Gods, 4th month, 21st day
I am starting this journal because I don't know what else to do. My husband was recently killed by a suspect that he was chasing. I used to ask him for advice whenever I had a problem. Most of the time, his advice wasn't always helpful, but I appreciated it nonetheless. But now I must take care of Ayleen all by myself. I don't know if I can do it and keep up on my responsibilities as a druid. I pray to Terra that she will give me guidance.
Nanya Ebella

Ayleen remembered the day her father died very well. She was only seven years old. Her mother was cooking dinner while she was in her room, playing with a new doll that her father had given her for her birthday just a week ago. When her mother called her for dinner, she heard a knock on the door. By the time she went downstairs to head to the dinner table, she saw her mother on the floor crying and begging the man at the entrance to tell her that 'it's a lie'.

At this moment, Ayleen wished that her father was still alive and could share his knowledge and could help her with the investigation. Her father was the biggest inspiration she had in becoming an investigator. Before her mother died, she had dreamed of being a druid just like her. After she died, Ayleen feared magic and refused to use it after that day. The only reason she tried using magic against the creatures was she had no other choice. She didn't want to use magic, but physical weapons weren't hurting the monsters. She needed a magical guardian, like her mother taught her. Ayleen flipped through the journal; this time, she read an entry from a happier time.

5921 of Third Gods, 10ᵗʰ Month, 11ᵗʰ day

Today I took Ayleen to meet the druid circle to find out if she has powers like I do. I'm happy to report that she indeed does. Ayleen is so thrilled she can't wait to start practicing magic. I have to wait until she is ten years old to officially begin training her and for permission from the circle to be her official teacher. I have no doubt in my mind that the circle will approve of me training my daughter. There have only been a few cases where the circle has denied a parent the right to train their child. I can't wait to start training Ayleen.
Nanya Ebella

Ayleen couldn't forget how excited she was when she learned that she was capable of using magic like her mother. Back then, even though her father was gone at that point, everything seemed to be going right for her and her mother. Between this entry and the final entry, she remembered her mother talking to her friends about looking forward to the future and being excited for the opportunity of training her daughter to become a druid. Ayleen assumed that this meant her mother was happy but didn't know for sure and never had the chance to ask her.

She turned to the last entry in her mother's journal. She'd read this entry so many times that she had it memorized. She knew that looking at this entry was unhealthy for her mental state but could not refrain from rereading it. Years ago, a friend of hers had offered to remove the last page of her mother's journal in order for Ayleen to heal. Part of her wished she had accepted her friend's offer while the other part of her knew that if that entry went missing, she would regret it. She took a deep breath and turned to the last page of her mother's journal. She read the last thing her mother wrote before she died.

5922 of the Third Gods, 13th Month, 8th Day

Ayleen has grasped the basic concept of elemental magic. Today I'm going to teach her how to summon animal spirits. I do not doubt that she will excel in this as she has done in the elemental magic. Last night she told me that she is terrified of summoning a scary animal like a bee. I assured her that I would be there to defend her if she summoned anything scary. We are currently staying at my father's cabin in the far North of Giana. I will be teaching her while my father is out hunting for our dinner. Ayleen has nothing to worry about. She will succeed, I know she will.

Nanya Ebella

It was her grandfather that found Ayleen crying over her mother's corpse. The young Ayleen didn't speak for weeks after the incident. Her grandfather raised her from the moment of her mother's death. He tried to convince her to go back into training with magic to no avail. There wasn't anything he could say to convince her that her mother's death was not her fault. Her grandfather died shortly after she became an adult; thirty-three, if she remembered correctly. Unlike her parents, she never felt that her grandfather was taken from her. His long life left a sense of completing his purpose.

By the time she finished reading her mother's journal, she had realized that the sun was beginning to rise. There was no point in her going back to bed. It was still too early to talk to anyone about her investigation. There were only two people she knew who would listen to her at this hour. For the next fifteen minutes, Ayleen got herself dressed and prepared for the day. Before she left her quarters, she felt compelled to look at the amulet that she bought from the weird man in red. She left her quarters and headed out.

Ever since the encounter with the illusion from his contact, Mobious had been on edge. He knew that he did not have much time to formulate a plan to keep the Cube of Destiny. Luckily for him, Brother Isaac, a monk of the Order of the Cube was due to arrive at his estate this morning. Whether the monk would bring the Cube with him, Mobious couldn't tell. This night was meant for gathering information. When Brother Isaac loses his usefulness, Mobious would indeed kill him. He hated loose ends.

The monk arrived at the estate mid-morning. The butler met him at his carriage and escorted him to Mobious' study. As the monk entered the room, Mobious noted that the monk had the purple skin. Even though Mobious had caused the events that changed the elves, it still jarred him to see the changes. Mobious wondered if the monk knew anything about who caused the event that changed the continent. But then again, based on his skin colour, he was likely at or near the capital and not the Cube at the time.

Mobious stood up and greeted the monk with a bow, and the monk returned the bow. "Brother Isaac, I hope you had a pleasant journey despite the circumstances. The recent changes are so out of the blue, my magic was unable to avert the disaster. Afterwards, my research led me to you. I knew I had to talk to your Order and perhaps get information from the Cube of Destiny. I am so grateful that you were able to make it on such short notice."

The monk took a seat. Mobious offered Brother Isaac wine before sitting down. He politely declined the offer and said, "It was very odd that the trip here coincided with what has happened to the land and the people. I'm unable to comment on what the Cube suggest we do about this event. I have been away from the monastery for more than a week."

"Fair enough." Mobious leaned back in his chair, nursing the wine in his hand. "As head advisor to the Queen, I recently was involved with discussing the safety of the continent and how to defend ourselves from the creatures that appeared right after the change. While at that meeting, I learned of a movement that claims that this change is a gift from Terra. To be honest, I think that the idea is nonsense, but I am curious as to what is your take on the situation."

Brother Isaac pondered the question for a while. "Whether this is a gift or divine punishment, I cannot say. What I do know is, while I was in the monastery, before I left for the capital, I know that the Cube warned us of a coming event. Unfortunately, none of my brothers could decipher the Cube's vague words enough so that we could warn the Queen."

Mobious was delighted that his duplicity had gone undiscovered. Now with that worry out of the way, he could finally ask the monk the questions he wanted to ask. "Brother Isaac, forgive me for changing topics, I just wanted to learn about the Cube of Destiny. Over the past year, I have been looking for a new purpose in life, and I think becoming a member of your Order would fulfil my new life's purpose. I believe I may be able to converse with the Cube and find the best solution for Giana."

"You have no idea how happy I am to hear those words." Brother Isaac seemed elated. "My Order has been observing you, Lord Mobious. We would be honoured if you would join us. To have someone like you as part of the Order would allow us to make progress in our research of the Cube of Destiny. While we know much about how the Cube functions, there are several aspects of the Cube that we don't understand yet."

Mobious' curiosity increased. He thought the monks knew everything about the Cube. He had to ask more questions before joining the Order. "If you don't mind, Brother Isaac, there are some questions I would like to ask. The first question I have is, what exactly is the Cube of Destiny? My research only came across partial answers and myths."

"That is a difficult question, Lord Mobious," Brother Isaac replied.

"What we know is the Cube is a physical object made by the first god. By the time the third gods got a hold of the Cube of Destiny, it was decided to divide into eight different cubes. The Cube we have at the monastery allows the user to ask questions about the elfish race and then the Cube will provide answers. The Cube has been known to show people the past or one of many possible futures. Only the initiated may talk to the Cube."

"You say there are eight cubes of destiny," Mobious probed, "I was only ever aware of six intelligent races on this planet. The Humans to the North of us just start building a society. Before that, they lived in caves from what I heard. I doubt they are ready to have an order of monks like us to view their Cube."

"The Humans to the North have destroyed and rebuilt their society repeatedly, it is true. But their Cube is safely guarded," Brother Isaac informed him. "On the topic of the eighth cube, it belongs to the race we refer to as the Lizardmen. A thousand years after the fall of the second god, the continents drifted, and the weather changed. The continent of the Lizardmen is no more than a frozen wasteland. Being cold-blooded, they would have all perished. As for the Cube, no one knows where it is. Likely, it is safely frozen under all that ice. I would discourage anyone from trying to find the lost Cube. Even if they were to find it, only a worthy Lizardman would be able to touch it, without the Cube disappearing. And there are none living."

Mobious stood up to put another log on the fire. As he tended to the fire, another question popped into his head. "What do you mean by saying that only a worthy person can touch the Cube, or it will disappear? Are you suggesting that the Cube is sentient? That it picks and chooses who it communicates with? When it disappears, where does it go? The monastery?"

"My Order can't tell if the Cube is actually sentient or has magically simulated sentience. Perhaps Terra speaks to us through it," Brother Isaac replied. "We know that if the Cube does not like the person touching it, it will teleport away from the person to a location it deems safe, not necessarily the monastery. We also know from experience that the Cube will erase all knowledge of itself from the unworthy person's mind. So many of our students forget why they are even in our monastery."

In his mind, Mobious was still confused as to what the Cube was. However, he figured that Brother Isaac had told him everything about the Cube that he knew. To better understand the Cube, he would have to come face to face with it. Mobious poured himself another glass of wine and sat back down. "Brother Isaac, do you think I am worthy of touching the Cube of Destiny? It sounds like only a select few could even hope to use the Cube."

"The road to being worthy is tough, but I think you can handle it," Brother Isaac replied. "At the monastery, the Cube will instruct us to put you through three trials. The first trial is the Trial of the Body. This trial consists of six hours of the worst pain you could ever imagine. The Cube wants this trial done, so that it knows you're physically able to handle the force that the Cube emits. The second trial is the Trial of the Mind. This will test your knowledge and your ability to accept the truth. The Cube doesn't want any closed-minded individuals to put their hands on it. The last trial is the Trial of Spirit. The Cube will go through your life, and you must justify all the actions it deems questionable. After that, if you succeed the Cube will allow you to use it."

Mobious pondered over this. He knew that the trials of the body and the mind would be no problem for him. The Trial of Spirit, on the other hand, he may have difficulties with. Mobious knew that he wasn't pure of heart, but he couldn't think of any living being that was. The idea of the Cube questioning him on the choices he had made didn't sit well with Mobious. Brother Isaac made it sound like the Trial of Spirit was a debate. If Mobious were to acquire the Cube, the Trial of Spirit would be his most challenging obstacle.

"Thank you, Brother Isaac," Mobious said as he stood back up. "I believe I am ready to head to your monastery. Given the location, I would like to offer you the use of my teleportation magic, so that you and I can arrive there and begin my trials as soon as we can. I should be ready to go within an hour or two. Will that work for you?"

Brother Isaac stood up and bowed. "Normally I would say you're a bit impatient, Lord Mobious. However, ever since the change in the land happened, I have been anxious to return to my home to see my Brothers. If your teleportation spell can also teleport my horse and carriage, I will gladly accept your offer."

"If my teleportation spell can't teleport everything that you need, then I would be a novice wizard." Mobious smiled as he led Brother Isaac outside the study. Soon he would have the power to resurrect his wife and daughter. Brother Isaac was just a means to an end. Once Mobious was done with the monk and his Order, he would dispose of them.

The morning air had a chill to it. Ayleen stood in front of her parents' graves. It had been awhile since she had visited these graves, but she didn't know what else to do. The graveyard itself was oddly quiet. She thought, due to the recent events, there would be at least one or two funerals taking place. Maybe volunteers had helped bury people after the New Year's Eve disaster. There were so many, and the staff here would need help. This was the sixth morning after the event. Part of Ayleen was grateful for being alone with her parents.

"Hello, Mother, hello, Father, it's Ayleen." She began talking to the graves. "Over the last few days a lot has happened, and I don't know how to proceed. I have a lead on the suspect, but until my informant can confirm he's the one who caused the disaster, I can't really act on anything. I just wonder what you would do, Father. You were always able to catch your suspect, or at least that was what you told me. I just wish you and Mother were here to help me through this situation."

As she talked to the graves, she felt someone come up behind her. At first, she thought it was another mourner. There were plenty of people buried in this graveyard, since it was the continent's most prominent. Her calm demeanour disappeared as soon as she felt a knife touching her back. She had dealt with this kind of situation before. She lost count of how many times a criminal had threatened her.

Ayleen raised her hands. She wanted information from this would-be assassin before she would take him down. "What do you want? If you wanted me dead, you would have killed me already. Did you not realize who I am?"

"Ayleen Ebella, Captain of Investigation," the assassin said. Now

Ayleen knew that this was a male; from where the voice was coming from, slightly taller than her. "My employer wants you to stop your investigation. If I don't convince you to stop, I am going to have to kill you. While I'm fine with that, killing a high-ranking officer of the law comes with the problem of having every officer on the continent after me. I'd prefer for that not to happen."

Ayleen slowly adjusted her stance to deal with the assassin. One wrong move and she would die. She had to move quickly without giving her intentions away. She took a step forward, whirled around to face the killer, and grabbed his knife hand with her left hand. With her right hand, she blocked his left-hand blow and kneed him in the groin. She forced him backwards and landed with both knees on his chest, winding him. She then slipped her knees off his chest and onto his arms, pinning them. She pulled out her own knife and held it to his throat. With the assassin on the ground, she could now tell that he had blue skin and shaved white hair.

Ayleen had to learn who sent the assassin to kill her. She had suspected it was Mobious, but had to make sure that she did not have another enemy. "Okay, now, you listen to me! By attacking the Queen's investigator, I have every right under the law to end your life! So, you are going to answer every question I have. Or Terra help me, I will plunge my dagger up through your throat and into your skull! Who hired you, and why?"

The assassin had a smirk on his face. "I don't know if you know this, but it's generally not polite for assassins to give away their employer's name. I'll never talk. I don't care if you kill me here because I will be dead by the end of the hour anyway for failing. I'd rather you kill me, than my employer."

Ayleen snarled at the man, "Maybe you didn't understand your situation. I have you pinned down, so you are going to answer every question I have or maybe I will just arrest you and wait for your employer to try to kill you. So, start talking! Was it Lord Mobious that hired you or was it someone else?"

The shock on the assassin's face told Ayleen that it was Mobious who hired the assassin. Clearly, he wasn't as good as he thought he was. "I will never tell you who hired me. You can torture me all you want."

Ayleen stabbed the assassin's knife-wielding hand and took his knife, as the assassin yelled and cursed. "Go back to your master and tell him you failed. Also, tell him that I will be coming after him. If you attack me again, you're dead. I have enough combat training to take out two or three assassins at once, and you're just not that good."

The assassin stood up and produced another knife in his left hand; he tried to attack Ayleen. She knew that the assassin would try to kill her again, which was why she was prepared with both his first knife and her own. As the assassin lunged at her, she dodged and plunged her dagger into his side and then got him in the back with the other knife. This was the part of the job she hated but understood that events like this happen every day in the field. He fell to the ground coughing and spewing blood.

"Thank you," he moaned. Then he died.

She had come to the graveyard for spiritual strength. Instead, she had an encounter with an assassin that seemed to confirm that Mobious was involved in the meteorite and the attack of the creatures. Why? She still didn't know. While she knew any evidence of the attack would be gone by now. She had a feeling she should go back to where this all began to see if she had missed anything. If nothing, it would confirm what she already knew.

Outside his manor, Mobious helped Brother Isaac prepare his horse and carriage for the teleportation spell. His goal was nearing completion. In a few moments, he would be at the monastery and one step closer to the Cube of Destiny. Before he could open the portal to the monastery, his butler, Jorrard came out to the courtyard signalling Mobious that he wished to speak to him.

"Brother Isaac, if you would excuse me for a moment, there is a matter I must attend to." Brother Isaac nodded. Mobious walked to his butler to make sure that Brother Isaac couldn't hear. "What do you want? I told you that I'm occupied with Brother Isaac at the moment. I don't have time for minor problems."

"Sorry, Master," Jorrard said hurriedly. "However, there are two issues that need your attention before you go. First, we have a new servant joining us in a matter of hours. I would like to know where he is to be stationed."

"Just put him anywhere we need. I don't care," Mobious angrily told the butler. "You told me there were two problems. What was the other problem? If it's as minor as your first problem, don't bother me with such pettiness."

"The gem you told me to watch has stopped glowing," the butler informed his master. Mobious knew what this meant, and he was furious. He had hired an assassin to either stop Ayleen's investigation or to kill her. He also put a spell on the assassin to tell if he had succeeded or failed. With the gem no longer glowing, he knew that the assassin he hired had failed. That bastard said he was the best!

"Get out of my sight now!" Mobious snarled quietly at Jorrard. He knew that he couldn't take out his rage on the butler while in the company of Brother Isaac. He turned around and stormed over to rejoin the monk. "Forgive me, Brother Isaac, there was a problem I had to deal with before we go."

"That is quite all right, Lord Mobious," Brother Isaac said as he finished preparing his horse for the journey. "Are you ready to summon a portal? I must be honest with you. This is the first time I have ever travelled via teleportation. I'm kind of nervous."

"There is nothing to be nervous about, Brother Isaac," Mobious told the monk as he opened a portal to the monastery. Mobious had already learned the location of the monastery earlier; it was in the Northwest. He had to choose the destination carefully due to the hot nature of the destination. Once the portal was open, the two men hopped on Brother Isaac's carriage and rode the whole thing through the portal.

Brother Isaac had told Mobious that before the events of New Year's Eve, this part of the continent was heavily forested and mountainous. The monastery used to be covered by vines and surrounded by a thick forest but now a moat of lava surrounded the monastery. Mobious was told that this was a place that the monks felt like they could hide their monastery and the Cube.

As the two men wound their way from the portal over a newly created bridge that crossed the lava moat, Mobious felt anxious. He was so close to his goal. His only worry was he had no idea how powerful the monks were in the art of magic, if at all. He barely knew anything about these monks since there was next to no information available. The only information he had was from his friend, Professor T'mass and even he wasn't sure about the information he had gathered. Only time would tell if Mobious could successfully leave the monastery with the Cube. He knew that he would die trying and take everyone that tried to stop him with him.

V

CHAPTER

AYLEEN CHOSE TO hire a local wizard to open a portal to Thaldor to avoid the two-day ride back to the Tree. She knew that all the evidence from the site of the attack was already collected or compromised. However, she had a feeling deep within her soul that she needed to return there. She had no idea if Terra was guiding her or if it was her own instincts. She parked her horse and carriage in Thaldor and walked to the meteorite site. If there was any more evidence to be found there, she didn't want her horse to disturb it. She did not expect to see any new evidence though; it would be too late for that. She just came here to confirm what she knew and to satisfy herself that all the evidence had been gathered.

Another reason why she came here was to get her mind away from the fact that someone just tried to kill her hours ago. There had been plenty of people that had decided to try and take her life in the past. This time, however, it was the first time that someone had paid an assassin to kill her. Assassins weren't uncommon in Giana, but they were usually used by nobles with plenty of money and desire to climb the royal hierarchy. She had no proof who sent the assassin but was disturbed by the fact that an assassin would kill anyone outside the nobility. This was the downside of working alone on a case; she had no one watching her back.

As she entered the clearing where the sacred tree used to be, she expected to see the meteorite still floating above the ground. To her amazement instead of a meteorite, there was a brand-new full-grown tree in its place; same size! She ran towards the new tree to examine it closer. The Tree itself was divided into three sections, each with its own colour and unique features. The first section she saw was black and purple bark with leaves that reminded her of smoke and shadows. As she moved counter-clockwise, the Tree changed and looked like the bark was frozen; white with blue and ice crystals forming where leaves should be. As she continued around the Tree, the bark looked as if it was made of lava with tongues of flame for leaves. She studied the ground where the Tree stood, and on each side of the Tree the ground matched the Tree and spread out over the continent. She called on her druid knowledge to determine everything she could about this tree.

This four-day-old tree had the appearance of a tree that looks a thousand years old or older. This both amazed and frightened Ayleen. Druids would use magic to restore trees that had been damaged or cut down by people. If the tree were destroyed by nature, druids would not be allowed to restore the tree. Ayleen put her palm on the tree in the purple section to feel if the tree had been grown using nature magic. As soon as she touched the Tree, she had to immediately pull her hand back. The magic radiating off the Tree was not part of the nature magic family but of one of the many dark forms of magic.

Part of her was glad the Tree was back, but not this way! Not with dark magic! She didn't know enough about the dark arts to identify which kind of magic it was. She wondered if the dark magic that was coming off the Tree was the reason why elves were acting differently, but in her heart, she knew that this change allowed them to show their true nature.

Her train of thought was interrupted by the argument of three men. Ayleen had forgotten whether she had seen them as she had entered the clearing. Each one of the men was a different colour. She recognized the purple one as Laeroth Waesmaer, an Earl in charge of a small town far to the South of the continent. The only reason she had heard of this Earl is that the local guard was called to his home after he drunkenly hit his wife. As for the other two, Ayleen assumed that they were part of his drinking party.

"Laeroth, I implore you to shut up," the red-skinned elf said as Ayleen began to listen in on the conversation. "You damn well know that you do not have a hope in the world with the Princess. You may be a noble, but you're literally the lowest type of noble on the continent. Even the High Priestess gets more respect than you."

"I believe you are wrong, Landmar," Laeroth shouted back at the orange-skinned elf. Ayleen could tell that the Earl was very drunk which was typical. "See, you two I may accept that you are low-level nobles, but if I act like a high-ranking noble, maybe the Princess will be so impressed with me that she will have no choice but to marry me. You agree with me, don't you, Jeven?"

"That literally made no sense at all," the blue-skinned elf replied. "Even if that remotely made sense, you realize that the Princess wants to kick out every blue-and-orange-skinned elf in the Southern part of the continent. That means that Landmar and I can't go drinking with you anymore. Also, what happens to our village if you leave? Who will run it? Not only that, you are already married! Or did you hit her again and she finally left?"

"Jeven is right, Laeroth." Landmar was clearly annoyed. "The very idea of you siding with the Princess goes against everything that our little village stands for. It may be the alcohol talking, but I think you should reconsider before you have to rule over an empty town."

"If you two were really my friends you would agree with me," the Earl slurred. "Everyone in my town that doesn't have purple skin are the ones that don't work: that includes you two losers. You just hang out with me so that I can buy your drinks. Well, I am sick and tired of being used like that. In fact, you can get out of my town now and don't come back with me."

The drunken Earl staggered off towards Thaldor as Landmar and Jeven stared at the man, confused as to what just happened.

Ayleen approached the two elves to ask them why they were in this area so soon after a disaster. "Excuse me, I am Captain Ebella, and I was just wondering why you three were here, given the circumstances."

Landmar and Jeven turned around to make eye contact with Ayleen. She could see that they were surprised by her appearance on the field. She imagined that they also thought they were alone in this field, like she had believed she was. Jeven was the one who started to talk first. "Sorry, Captain, we used to be the friends of that piece of trash that just walked off. And if he really meant what he said, we are now homeless."

"Our former friend wanted to see the meteorite that we had told him about," Landmar added. "We tried to convince him not to ingest any more alcohol on our trip, but that worked as well as teaching a fish to walk. Is there anything we can help you with, Captain?"

"Gentlemen, I am investigating the events of New Year's Eve. I don't know yet if it is safe for you to be in this area. I'm going to have to ask you to move along," Ayleen told the men. "Unless one of you has any knowledge of anything you might have seen or heard the night of the incident."

Landmar and Jeven looked at each other. Jeven gave a quick nod to Landmar. Landmar took a deep breath. "Captain, while I don't have anything to report about the night itself, I know a little bit about magic. A little less than a year ago, my cousin was asked to send thirteen giant diamonds to an estate in the Northeast. Thirteen! The buyer asked my cousin to deliver the diamonds within forty-eight hours. I only ever thought that the Queen had that much money. Don't major magical spells require thirteen ingredients? Was it a spell that brought down the meteorite?"

Something in Ayleen's mind clicked. Demonic magic users used giant diamonds to store one soul per diamond. If whoever cast the spell used souls as ingredients, then he or she would never run out of magic as they could use the souls repeatedly. Ignoring his question, Ayleen had to find out if Landmar knew anything more. "Did your cousin ever give you the name of his client?"

"Let me think." Landmar scratched his head for a moment. "I think the name was Linda Dobious? No, that's not right. Oh, I remember now. It was Linda Mobious. That sounds right."

"Lindar?" Ayleen retorted.

Landmar nodded. "That's it! Lindar! Seriously, who names their daughter Lindar!"

Ayleen had been sure it was Lindar Mobious, but now she had confirmation. She had to investigate this information further. She bid farewell to Landmar and Jeven after asking for the cousin's name and then asked them to leave the area as soon as they could. The two men agreed and left the field where the meteorite had been; now replaced by a tree. Two questions raced through Ayleen's mind. Was Mobious planning any more attacks? And, what type of dark magic was radiating off the Tree?

Tyran sat on a bench in the park, waiting for Klep to arrive. He was very annoyed at this moment. Klep said he would meet Tyran in six hours. It had been ten. The amount of Tyran's time Klep had wasted was enough time to hire his own wizard and portal to Mobious' estate by himself. The only good part about waiting this long for Klep was that Tyran managed to get his nerves under control. Unlike any other day, the park was very quiet. When Klep finally arrived, the sun had been up for several hours.

"You said six hours, Klep!" Tyran yelled at the man. He saw that Klep had brought another person along with him. A purple-skinned man Tyran assumed to be a wizard. "What took you so long? Didn't I make it clear how urgent this was? It's nearly noon!"

"Don't get your shorts in a knot," grunted Klep. "I had to contact my friend at Lord Mobious' estate and find a wizard that knew how to teleport people not just messages. I also had to find one who wouldn't make me to go bankrupt. I would have been here sooner except for the fact that my mistress caught me walking out of Madam Charlottine's. That argument lasted two hours in and of itself. Don't worry, I will make it up to you."

"Fine. Just let's get this over with," Tyran snarled. Klep gave the wizard a nod. Within seconds a flash of light appeared and disappeared. There in front of them was a portal to Mobious' estate. Tyran and Klep stepped through the portal as the wizard kept it open waiting for Klep's return. On the other side, three blue-skinned elves waited for the pair. In the centre of the group of three stood a man six-foot-tall wearing a butler's uniform. The two standing on either side of him were young ladies dressed in maid's outfits.

"You are lucky I don't punch you right here and now, Klep," the butler stated. "The last time we met, I do believe you said you would pay me back my two hundred gold pieces. Here we are three years later and no repayment, but you managed to talk me into helping you again. I must be a saint or an idiot."

"I have your money here, Jorrard," Klep said as he gave the butler a sack. "I am so grateful that you are willing to do this for me. This is my good friend, Tyran Dori. He is so excited to work for Lord Mobious that he begged me to get him a job here as soon as possible. That is why I was in a rush when I spoke to you through a portal earlier."

"I hope your friend is more reliable than you," Jorrard sneered then he shifted his gaze towards Tyran. "Mr. Dori, why are you interested in serving Lord Mobious? I assume you have the necessary skills I will require. I just hope you're not trying to pull a fast one on me by trying to get a job you are not qualified for."

"I can assure you, sir, that I'm a good worker." Tyran had to pick his words carefully. He didn't want the butler to know why he was really there. "I was a minor servant in the royal palace before the meteorite hit. I worked alongside my brother in the kitchen, prepping food for the cook. My brother and I had the day off on New Year's Eve. We both went to the celebration at the centre of the continent. However, my brother did not survive the night and working at the palace just brings back painful memories."

Tyran gave Klep a look that told him to keep quiet. Klep knew that Tyran had just lied to Jorrard but knew Tyran well enough to support him. One of the maids had tears running down her cheeks. Tyran suspected that she had lost someone in the attack as well. Jorrard remained motionless as he pondered Tyran's story. Tyran hoped that Jorrard bought into his lie.

"Mr. Dori, I am so sorry for your loss," Jorrard said casually. "Miss Cholwell here has also lost someone recently. She found out that her sister passed away under mysterious circumstances a couple months ago. Since you have experience with kitchen duties, I am going to have you partner with Miss Cholwell. As the kitchen is in her part of the house, she is responsible for cleaning; she will familiarize you with the area so you don't get lost."

"Thank you, sir," Tyran said. "I will try to work my hardest to please you and Master Mobious. Klep, I want to thank you for getting me here. You are such a good friend. I will contact you if I need anything else."

Tyran had to force himself to keep himself from vomiting when he called Mobious 'Master'. He wanted to be here, but he was unhappy about his fake job. The thought of working for Mobious offended him, but he knew it was the only way to find out if he was connected to the attack.

Tyran bid Klep farewell. The two men shook hands, then Klep walked back through the portal. It closed behind him. Jorrard told Tyran to follow him and the maids. While the four of them were heading to the manor, Tyran found himself walking beside Miss Cholwell while Jorrard and the other maid walked ahead of them.

"Mr. Dori, I want to say how sorry I am for your loss,." Miss Cholwell said demurely, not looking at Tyran at all. "It was very hard on me when I learned my sister had committed suicide. As we are working together, I would appreciate it if you would address me by my first name, Zalissa. Feel free to talk to me about anything you want."

"Thank you, Zalissa," Tyran replied. He had a feeling that Zalissa would be a great asset to his investigation, but he needed to earn her trust. "Tell me, do you enjoy working here? I know this area was beautiful before the meteorite hit. I feel a bit out of place here. This is only my second time seeing ice and snow."

"That is understandable," Zalissa said, still not looking at Tyran. "The staff of the house are still getting used to the changes. It's a little easier for me because I grew up in the mountains where we would get some snow in winter. As for the estate, before the meteorite hit, it was indeed one of the most beautiful places on the continent. The meteorite wasn't the only event that changed the estate. Just over a year ago, the master's wife and daughter died of the plague. Everyone working here was in mourning."

Tyran had heard about Mobious' wife and daughter. He would have felt sorry for Mobious if he didn't suspect that he was behind the disaster. Tyran had also lost someone to the plague, but not many people knew about him. The lie he told to Jorrard wasn't a complete lie. His brother did die; not because of the attack but because of the plague. Even Ayleen didn't know that Tyran had a brother and he wanted to keep it that way. For the rest of the morning, Tyran followed Zalissa around as she instructed him on the layout of his section of the estate. It would only be a matter of time before Tyran earned everyone's trust and found the information that he needed.

Before Ayleen booked a portal back to the capital, she decided to inspect her carriage. To her surprise, she found that half of her rations were missing. Usually, she would be furious at this revelation, but because of the events of the past several days, this was the least of her worries. She had enough food for a couple days but not enough food if she was delayed. She debated about staying in the area and going for a quick hunt, but she needed to get back to the capital to follow up on some leads.

"Really, Terra! You want me to learn a lesson at a time like this?" Ayleen said to herself. "I do not have time to be delayed. What should I do now? Fine. I'll head into the woods, kill a few hares and be back within an hour. Then, find a wizard to portal me back home."

She rode the carriage to the edge of the woods in hopes that being out of the city meant it wouldn't be ransacked again. Before she could climb off the carriage, a little girl no older than ten years old ran out of the woods screaming for help. What was a little girl doing out here all alone? She ran to the orange-skinned little girl. "Are you all right? What happened?"

"My mommy had a tree fall on top of her!" the little girl cried. "Please, miss, you've got to help her. I have been running in the same direction trying to find someone, and you're the first person I've seen. Please, you've got to help me save my mommy."

"All right, direct me to your mother," Ayleen replied to the girl as the girl ran in the direction she had come from. While Ayleen needed to head back to the capital, she couldn't let another elf die on her watch.

Ayleen followed the little girl back into the woods to a spot where white-ish blue trees met up with purple trees. The girl ran to a fallen tree where Ayleen saw the mother under it. Looking at the situation, she wanted to make sure that moving the tree off the woman was safe to do. If she was crushed, moving the tree would kill her instantly. If there were other items propping the tree up a bit, she could help her out and check for injuries.

"Mommy, I found someone to help you," the little girl cried, tears still in her eyes.

"Hello, ma'am," Ayleen said as she knelt down to see the woman's face. Like the little girl, she also had orange skin and red hair. To Ayleen's assessment of the situation, the woman looked as if she would be fine if Ayleen could just move the tree enough for her to wiggle out. "Before I try to move the tree, I have to ask do you feel numb anywhere? Do you feel any pain at the moment?"

"No, ma'am, I think I'm all right, just pinned," the mother of little girl replied. With that confirmation, Ayleen felt that it was safe to move the tree from on top of the woman. First, she used her knife to cut away some of the smaller branches.

Ayleen asked the little girl to step back a couple of feet as Ayleen grasped the tree trunk and barely lifted it to allow the mother to crawl out from underneath. Ayleen let go of the tree as soon as the mother's feet were clear. Holding the tree felt like minutes for Ayleen when it was only seconds. The weight of the tree was about the maximum weight she could lift, but a surge of energy added to her strength. When she turned around to check if the woman was all right, she saw the little girl embracing her mother with the tightest hug Ayleen had ever seen.

"You should be proud of that little girl," Ayleen remarked. "She ran a whole five minutes through dense woods to find me. I am Captain Ebella of the Investigation Department. I just want to know what you were doing out here in the woods, and how did the tree fall on you?"

The woman stood up and leaned on her daughter. "First of all, thank you, Captain, for saving me. The reason I was out here with my daughter is we were hunting for food, and I got careless and ran after a deer. I didn't pay attention to my surroundings and didn't realize that the tree was ready to fall. While I was under the tree, a purple-skinned elf staggered by and ignored my cries for help. He was clearly drunk, but I thought he would go for help."

Ayleen realized it was the drunken Earl she saw earlier, but this attitude from purple-skinned elves made her ashamed to be one. She didn't know how many elves would help those of different skin colour. Part of her didn't want to know, but she knew she was destined to find out. She decided not to mention any of this to the huntress or her daughter. It was not their problem.

"We all make mistakes," Ayleen commented. "Maybe next time you should bring a second adult with you just in case this happens again. When hunting, there is never such a thing as being too safe."

"You're probably right, Captain," the huntress said. "Allow me to repay you. My camp is another ten minutes into the forest, and my daughter and I have caught enough meat to spare. Please come and take some as repayment for my mistake."

As much as Ayleen wanted to refuse the woman's offer, she knew that she had to have more food for the trip she knew she'd probably be taking to the Mobious estate. She was betting he wouldn't show up to the next meeting and be conveniently interrogated.

. When the three of them got to the camp, the woman handed Ayleen a pair of rabbits. Now Ayleen knew she could not make it back to the capital today as she still needed to hire a wizard and it was getting late. With the gift she had received from the huntress she wouldn't need to hunt for her dinner, but it was more likely she'd be staying in Thaldor.

Then Ayleen had a thought. Perhaps she should spend another day in Thaldor. Perhaps with this new information, she should re-interview the families of the thirteen victims. Perhaps they would remember something that would strengthen her case again Mobious. She could still be in the capital in time for the second meeting to convene.

Mobious sat in the chambers of the Abbot of the Monastery of the Cube. While waiting for the Abbot, Mobious contemplated how he would take the Cube from the monastery. He knew that he had to complete the trials to even touch the Cube. If everything Professor T'mass told him was true, then the Abbot would know the most about the Cube of Destiny and every vision that the Cube had. Mobious hoped that the Cube didn't see how many people he had murdered. As he pondered this the door of the Abbot's chambers opened and in walked an elderly, balding orange-skinned elf. Without saying a word, the Abbot offered Mobious a glass of wine. When Mobious accepted, the Abbot sat in a chair across from him.

"Lord Lindar Mobious, it is interesting to finally meet you," the Abbot greeted Mobious. "My name is Father Marick, and it's my duty to welcome you to the Brotherhood of the Cube. Please feel free to ask me any questions. Your first trial will begin tomorrow morning."

"Thank you, Father Marick, I'm eager to start," Mobious replied. "I do have a few questions. Brother Isaac answered most of my questions, but I have a few more that I feel only you could answer."

"I'm assuming that one of your questions is, why we have let a serial killer into our monastery?" Father Marick said dryly to Mobious' shock. "Don't worry, Lord Mobious, I have no intention of handing you over to the authorities. The Cube itself asked me to allow you into our home. It believes that you will be a valuable part of the events to come. Let me assure you though, if it were just up to me, I would have imprisoned you the moment you arrived. While you are in my monastery, I expect you to follow our rules."

Mobious' mind raced. As surprised as he was that the Father knew of his past deeds, he was more surprised that the Cube itself wanted him here. For what purpose, he had no idea. First a Time Magic master trying to use him, now a Cube? "Father Marick, I promise you that I will not harm you or any of your brothers while I am here. I am curious though, as to why the Cube wants me to be in this monastery when it knows what I've done to get here."

"I'm unable to answer why the Cube wants you here," Father Marick stated. "I do know that the Cube has a plan for you. What it is, I have no idea, but it had requested me to allow you to take the three trials. To be completely honest, I don't think you are worthy enough to complete the first trial, but you may prove me to be wrong. That's all I will say on this matter, but if you have any other questions, I will answer them to the best of my ability."

"I do have two questions," Mobious continued. "I noticed you called your order the Brotherhood of the Cube. I find it a little odd that there is a religious order with all men in the continent of Giana, when the temple of Terra has only females as attendants. Are you not worshippers of Terra?"

"Great observation, Lord Mobious." Father Marick took a sip of his wine before continuing. "To be completely honest, there have been a few female members of the monastery, however, most of the time when the Cube finds a worthy female member they are immediately taken by the temple of Terra and trained to be a priestess. As for our religious affiliation, most of us pray to the first god. No one remembers his or her name, but since the Cubes of Destiny were created by the first god, that is the god we choose to worship."

"Interesting," commented Mobious. "My last question is how much of the Cube's visions do you relay to the Queen?"

"Only the visions that the Cube tells us to," Father Marick replied as he stood up. "Like I said, you have no reason to worry about your past crimes. I took a vow to obey every word the Cube says. Now, if you have no more questions, we will have dinner and then retire for the evening. In the morning, we start your trial so that you can leave my monastery as soon as possible."

Mobious nodded and stood up from the chair he was sitting in. Father Marick led Mobious out of his chambers and through what felt like a maze of corridors. Their journey passed by a pair of gold-plated doors. Mobious paused in front of the doors; he noticed how massive the doors were. Mobious felt a little bit intimidated by the size of the doors, but he had come this far to claim the Cube. He wondered what tomorrow would hold.

Duke Edwin Morgwyn waited outside the chambers of Princess Dariusa, as requested. Last time he saw her, it was a week before New Year's. He was worried that she had heard about his performance at the council meeting and would think he should have done more, spoke up more. Would she select another duke to be her husband when she became Queen? Edwin knew that there was another duke the Princess had considered, but he was orange now. Orange! With a deep breath, he knocked on the Princess' chamber door.

Seconds later, the Princess opened the door and smiled at the Duke. Edwin nearly made a fool of himself when he saw that the Princess answered the door in her nightwear. The Princess had asked him to come to her chambers at this late of an hour for a discussion. He had no idea that this discussion would involve the Princess wearing a see-through nightie, not that he minded. Dariusa took the Duke by his hand and led him to her bed. They both sat on the bed, looking at each other. Edwin felt like it was his duty to start the conversation.

"Your Highness, when you asked me to meet with you, I wasn't expecting this kind of encounter," Edwin said as he gulped. "How can I be of service to you, my future Queen?"

"Depending on how this conversation goes, you may get what I know you're thinking about," Dariusa answered smugly. "Tell me, Edwin, how bad do you want to become my husband? Would you do anything I asked of you? Or if I asked something you disagree with, would you betray me?"

The Duke was taken aback by this question. What was Dariusa talking about? "Your Highness, I would obey any order you gave as if you were already my Queen. Even now, I would obey you and do anything you ask. I give you my word. I am loyal to you and only to you."

"That's a good boy," the Princess simpered as she stroked Edwin's face. "There is something I need your help with. But if we do not do this carefully, I will be charged with treason and won't be able to obtain the throne. Are you willing to risk being executed with me, my love?"

"I would risk death or dismemberment for you, Dariusa!" Edwin stated, still completely bewildered. With the way the Princess was dressed and was acting, he assumed that she wanted him to take her virginity before marriage. Those devoted to the goddess, Terra, would not allow sex before marriage but Terra would allow for a couple to consummate once they were engaged to each other. In Terra's eyes, an engagement was a pledge to marry and that kind of pledge was not to be broken.

"I need your help overthrowing my mother," Dariusa answered

in a sultry voice. "She doesn't realize that the old way of the elves died when the change occurred. If we continue to live alongside the blue-and-orange-skinned elves, there would be fighting in the streets. Brother will turn on brother, and our great kingdom will be torn apart. If you can do this for me, Edwin, I will accept your proposal here and now and we can rule the new kingdom together."

"Do you have a plan in mind, my love?" Edwin asked. "If you don't, may I suggest we find a way to discredit your mother. It will be the simplest method of taking the throne from her and it will not cause any needless bloodshed, nor will it reflect on us."

"Oh Edwin, don't you worry about that. I have everything under control," Dariusa replied. "I have recently acquired a potion that, when taken, my mother will be susceptible to suggestion. All I need you to do is gather one final ingredient tomorrow morning. This way it can't possibly be linked to me. After my mother drinks the potion I will ask her to start rounding up the blue-and-orange-skinned elves and send them into exile in the mountains to the North. The civilians will no longer trust her after she does this. Then the Council of Dukes will make me the new Queen."

Edwin had to think about this for a moment. What the Princess was asking him to do was definitely treason, but he agreed that the Queen was doing nothing to solve the continent's problem, yet again. "You ask me to do a huge favour for you. I hope you realize that if this goes south, everyone who is involved with this will be an enemy of the kingdom. I think you already understand that and that is why I will accept helping you overthrow your mother. I can't sit back and watch as Terra's chosen elves are being hurt every day by those blue and orange heretics."

"I couldn't agree more, Edwin." Dariusa kissed the Duke on the lips. "I want this transition of power to be as fast and peaceful as possible. I admit there might be some casualties, but they will all be the ones that are blinded by my mother's incompetence. That is a worry for tomorrow. Tonight, we celebrate our engagement."

The two purple-skinned lovers embraced. Soon the continent would change for the better, Dariusa thought. She knew that she could use

Edwin to do whatever she wanted. Once she was crowned Queen and had her first daughter, she could kill Edwin if he was no longer useful. If Edwin gave her a son, she would kill the child and blame his death on Edwin. She had heard legends that the goddess, Terra, always had a demi-god in the realm of mortals. A woman that would be able to use the goddess' power. Princess Dariusa was convinced that her first-born daughter would be the next demi-god and she wanted the demi-god to be the Queen after her. What a perfect world it would be!

After a modest breakfast, Mobious was ready to start the first trial. Father Marick had collected him and led him back to the massive gold doors. He was instructed to go in and wait for the Cube to acknowledge him. The massive door was heavy as he pulled it open.

Mobious entered a pitch-black room as the door closed behind him. The only light source there, was at the centre of the room emanating from the Cube itself. Finally, Mobious had come face to face with the Cube of Destiny. Mobious could see that the Cube itself was made from gold with unknown inscriptions on the sides of the Cube. He circled the Cube, studying the symbols. As Professor T'mass had stated in his report, each side of the Cube was exactly fifteen centimetres in length and height. Mobious stopped back in front of the Cube, not knowing what would happen as he waited.

"Lindar Mobious, put your hand on me," a thousand voices commanded. Mobious had no idea where these voices were coming from. He assumed it was the Cube talking but couldn't be sure.

"Are these the voices of the Cube?" Mobious asked. "I would like to know what this first trial entails before I submit to it."

There was moment of silence before the Cube repeated, "Lindar Mobious, put your hand on me!"

Obviously, Mobious wasn't going to get an answer. He slowly moved his hand towards the Cube, unsure what was to happen next. The second his hand connected with the Cube a jolt of energy surged through his hand and down his body. The electricity caused his muscles to contract and kept him connected to the Cube. As soon as one jolt passed through his body, another jolt was released from the Cube. Mobious thought that he could use his magic to ease the pain, but there was no way he could focus on a spell. Even if he could concentrate, his jaws were clenched, and he was unable to speak the incantation. How could he survive six hours of this?

When he became more used to the pain, memories began to flood his mind replaying each and every physical injury he had ever experienced. Everything from a simple paper cut to the time when he broke his leg as a child. The pain was so much that he wanted to cry to release the tension, but even that part of his body was paralyzed. He had no idea how long he had been standing there. To him, it had already felt like six hours had gone by, but he knew that was an illusion.

When the Cube finally released him, he collapsed to the floor. He felt as if days had gone by. Whether he was being tortured for the full six hours, he couldn't say. He had to take a few deep breaths to gather himself before he could move.

"Leave now!" the Cube shouted. "Return to Father Marick and rest. The next trial starts tomorrow."

Mobious was grateful that he was going to get a night's rest before the second trial. He didn't know if he could pass the other two trials in his current state. At least his memory was still intact. He got up off the floor and made his way to where he thought the door was. He left the chamber of the Cube and saw Father Marick waiting on the other side of the large golden doors.

"That was intense," Mobious said, shaking slightly. "Was I truly in there for only six hours? It felt like six days."

"I assure you, Lord Mobious, you were only in the chamber for six hours, as discussed," chuckled Father Marick. "If it were up to me, I would have loved to have seen you suffer longer, for all the crimes you have committed. But as I said before, I cannot disobey the Cube's orders, and it has ordered me to keep you safe. Now, let me show you to your room so you can rest before dinner. You have only completed the first and easiest trial of the Cube."

Father Marick led Mobious back to his room in the monastery. As Mobious entered the room, Father Marick shut the door behind him and left Mobious to himself. He collapsed on the bed immediately. He was too tired to care that his room for the night was barely bigger than the average prison cell. There was only one thought going through Mobious' mind. If what he had just experienced was the easiest trial that the Cube had, how in Terra's name was he going to survive the other two?

VI

CHAPTER

ARLY IN THE morning, Tyran awoke in his new bedchamber. He had an hour until his shift started so he had a little time before Zalissa arrived to take him to the kitchen. After he got into his new uniform, he decided to take a quick walk around the grounds where Jorrard told him he could wander. He didn't want to go into any restricted areas yet. He needed to scout the space to figure out how to enter the restricted rooms without being caught by Mobious' personal guard. Half an hour into his walk, he noticed two muscular men guarding a building that was not attached to the main house. He almost debated on trying to get a glimpse into the building when he felt a tap on his shoulder.

Tyran almost jumped two feet off the ground. He turned around to find out who had sneaked up behind him. He came face to face with Zalissa. He didn't figure she would be out here at this time, but he knew he had to cover up why he was looking at the room. "Zalissa, you almost scared me half to death."

"I just was wondering why you were looking at the restricted building," Zalissa asked Tyran. "That is Master Mobious' ritual chambers. We are not allowed anywhere near that building."

"It is?" Tyran had to think fast. "I got totally lost out here. I was doing my morning exercises, and I forgot which part of the estate was off limits. Please forgive me and don't tell Jorrard."

"Don't worry. I won't tell him this time." Zalissa had bought Tyran's story. "To be honest with you, the first week I was here I got lost so many times that the other maid had to cover for me to prevent the wrath of Master Mobious. Now, Tyran, if you will be kind enough to follow me, I'll take you to the kitchen. There are a lot of rules the cook will need to teach you before you can officially start working."

Zalissa began to walk away, assuming Tyran would follow her. While he was following her, he noticed that she was not paying much attention to whether he was following or not. He could have wandered off, and she would not have seen until they arrived at the kitchen. However, he wanted to gain the woman's trust. When the pair entered the kitchen, Tyran had to control his reaction. This kitchen was the fanciest one he had ever been in but he did not want Zalissa to see how awed he was.

"As you can clearly see, this is the kitchen," Zalissa stated as she turned to face Tyran. "This is probably not as fancy a kitchen as you are used to. I am sure the one in the palace is a lot more lavish. Your job is to make sure everything in this room is clean, at all times. You will be cleaning dishes, washing the sinks, then the counters and finally the floor. Be sure to stay out of the way of the bakers and cooks. Nedu is the chief cook and will tell you the rules as you work today. Any questions?"

"I have one question, but it's a little off topic," Tyran said as he waited for her to nod in approval. "What exactly was that room that I saw before you crept up behind me? What is a ritual chamber?"

"I guess it couldn't hurt to answer that question." Zalissa sighed. "That is where he conducts all his magical experiments and keeps many magical objects. Therefore it is separate from the main building and for our safety, we are not allowed anywhere near that building. If you don't have any more questions, let us begin our duties."

Tyran did not have any more questions for Zalissa. He followed her instructions to a tee to make sure that she thought of him as a reliable worker. Mobious' ritual chambers were still on his mind as he worked.

He knew he had to get in there somehow. If Mobious was indeed the mastermind of the attack a few nights ago, then the evidence must be in that building.

As the day wore on, Tyran caught himself constantly looking at Zalissa every time their paths crossed. He knew this meant he was attracted to her, and this was a cause for concern. Every woman he fell in love with, he ended up hurting. Last time he fell in love was with a Duke's daughter, and that did not end well. This time he knew his job would make him untrustworthy or dead if he were ever caught. For both their sakes, Tyran hoped that his feelings towards Zalissa did not develop any further. He was determined to squash them.

Morning in the castle was quiet. Not many servants were working as this was the holy day of the week. This allowed Princess Dariusa to concoct the potion without anyone seeing her. She sat in the dining hall, waiting for Duke Edwin Morgwyn to deliver the final ingredient to her. Alone in the room, she reflected on what she was about to do. Her heart beat a little faster in anticipation. She knew she had to dethrone her mother because her mother couldn't see that the other two races of elves were inferior.

The Duke arrived at the exact time the Princess had told him. It was a long walk to where the Princess was waiting due to how large the dining room was. It was one of the biggest rooms in the castle. Sometimes holding up to five hundred guests. As Edwin approached Dariusa, she gestured for him to sit across from her.

"I have the ingredient you asked for, my love," the Duke said as he sat down. "Never realized how expensive fairy blood is. I'll be honest, I have never seen a fairy myself. I'm glad I have never met one; otherwise, this purchase would be harder for me to do. I hear they are quite lovely."

"I hope I'm not marrying a man with weak convictions. Fairies are nuisances," Dariusa snarled back at him. "We need this blood to secure my throne. So what if a few fairies must die. The more the better. It's not like they are actual people. My mother will be here any minute. After I tell her about our engagement, I would like you to leave us alone. I don't want any interference when she has drunk the potion."

"Understood, Dariusa," Edwin said as he watched her finish mixing the Queen's drink. "I will be nearby just in case you need anything. Your plan will succeed, and your mother will be out of your way."

Before Dariusa could say anything more, Queen Merri entered the dining hall. She was escorted by two royal guards. This didn't bother Dariusa at all. She knew that the guards would be sent to a corner of the room once the Queen had been seated. The room was utterly silent as she made her way to the head of the table. The rule was that no one should speak until the Queen was seated. As soon as the Queen took her seat, she directed the guards to move to their positions.

"Greetings, Mother, I hope you had a pleasant night's sleep." Dariusa smiled at her mother. "Before we begin breakfast, I would like to announce my engagement to Duke Edwin Morgwyn of Thaldor. He proposed to me last night, and I have accepted in the traditional manner."

"Congratulations." The Queen complimented her. "We approve of your choice of husband. He has been nothing but loyal to the kingdom for the past forty years." She turned to Edwin. "We are very pleased that you have been accepted by our daughter, Duke Morgwyn."

"Thank you, Your Majesty," Edwin replied. "I give you my word that I will respect your daughter, and when the time comes, I will make sure that she is protected while on the throne. If you would excuse me, there is a matter I must to attend to. I would have loved to share breakfast with you, but my duties call."

The Queen nodded, allowing the Duke to leave the table. The Queen waited a few moments to make sure no one was in earshot of her and her daughter. "You sure know how to find a good man, Dariusa. I assume he is part of your little cult. If you continue with your religious ranting when you are Queen, the people may revolt. They know that it is the job of the Priestesses to spread Terra's message."

"I have enough influence among the nobles who have purple skin," the Princess stated. "As for the blue-and-orange-skinned elves, if they stay in their part of the continent, I don't have a problem with what they do. This is Terra's will, Mother, I am shocked that you don't understand it as well as I do."

"We are not getting into this debate with you again, Dariusa," Queen

Merri said. "We would just like to enjoy our breakfast with the company of our daughter."

"My apologies, Mother," said the Princess as she handed the Queen a cup. "I have obtained a special juice from a Northern farm to celebrate my engagement. I had hoped Edwin would have been able to join us, but he is far too busy. I hope you enjoy this drink. The farmers were so happy when they found out that it was for a royal occasion."

The Queen accepted the drink from her daughter without any questions. As she took a few sips of the drink, the Queen's eyes changed colour. That meant that the potion was working. It pleased Dariusa as she leaned towards the Queen to whisper in her ear. "You should tell the guards to kick out all the blue-and-orange-skinned elves from the capital city and the south of the continent. Anyone who resists, should be executed. You should do this now."

The Queen stood up and beckoned her personal guards to come by her side. "Guards, we are going to the throne room to make a royal decree. Make sure our journey is safe."

As the Queen left the dining hall, Dariusa smiled. She knew that this would hurt her mother's reputation. The Princess hoped that all the dukes of the continent would pull out their military support, forcing her mother to step down as Queen and paving her way for her ascension to the throne. Part of her was disappointed that she had to go to this extreme to make her mother understand the dangers the blue-and-orange-skinned elves posed. The other part of the Princess felt pleased with what she had done. Now the continent would finally start to have some progress under her rule.

Ayleen arrived back in the capital city, Terra, in the mid-morning. She had learned a few new things from talking to the families. There seemed to be a connection between some of them and an abandoned house in Thaldor. Most were looking for work.

This afternoon was the second meeting of the war council. While she wanted to arrest Mobious at the meeting, Tyran had not contacted her with any confirmation of Mobious' actions. It infuriated Ayleen to no end but realistically, he'd had only one day to search. She knew

Mobious was guilty of the attacks but could do nothing about it. So long as Mobious was free, he could attack the citizens of Giana again.

She had spent the night in her ancestral home just outside the capital. She needed to feel close to her family. Too much had happened in too little time.

Her carriage drove through the main gates of the city. She expected a quiet ride between here and the castle. That was not the case, however. The second she passed through the gate, she saw purple-skinned guards going into citizens homes and throwing out blue-and-orange-skinned elves.

What was going on here? Why were there royal guards kicking out people from their homes on such a massive scale? She had to investigate why this was happening. She jumped off her carriage and headed to the nearest commanding officer she could see.

"You there! Can you tell me what is going on?" Ayleen shouted at the guard. As she got closer to the guard, she noticed the insignia on his armour. It told her that his rank was that of a lieutenant.

"Please stay back, ma'am, there is a situation being dealt with," the guard said as he turned around to face Ayleen. "Captain Ebella, I did not realize it was you speaking. The Queen has ordered all blue-and-orange-skinned elves out of the city."

"Why in Terra's name would the Queen make an order like that?" Ayleen asked as she started to get frustrated with the situation. "I need to get an audience with the Queen as soon as possible! I just can't believe that the Queen would order such an action."

"I'm afraid the Queen is unable to speak with anyone right now," the guard said. "I was ordered to direct any of the security personnel to General Ironbark to assist with clearing the city of unwanted persons. That is what I was ordered to say to all returning officers."

"What about General Bloodthorn?" Ayleen asked. "Isn't he the head of the army? We should not be forcing the expulsion of any citizen just because of their skin colour!"

"General Bloodthorn has been arrested for conspiracy against the crown," the lieutenant said as he beckoned for four other guards to join him. "Captain Ebella, you are expected to join us and follow your

Queen's orders. We have been instructed to arrest any returning officers that refuse."

The thought of General Bloodthorn conspiring against the crown was unfathomable. While Ayleen and the general hardly ever saw eye to eye, they had respect for each other. His loyalty was impeccable. She doubted that she could talk to Bloodthorn anytime soon. If Queen Merri had locked the General up, then who else had the Queen locked up? There had to be more to the situation than what was in front of her. Merri wasn't like that!

"I will not comply with any order that harms the civilians of Giana," Ayleen stated at the royal guards. "If you have a problem with that, you will have to take me in by force."

"Very well, Captain," said the lieutenant.

As the guards drew their swords, Ayleen put both her hands on the hilts of her two short swords. She was not going to follow any order that commanded her to hurt innocent civilians. If these guards were going to arrest her, she would die defending her moral standing. The five guards surrounded her, waiting for the lieutenant to give the signal. If the guards intended to take her by force, she wouldn't kill them, but there would be bloodshed. Ayleen knew that these guards had no idea who they were facing. In her training days, she was able to take down five opponents. Now she could probably take down eight at once.

"Captain Ebella," shouted the lieutenant. "This is your last warning. Head to General Ironbark or be arrested by the order of the Queen."

Ayleen refused to reply. The lieutenant took this as a sign of disobedience. The five guards slowly approached Ayleen with their swords pointing towards her. As soon as they were close enough, Ayleen slid between two of the guards and hamstrung them. The two guards fell to the ground, unable to continue the fight. Another two guards tried to swing at Ayleen, giving her the opportunity to stab one in the armpit while hitting the other in the side of his head with the pommel of her sword. Whirling around, she found the lieutenant sneaking up on her. She quickly disarmed him, kicking him to the ground and pressing the tip of her sword to his throat.

The next thing Ayleen heard was the sound of clapping from a distance. She moved her eyes to the side to see Princess Dariusa, astride her horse, accompanied by twelve purple-skinned soldiers. "Nice job, Captain Ebella, I see that the newest soldiers lack the proper training. I overheard that you refused to help the Queen. Why is that?"

Ayleen released the lieutenant. She knew that she did not have any leverage at this point. "Princess Dariusa, is it true that your mother has ordered the expulsion of elves based on their skin colour?"

"Unfortunately yes, she has, Captain," the Princess replied. "She has ordered me to oversee the operation. If you would follow me, I will take you to the palace and let my mother explain her reasons."

Ayleen knew something was up, but as long as she was out here, she wouldn't get any answers. She had to figure out what was going on. She surrendered herself to the Princess' guard, allowing them to disarm her. The Princess refused to let her guards bind Ayleen's hands. Ayleen knew this was the Princess' way of trying to gain her trust, but it wasn't working for her. She knew the Queen would never give her army an order that would hurt the civilians of Giana. She had to figure out what was going on even if it meant playing the Princess' game.

Tyran's second day of work went pretty much like the first day. He was so tired after his first day of work that he fell asleep after spending the evening with Zalissa and a few other staff. He hadn't seen Mobious all day. He learned from the group that he had gone away just before Tyran's arrival. And they didn't know when he'd return.

Tyran decided tonight would be the best time to try to get into that building. The place was too busy with people during the day for him to slip away. Why one man needs so many staff, was beyond him. If he was tired again tonight, he'd need to take a nap without eating dinner so that his hunger would wake him in the night.

Ayleen sat alone in a meeting room where the Princess had escorted her. Princess Dariusa told her that she would fetch Queen Merri so that the two of them could have a conversation. Ayleen needed to get answers from her. She had to have a good reason for the expulsion of every blue-and-orange-skinned elf from the capital. When the door to the room opened, just the Princess entered. Ayleen wasn't sure if she had lied about getting the Queen or whether the Queen was yet to come. She had to tread carefully when talking to Dariusa. Part of her felt like she was up to something but she couldn't put her finger on what it was.

"Captain Ebella, I want to apologize for the way the royal guards treated you back there," Princess Dariusa said before Ayleen could get a word in. "My mother has been very busy and will join us shortly."

"Your Highness, what in Terra's name is going on here?" Ayleen asked hoping to get answers but she had a feeling she wasn't going to get any. "Why is your mother evicting every elf that doesn't have purple skin?"

"I have no idea, Captain," Dariusa lied. "We were supposed to have breakfast this morning. But after I told her of my engagement, she went to the throne room to make a royal decree. Next thing I knew she put me in charge of the expulsion of the elves from the capital. While I don't agree with this course of action, I had no choice but to comply. I will summon the Council of Dukes to see what we can do about this overstep of power, but it may take a couple days for them to get here. Due to the upheaval today, the meeting that was scheduled for this afternoon is cancelled."

"Best wishes on your engagement, your Highness," Ayleen commented still unsure as to what the feeling she had was about. "The Council of Dukes has never voted out a Queen in Gianas' history. Sure, there was one time when a third of the Dukes pulled out their military support, but for the Queen to resign, ten out of twelve Dukes or Duchesses must pull out their military support and then you risk sending the continent into civil war. I hope there is a solution to this problem that does not result in bloodshed."

"I agree with you, Captain," Dariusa lied further. "I know my mother well. If she realizes how much of a mistake she has made, she will resign and appoint me as the new Queen. I just hope I can rectify her mistake. She has already done so much damage to the people of Giana. I wonder if it's possible to unify the elves after this tragedy. I will do my best to try."

Before Ayleen could comment on what the Princess said, a guard came into the room and asked the pair to follow him to the throne room.

This was a bit odd to Ayleen. She thought Dariusa said that Merri would meet them here. Something was up. Merri usually preferred to talk to Ayleen in a private room, alone. Whenever the Queen summoned people to the throne room, it was usually to address a massive amount of people or to make official statements.

As the group entered the throne room, Ayleen noticed another indication of something out of place. Queen Merri would usually stand up as people entered the throne room. This time she remained seated on her obsidian throne. It made Ayleen feel uncomfortable. She preferred the Queen standing up, as when she did so, the three windows behind the throne shone light upon the Queen as if a blessing from Terra. Without this imagery, Ayleen felt something was very wrong. As they reached the foot of the throne, they all bowed their heads and waited for acknowledgement from the Queen. When Queen Merri acknowledged them, she asked Princess Dariusa to come up beside her throne. As soon as Dariusa reached her mother's throne, Ayleen noticed that the Princess whispered something in her ear.

"Captain Ebella, we understand that you have refused to follow our orders," Queen Merri stated. "You know that disobedience of this kind can be seen as treason. There is also the matter of you attacking the guards that were trying to do their duty. What do you have to say for yourself?"

"I am sorry, Your Majesty," Ayleen replied as she looked up to her friend's face. She noticed that Merri's eyes were different. It could only mean that the Queen was an imposter or under a spell. Either way, now was not the time to challenge the situation. "When I heard what you had ordered, I wanted confirmation that the order really had come from you."

Princess Dariusa whispered in the Queen's ear again. Ayleen had no idea why but suspected that the Princess had something to do with Queen Merri's odd behaviour. What was Dariusa up to and would she put a spell on her own mother? She had to find out the answer but knew that any action now would cause a fight. Was she trying to usurp her mother by discrediting her?

"Captain Ebella," the Queen said, raising her voice. "By the power given to me by the goddess Terra, you are hereby temporarily stripped of your rank and confined to your quarters until further notice. Do you understand?"

"I understand, Your Majesty," an annoyed Ayleen replied. She now believed that the Queen was compromised. She needed to be alone to formulate a plan. If she was taken to her quarters, she knew how to escape the castle from there.

Four royal guards surrounded her, as was the custom in this situation. She wasn't about to fight anyone who was obeying the Queen even if that order was suspect. There had already been enough bloodshed today. She didn't want to become a fugitive. For Ayleen to solve this mystery, she had to obey the Queen for now even if that meant following orders that she didn't agree with. She would only flee from the castle if she had no other option.

Unlike his estate, Lindar Mobious found the monastery very hot and humid. Not that he minded. He had been all over the continent when he searched for ingredients for the cure that was made too late to save his wife and daughter. He was capable of adapting to different climates and it was a nice change from waking up in the frigid cold his home had become. He decided to have breakfast privately in his room. He didn't want to bond with any of the other monks. They were a means to an end. He didn't need any "friends" chasing after him when he made his escape with the Cube. After he finished eating, he met Father Marick outside the golden double doors behind which the Cube waited.

"Good morning, Lord Mobious," Father Marick greeted him. "I would usually ask how well you slept, but in this case, I couldn't care less."

Mobious was offended by the Abbot's attitude and made a mental note to kill him later. "Good morning to you, too, Father Marick. This morning I was looking back at everything you said to me since I got here. I'm wondering why you're so cold to me even though it was the Cube itself that wanted me here. Have I offended you in some way?"

Father Marick's face contorted, showing his anger. After a few deep breaths, he replied to Mobious. "Of course I'm offended by your presence here. My sister was one of the thirteen people you murdered. The Cube told me your plan when you started your killing spree and told me that you killed my sister the night you cursed her. However, the Cube made me swear to let you come to the monastery. I am also not allowed to hand you over to the authorities or to take any action to avenge my sister. I will not disobey the Cube."

"Interesting." Mobious smiled as he stepped closer to the Abbot. "I don't know whether you are a strong person or a weak one. You allow an object to dictate what you can and cannot do; that is weak. On the one hand, you have chosen not to act on your darkest desires of revenge for your sweet sister. This proves that you have a strong moral compass. I wonder what it would take to break that compass."

"I will not be provoked by the likes of you," retorted Father Marick. "I know you were a good person once in your life. I just pray that with the Cube's help, you will return to be a good person before your scheming gets more people killed. In the end, Terra will judge you and either send you to the Field of Tranquillity or the Frozen Waste of Damnation."

"I do not care how Terra judges me." Mobious stared directly into Father Marick's eyes. "My actions will bring back my family. After I die, it won't matter what happens because, in life, I will succeed at everything I set out to do. Even if Terra condemns me to damnation, I will be laughing every moment I'm there. To gain your wish when you're alive is the ultimate goal of any man. You don't have the guts to fulfil yours."

"You really think that the Cube will bring your loved ones back?" Father Marick asked in disbelief. "I have never heard of the Cube ever bringing anyone back from the dead. I don't know if it's even possible. The eight Cubes combined, perhaps."

"I know it's possible, Father Marick!" Mobious shouted. "I was told by a very powerful ally that it could be done. Maybe you don't have as much faith in the Cube as I do, but I know I can bring my family back."

"Don't you dare question my faith!" Father Marick shouted back. "Now go through those doors and complete your next trial, if you can. The sooner you are done, the sooner you can get out of my monastery."

"Very well." Mobious smiled. "I assure you when I finish my trials and use the Cube, I will make sure that my family will come back to me and I will prove everything you think you know about the Cube is wrong just to spite you."

Father Marick didn't say another word. Mobious took his time to pass through the golden double doors again. Mobious wondered if Father Marick was telling the truth about the Cube not being able to bring back the dead. While he had told Mobious that he didn't know if it could, Mobious assumed that this meant he just never saw it happen. He had to find out if the Cube could bring back his family. If it couldn't, the man who told him about the Cube would die slowly, even if it took him the rest of his life.

Once again, Mobious entered the pitch-black room of the Cube. Nothing about this room had changed since the last time he was there. As he entered the room, the Cube once again told him to touch it.

He reached out to the Cube with a little more hesitation. Mobious had no idea what the Cube would do to him this time. As soon as Mobious touched the Cube, the darkness disappeared, and he was in a bright white room with a table and two chairs. Sitting in one of the chairs was an old elf with pale skin, white hair and a beard. His appearance was that of an elf prior to the meteorite. The old elf motioned for Mobious to sit down across from him. It seemed safe, so he sat down.

"Where is this?" Mobious asked. "I know this is supposed to be the trial of the mind, but I wasn't expecting to teleport elsewhere. I thought that the Cube would ask me a series of questions, and we would have a debate."

"You are inside the Cube. You are inside us. According to my calculations, mortals feel more comfortable if they are talking to a living being rather than an object." The words entered Mobious' mind; the old elf's mouth never moved. "Lindar Mobious, you are entering the Trial of the Mind. I am the Elvish Cube of Destiny. When my mother created the original Cube, I was part of a greater purpose. Now that I'm separated from my siblings, I solely focus on the development of the elves. I will test your ability to accept knowledge."

"How intriguing," Mobious mused as he scanned the room. "How considerate of you, but what do you mean by 'accept knowledge'? What does this trial entail?"

Mobious heard the voice again. "I will ask you three questions. After each question, you will provide an answer, and I will ask a follow-up question. Your first question is 'what is life?'"

Mobious only had to ponder this question for a few seconds. "A fragile existence that can be taken away at any time." Memories of his wife and daughter flooded his mind as he tried to suppress them.

The idea of the Cube asking Mobious a question such as 'what is life' was a joke. The Cube had to know that there are a billion different answers for that question. There was no telling which answer the Cube would accept. He believed his answer was good enough but knew that the Cube was vastly more intelligent that he would ever be. If so, many monks had passed this trial before so maybe it wasn't the answer itself that the Cube was looking for, but rather a good argument. He waited for the Cube to reply to his answer.

The old elf said, "Based on your answer, I calculate that you speak from experience. Your view may be biased. Many mortals have given me very similar answers, but I will accept this answer because your argument is sound. My follow-up question is: do you think it is possible that some people choose the way their life ends?"

"Life itself is a choice," Mobious replied. "Life is precious. It can be taken away at any minute. My wife and daughter did not choose the way they ended their life. It was taken from them."

"One in a hundred people I have interviewed has given a similar answer," said the old man. "Life is indeed about choices such as what you do for a living, who you marry, and what you eat for breakfast. I will accept your answer for the first question."

"My second question is 'what is death?'"

Mobious did not have to think about this question at all. He had more than enough experience with death to answer the Cube's question. "Death is an illness that is waiting to be cured. If life is about choices, then death is the one aspect of life you can't choose. It's a curse from the gods mocking our existence."

Mobious considered himself an expert in death. He had witnessed and caused so many deaths in the past that if he didn't provide an adequate answer, then the Cube had to be mocking him. Given the type of conversation he had been having with this object, he doubted the Cube had the capability to feel emotions. He wondered what the point of these questions was. From the information he gathered from Brother

Isaac and Father Marick, the Cube was supposed to be testing if he had an open mind. Whether these questions would prove that to the Cube, he had no idea.

"You have an interesting of view of death. But I have heard it all before," the old elf commented. "I heard this answer from many of your kind. I find the argument that you mortals think that you can overcome something so final as death illogical. Everything dies. The preservation of life is also illogical. My follow-up question is this: if mortals didn't have death, then how can you make room for a new life?"

"I think you misunderstand my answer," Mobious replied. The old elf looked up, intrigued by this statement. "If mortals were capable of controlling death, we would only allow the people who deserve to live to escape death. You are right that if we allow everyone to live, there would be a population problem or worse. But there are a few people that don't appreciate life and refuse to use the tools they were given to live at their full potential. If mortals were able to control life and death, society would only have people that contributed to and furthered the progress of that society. Death is meant for the wicked and the unworthy."

"I will accept the answer you have given." The old man continued to sit in his chair. "You provide a decent argument. Whether you honestly believe the answers you are giving to me as fact, I can't calculate. I will have to go through my data after the trial and determine the validity of your answers."

"My final question for you is 'what is time?'"

Up until this moment, Mobious had contained his emotions. How dare the Cube ask him such questions as "what is life" and "what is death". The Cube knew all about the events in his life. It knew all the suffering and pain he had endured. However, he knew that getting mad at the Cube of Destiny was pointless and could cause him to fail the trials. The Cube was asking Mobious these questions out of pure logic and not to provoke him. The last question that the Cube had just asked him was the most fascinating one out of the three.

"Now that is a question worth answering," Mobious commented. "Time is a concept made by mortals. It is used by the weak to cherish the life they have. We mortals think that time is a real concept, but time is just an illusion. Just like death, it's a disease given to us by the gods to laugh at our misery."

"You are the first mortal that has answered the question in that way." The elderly man stood up for the first time. "If you truly believe time is an illusion, then you must know the truth. For every illusion, there is the reality. My follow-up question is: what is the reality of time?"

Mobious had to ponder this for a while. He knew time was the illusion but never thought of what the reality was. "If time is the illusion, then life is the reality. Time is an imaginary concept that we use to budget our actions. Instead of worrying about running out of time, we should just act without hesitation. Time is the chain that ties us down. Life is the reality."

"Lindar Mobious, you have passed the Trial of the Mind," the elf said as the room faded to black. "Touch me again when you are ready to begin the Trial of Spirit. It will be the quickest trial out of the three, but it will also be the hardest one."

Mobious once again found himself in the pitch-black room with the Cube. There were millions of thoughts going through his head. Most of them dealt with whether the last few minutes he had spent inside the Cube had been real. Mobious knew that none of that really mattered right now. He knew he had one more trial before he could take the Cube. Soon his goal would be complete. He just prayed that everything he learned about the Cube was accurate. If it weren't, he would force the Cube to help him find the answers he wanted.

VII

CHAPTER

WHAT GREAT LUCK! Tyran thought. He had been given an hour's break in the early afternoon since the kitchen was preparing for Mobious' return and he would work later than normal. What's more, he had learned the guards watching the restricted building would be changing at the same time. He'd have maybe ten minutes to have a look.

Before he left the kitchen, he made sure that all the work that he had been asked to finish was done. He didn't want any chance of anyone noticing that he was sneaking around the estate; even if he was on his break. Part of him enjoyed this simple job. The rest of him knew that he wouldn't stay long enough to let anyone give him harder work.

Tyran made his way to the door of the restricted building and waited until the guards left. What surprised him was that they always left before their replacements arrived. Before he tried to enter the room, he made sure that no one was approaching the area. He then examined the lock securing the door. This gave him another surprise that he never accounted for. The lock itself was an antique style that hadn't been used on Giana in over a hundred years. Back when this type of lock was popular, it was very easy to pick. Nowadays, not many thieves knew how to pick this kind of lock. Thankfully it was an easy one for Tyran.

As he entered the room, Tyran made sure that the door was shut behind him; he locked it for safety. If anyone tried to enter the room, he would hear the lock being turned and have time to hide. In the room were thirteen diamonds the size of his fist, floating above pedestals. He was amazed that Mobious could afford to get thirteen of these. He looked around the room to see what else was there. The only thing noteworthy was a book on a table at the back of the room.

Picking up the book, he decided to flip through it to determine if there was any useful information that Ayleen could use. Fear overtook Tyran as he realized what the book was. It was a demonic spell book usually only seen in underground cults. One page he looked at detailed how to trap a soul in a diamond. According to the book, to make sure that the soul was successfully trapped in the diamond, the diamond would glow a faint green. He turned around to stare at the diamonds. When he first entered the dark room, he had not noticed the colour of the diamonds but since reading the book he was sure that there was a faint green glow.

Knowing that he couldn't steal the book without anyone noticing, he saw that there was a quill and some paper on the table. He took one sheet of paper and the quill and copied as much of that spell as he had time for. Ayleen had to know about this. It was confirmation that Mobious was both the Mad Wizard of Thaldor and the man responsible for the attack at the celebration. After making sure everything was in the same place as when he entered the room, he left the room and made sure that the door was locked again.

Tyran made his way back to the kitchen. Before he could turn the final corner to the hall of the kitchen, he overheard Zalissa talking to another maid. He knew if he turned the corner now Zalissa would ask him where he'd gone. Tyran knew that there was another entrance to the kitchen. It would only take him a minute longer to get to that area. Before he could make his way to the other door, he overheard the two maid's conversation, and they were talking about him.

"I don't know. I'm a little scared," Zalissa said. "Last time I was involved with another member of the servant staff, that man used me to get my late mother's money that she left for me in her will. How can I trust anyone after that?"

"Oh, come on, Zalissa, don't say that," the other maid replied. "It was you who kept me up half the night talking about this new fellow Tyran. You went on for two hours about how attractive he was and how nice he seems. Now you're not going to pursue him because you are worried you will be hurt again. Give me a break."

"First of all, Saria, I had a little too much alcohol last night," Zalissa confessed. "Second, he is probably not attracted to me. He has orange skin, and I have blue skin. Before the change, maybe we could have been friends. Now we don't know if orange-skinned elves can be attracted to girls like us. Finally, this is not the time to be worried about my future husband. Master Mobious has requested that we be ready at a moment's notice for an important event. I cannot pursue anyone until Master Mobious is done with whatever he is planning."

"Fine. Be that way," the other maid commented. "It's only going to be your fault when you realize that you let a perfect opportunity slip through your fingers."

Tyran didn't want to hear Zalissa's response. He knew that he wasn't interested in pursuing his feelings. He made his way to the other entrance to the kitchen and started to look busy. This way, when Zalissa checked up on him, she wouldn't have any idea that he hadn't been there all along.

When Zalissa finally re-entered the kitchen, she told Tyran to wash himself up as the servants would present themselves to Lord Mobious on his return to the estate. Tyran had no idea how to feel about this. He would indeed follow Zalissa's orders, but when it came to meeting Lindar Mobious, he had no idea if he could restrain himself. The two left the kitchen to meet up with the other servants.

After lunch, Mobious stood alone in the dark room with the Cube. He knew what trial was next and knew what it would entail. The moment he touched the Cube, the Cube would scan his entire life to judge whether or not he was a good person. To him, all his actions over the last two years were justified. Every murder he committed had a purpose.

He had prepared long and hard for this day. In his mind, the killings were necessary for him to gather the souls needed for use in making a powerful spell. By casting the spell, he summoned the shadow creatures to attack the New Year's Eve celebration. He had caused so much of a distraction that no one knew he was seeking out the Cube. He had gone too far to stop now.

After a few deep breaths, he reached his hand out to touch the Cube. This time there was no pain or teleportation. His entire life flashed before his eyes. Was the Cube going to kill him? Wipe his memory? The images of every evil deed he had done passed slowly before his eyes. The Cube obviously wanted to highlight these moments. Whether or not the Cube was judging him based on these actions, he wasn't sure. When the images stopped, Mobious removed his hand from the Cube.

"You have lived a unique life, Lindar Mobious," the thousand voices of the Cube sounded in Mobious' mind. "The monks that come here lead simple, pure lives. We find you fascinating. We have seen the future, and we will need to travel with you. We are unable to tell you the reason why this is necessary as it does not concern you. Do you understand, and do you accept our terms?"

"I understand." Mobious was elated. This was too easy! "I know that the monks of the Cube will prevent me from taking you with me. As I cannot use magic in this room, how do you wish for me to deal with the monks?"

"That choice is up to you," the Cube replied. "We would prefer it if there was no bloodshed. However, we don't see a possible future where this outcome can be achieved by you. If you need to kill the monks, then do so."

Without responding to the Cube, Mobious grabbed the Cube and left the dark room. As he passed back through the golden double doors, he saw that Father Marick and Brother Isaac were waiting for him along with the rest of the Brotherhood. It was a little hard for Mobious to count how many monks there were since their gray robes blended into the stone that the monastery was built with. He could make out most of the monks' faces. Most of the Brotherhood, from what Mobious could tell, were orange-skinned elves. There were one or two blue-skinned elves and the same with purple skin.

"Congratulations, Mobious, I see you have successfully completed your trials," Father Marick commented. "I must have forgotten to mention this, but no one is permitted to remove the Cube from its chamber. Will you please turn around and place the Cube back into its room?"

"I'm sorry, Father Marick, I simply cannot do that," Mobious replied. "The Cube itself asked me to take it with me. I am doing so to bring my wife and daughter back from the dead. If you want to confirm with the Cube yourself, you are welcome to come here and communicate with it."

"That is absolutely ridiculous, Mobious!" Brother Isaac shouted. "The Cube had ordered us to make sure that it is not removed from that room. How can you possibly expect us to believe that the Cube asked you to remove it?"

"Calm down, Brother Isaac," Father Marick ordered the monk. "Lord Mobious, I will ask you this one more time. Return the Cube to its chamber now, or we will have to force you to do so."

Mobious let out a chuckle. "I will not return the Cube to you at all. I am going home with it. You will have to stop me if you want the Cube to remain here. I don't see anyone in this room with the power to make me yield. All I see is a group of weak men who rely on an object to tell them what to do."

With a nod from Father Marick, the rest of the Brotherhood start to move forward towards Mobious. The second they took a step Mobious began muttering an incantation. Within seconds every monk except for Father Marick was set on fire. Father Marick took a step back in shock. One by one, the monks fell over as they burned to death. Mobious slowly walked towards Father Marick as he muttered another incantation. Father Marick could barely escape as he tripped over the bodies of the fallen monks. As he tried to pick himself up off the floor, he felt a sharp object move through his stomach. Mobious had stabbed him with a magical constructed sword.

"Why, Lord Mobious?" coughed an injured Father Marick. "If you wanted to kill us all, then why did you leave me alive at first? Why not let me die with my brothers?"

"The answer is simple, Father Marick," answered Mobious. "Deep down, you wanted revenge for the murder of your sister. You did nothing to stop me from entering your monastery. I just wanted to show you how weak and pathetic you really are. You are not a man. You're nothing but a coward, and you deserved to die like a coward."

"Curse you, Mobious," groaned Father Marick. "May the gods, Terra or the others, take you to damnation where you belong. May they torment you for the rest of eternity."

As Mobious' spell fizzled out, Father Marick lay dead. Hopefully, this would be the last murder that Mobious needed to commit. If it wasn't, though, he prepared himself for more mass bloodshed like this. Now he had the Cube of Destiny in hand. Tomorrow night he would contact his mysterious friend and find out the way he could bring Elnora and Tavia back. He opened a portal to his estate and stepped through it not looking back at the massacre he had caused. There was no point in dwelling on it. All of them were cowards in his opinion.

Lying on her bed, Ayleen contemplated what her next move should be. She did not have enough evidence that the Queen was under a spell. All she had was a suspicion that Princess Dariusa was somehow involved. The one thing she knew for sure was the Princess had whispered something in the Queen's ear before the Queen had acted. She knew that the Queen would not have placed her under house arrest before today. They were friends! They would have talked privately! She had to figure out what was going on before the kingdom was sent into chaos.

About two and a half hours passed before Ayleen heard a knock at the door. Ayleen answered the door and to her surprise Dariusa stood outside her room, wishing to speak to her. Ayleen allowed the Princess to enter her room. If she wanted any answers, then Dariusa would be the best source of information. She offered her guest some old wine she had in her room. As expected, Dariusa refused the wine. Not like Ayleen would even drink the wine herself. She decided to sit on her bed while Dariusa sat in the only chair in the room.

"Thank you, Captain Ebella, for speaking with me," Princess Dariusa said. "These last few hours have been very strange for me. I have never seen my mother act so coldly before. The Council of Dukes has agreed to convene tomorrow. I want to assure you that you will be allowed to go to the Council's security meeting as soon as we can rebook it. We have not been able to get in touch with Lord Mobious. My mother and I agree that you are a key part of the defence of Giana. She also said that all charges will be dropped if you successfully find answers regarding who attacked us the evening of the New Year's Eve celebration."

"But your Highness, that will be a problem," Ayleen commented. "I am currently under house arrest. While I'm allowed to go to the meeting of the Security Council, I won't be able to conduct my investigation if I am confined to my quarters until the meeting."

"I discussed this with my mother," Dariusa answered. "She will allow you to conduct your investigation and leave your quarters provided you are accompanied by two royal guards of my mother's choice."

"Thank you, your Highness," Ayleen stated. "It was never my intention to disobey the Queen's orders. I was just surprised that your mother ordered the guards to kick people out of their homes just because of their skin colour. It's so unlike her. When I finally saw the Queen in the throne room, I did notice that her eyes were different. Do you know anything about why this has occurred?"

"That's nonsense. That would mean that my mother is under some sort of spell," Dariusa replied. Ayleen noticed that the Princess jumped to the spell conclusion right away. That made Ayleen even more suspicious. She decided to let her continue talking. "The only wizard that would have that kind of power is Lindar Mobious. He hasn't been seen in the palace since before the creatures attacked us. The only way that my mother could be under a spell is if she drank a magical potion."

"Really? Very interesting, it appears I know far less than you about these things. Tell me more," Ayleen commented. She knew that Dariusa had just confessed to her, but why would she want her mother to do these terrible things? "Who would want to drug the Queen? She has enough guards at her side that any enemy would be intercepted right away, unless they were very clever. If she is indeed under a spell, then the people must know."

"Normally I would agree with you, Captain." Princess Dariusa gulped. She knew Ayleen had caught her in her lies. "With everything going on, I think it's best if we wait for the Dukes to decide. If the

Dukes pull out their armies from the Queen's support, my mother will have two choices: to step down or start a civil war. However, if we bring this theory of yours to this meeting, then the council might open an investigation and find the culprit. That is something we cannot have at this point in time."

"The longer we wait, the more likely they will get away, your Highness." Ayleen decided to play along in hopes that the Princess would divulge more information. "But perhaps you are right, after things have calmed down, we should investigate the potential tampering of the Queen's integrity. Do you think you could create an antidote? And may I suggest that you delay the meeting of the Council of Dukes for a week?"

Of course, Ayleen didn't want to do this, but if this were the only way to get confirmation that the Princess was involved in a conspiracy, then she would take this risk. The Princess pondered Ayleen's request for a minute. "I'm sorry, Captain, I cannot delay this meeting at all. If my mother is unfit to rule anymore, then the council must decide as soon as possible before more lives are ruined. Besides, potions wear off with time."

That was all Ayleen needed to know. If she could stall the Princess for a bit, the Queen might regain her senses. Ayleen turned her head to gaze out the window and noticed the sky had a greenish cast to the clouds. What in Terra's name?

When he arrived in the main hall of his estate, the portal closed behind Mobious. As he expected, all his servants were lined up to greet him. He examined his staff to make sure that everyone was in attendance. He noticed that there was an orange-skinned elf in the sea of blue. While he was away, he knew that the butler, Jorrard, had hired a new servant. He didn't care what colour skin his new servant had, just as long as he obeyed every command. As per usual Jorrard was the first to greet Mobious.

"Welcome back, Master Mobious," greeted Jorrard with a bow. "I trust your trip was a success. Is there anything I can do for you at this moment, sir?"

"Nothing at the moment, Jorrard," answered Mobious as he walked towards the butler. "As for my trip, I acquired exactly what I needed."

Mobious held up the golden Cube and looked at it lovingly. "I assume the ritual room is prepared."

"Yes, sir," said Jorrard. "Everything that you asked for has been set up. Unfortunately, there was ten minutes where it couldn't be guarded. Forgive me, Master, it was a scheduling oversight that I should have seen earlier."

"That is all right. Ten minutes unguarded won't cause any trouble." Mobious gritted his teeth. He had told his butler to always have two guards stationed there at all times. To punish him here and now in front of all his servants would damage his image. "You are to meet me in my study tonight for a private meeting. We will discuss how to avoid this going forward."

"As you command, Master Mobious." Jorrard gulped, knowing that he had made a dreadful mistake. He should have kept his mouth shut. Mobious would never have known otherwise. None of the servants would have gone near the building. "I would like to introduce you to your newest servant. This is Mister Tyran Dori. He came from the capital city to work for you. After his brother died in the New Eve's Year celebration massacre, he couldn't bear the thought of working where he had worked with his brother."

Mobious walked towards the back of the room where Tyran was standing in silence. Looking Tyran up and down, he found no apparent problem with his appearance. "Mister Dori, I am so sorry for the loss of your brother. I hope you will be of great service to me. Feel free to ask Jorrard any question you have. And remember, loyalty to me will be greatly rewarded."

Tyran wanted nothing more than to kill Mobious here and now but he knew that he needed to contact Ayleen with what he'd seen. This was enough evidence so that the Queen would imprison him. Despite every thought he had, Tyran could only reply with a bow and say, "Yes, Master."

Mobious examined the orange-skinned elf for a few moments. He could see that this new hire was physically capable and well fit to defend himself in a skirmish. Whether or not this would be a benefit to Mobious he could not tell, yet. He didn't care that the man in front of him had a different skin colour than the rest of his staff. Little issues like that didn't matter to Mobious. All he cared about was how useful a person would be to him.

"You know how to pick a good worker, Jorrard," commented Mobious. "But don't mistake that for a pass on neglecting your duties. Servants, you are dismissed to return to your duties. Jorrard, you are to follow me to my special room and this time make sure that no one disturbs me."

As the servants left the hall, Mobious and Jorrard walked towards the restricted room. While Mobious had the Cube of Destiny in hand, news of the massacre at the monastery might spread fast. He had to make another distraction before the Queen knew he had murdered dozens of monks. Arriving at the room, Mobious noticed there was something a little off about the lock. He had put a spell on the lock, knowing it was easy to pick.

"Jorrard, no one except my guards have been in this room, right?" Mobious asked the butler. "I would hate to punish my head butler for disobeying a basic order. If you could explain why the lock is only partly locked, I would appreciate it."

"My apologies, Master," answered a worried Jorrard. "The last two guards I had assigned to this room are not the brightest. They must have misunderstood and tried to get into the room to guard it."

"That is why you don't hire idiots to do important jobs, Jorrard," Mobious said as he opened the door. "After today, we won't have to hide what we are doing here. I have received the Cube, and while you have made a few mistakes, overall you have been very supportive and a great help to me ever since the accident with Kenei." Mobious emphasized the word accident. "I trust that you haven't told any of the other staff what is in this room."

"No, sir, I haven't," assured Jorrard. "I appreciate you letting me in on your secret."

The two men entered the room, locking the door behind them. Little did they know that Tyran was around the corner outside the room watching them. He knew that Mobious could be preparing another attack, but the problem was the door was the only way in or out of that room and it was guarded. He had to find a way to watch what Mobious was doing. He circled the building and noticed a small window partially obscured by bushes. It wouldn't let much light in, so perhaps that was why he didn't notice it when he was inside earlier.

Inside the room, Mobious placed the Cube on the table at the back of the room and then stood inside the circle of diamonds to prepare his spell. Jorrard stood with his back to the door, observing his Master. "I never thought the Cube of Destiny was real. I'm surprised, Master, that the monks allowed you to take the Cube."

"They didn't allow me," Mobious calmly replied. "I had to liberate the Cube. The day after tomorrow I will be expecting a guest in the evening. After that, I will have the knowledge to use the Cube how I see fit. I will finally be able to see Elnora and Tavia again. Would that please you, Jorrard?"

"Of course, I would love to see your wife and daughter again," answered a confused Jorrard. "Forgive me, but I do not understand why you ask such a question."

"I'm just testing your loyalty," Mobious stated. "I am so close to my goal that I don't want anyone to get in the way of seeing my family again. Just so I'm clear, Jorrard, if you are lying to me at all, I will kill you, and you know that. Now stay back as I cast my spell."

Jorrard knew that he shouldn't reply to Mobious' remark, not that he even had time to do so. As soon as Mobious stopped talking to the butler, he began mumbling an incantation. Unlike other spells, Mobious had to repeat these words constantly for the spell to work. Inside the room, it felt like a hurricane. Wind from nowhere began to whirl around the room. Inside the circle of diamonds, a black tornado enveloped Mobious. Jorrard could no longer see his Master. He knew that Mobious was casting the same spell as he did on the night of the New Year's Eve celebration. Peering through the window, Tyran watched the spell being preformed but had no idea if or how he could stop it.

Another knock at the door interrupted the discussion. Ayleen got up and answered the door. To her surprise, a royal guard stood before her with a panicked look on his face. Ayleen wondered why a veteran royal guard was so scared at this moment. "Yes, how can I help you?"

"I am sorry to bother you both," the guard said with a tremble in his voice. "But there is something outside that the Queen has asked both you and the Princess to look at. It doesn't look good."

Both Ayleen and Dariusa agreed to follow the guard outside. What could possibly have happened to unnerve this veteran guard? Ayleen did not have a good feeling about this. She knew that something terrible must have happened or was happening. The only thing she could think of was another attack from the shadow creatures. If that were the case, there would be little she could do to help the citizens of the city.

Ayleen and Dariusa followed the guard to the outer walls of the castle. The moment the group stepped outside, Ayleen saw the sky getting greener. It was at that moment she realized the shadow creatures were going to attack again. Ayleen had no idea when the attack was going to start. All she knew was that it was imminent. The Queen joined them on top of the wall. It was then that Ayleen noticed Merri's eyes slowly returning to normal. Now wasn't the time to be concerned about her. If there was another attack about to happen, she had to make sure that the citizens of the city of Terra were safe.

"What in Terra's name is going on?" Princess Dariusa cried, turning to her mother for help. "Mother! Surely you know what is happening? This looks like a storm is brewing, but I have never seen the sky like this before!"

The Queen shook her head. "We don't know what is going on either. We were only told a few minutes before the guards were sent to escort you here. I feel so confused. I can't think. Captain Ebella, you were there at the New Year's Eve celebration. Is this similar to what you saw then?"

"It is indeed similar but not exactly the same," Ayleen replied as she looked out towards the city hoping to get a clue to what was happening. "My Queen, on the night of the last attack, a meteorite struck the continent. Whether between that and the attack by the shadow creatures, I don't know if the sky turned green. It was dark then. But I have a feeling that we are going to be under attack very soon."

The Queen stood in silence for a moment, pondering what the Captain had just said. "Then there is a chance this may not be an attack. We would not like to take that chance. We have ordered all our guards to go into the city and patrol the streets until whatever this is passes over."

"Mother, do you think that's going to be enough? Shouldn't we evacuate?" Dariusa questioned her mother. As soon as those words came out of her mouth, the group heard the sound of thunder coming from the direction of the city. As the group turned to look at the clouds, they saw lightning flashing down on the city. In the clouds, every time a new lightning bolt struck a shape would light up. Ayleen knew this shape well. It was a wolf skull with its jaws wide open and an eyeball in its mouth. It was the magical signature of Mobious.

What was Mobious thinking? How did he benefit from this? The two thoughts raced through Ayleen's mind. What was he up to? The only possible explanation that Ayleen could come up with was that Mobious believed this magical storm could benefit him in some way. This had to be a distraction. For now, Ayleen knew that she had to do something to save the civilians of the city.

"Your Highness, this is an attack! I'm sure of it! And yes, we should evacuate!" Ayleen shouted over the noise of the storm. "The symbol in the clouds is none other than Lindar Mobious' magical signature. I know you asked me to provide more evidence, Your Majesty. I have been trying to get said evidence over the last two days. What you see in the sky is the best evidence you could get. Please allow me to go to the city to help protect the civilians and then after that I will bring Mobious to justice."

The Queen looked confused by Ayleen's request. She vaguely remembered the charges that she had laid on the Captain earlier but could not remember why. "Very well, Captain Ebella. All charges are dismissed on one condition. After the attack has been dealt with, you are to report to us immediately. Alone."

"Understood, Your Majesty, I won't let you down," Ayleen consented as she ran toward the castle's exit. Merri was beginning to sound like herself again.

Princess Dariusa now realized her spell on her mother was wearing off. Would she remember everything that she ordered her to do? She had to play it safe. There was no way for her to tell if she was still in control. "That was very kind of you, Mother. Normally you wouldn't let a criminal walk free."

"Captain Ebella is no criminal, Dariusa," the Queen stated. "The past twenty-four hours have been a blur for us. We remember ordering the expulsion of elves from the capital, but we don't remember why. We also remember ordering the arrest of our friend but cannot explain why. Would you know anything about that?"

"I have absolutely no idea, Mother, but you haven't been yourself," the Princess lied. "Unfortunately, the Council of Dukes has called a meeting tomorrow to discuss the orders you have given. I will do my best to defend you, Mother, but if the Council withdraw their armies, there may be a civil war. This is not the time for that."

"You are right, Dariusa," the Queen acknowledged. "It is odd though that we have felt confused and disorientated, like we were under some sort of spell. With our head magical advisor nowhere to be seen for days, the only other person with alchemical knowledge is you, Dariusa. Of course, that is ridiculous that our own daughter would put a spell over us. If we were to find out that you had anything to do with this, we would have no choice but to remove you from the line of succession to the throne."

"I assure you, Mother, I would never do such a thing," Dariusa assured the Queen. "I will personally investigate this myself. If you would excuse me, I think I should go inside before the storm hits the castle."

Dariusa turned to head inside the castle. She didn't look to see if her mother followed her or had any more questions. She knew that if she weren't careful, she would be caught. She thought the potion would have lasted longer. She'd come too far to be stopped now. If her mother removed her from the line of succession, then her cousin, Duchess Norin, would be the next Queen. There was no way on this planet that she would let that witch become Queen. Duchess Norin was of the orange-skinned elves now, and Dariusa refused to allow anyone other than a purple-skinned elf to sit on the throne. To her, the purple-skinned elves were Terra's chosen and the other two were no more than heretics.

As Ayleen ran out of the castle gates, she saw guards staring at the sky. She knew that none of them had been near the area at the New Year's Eve celebration. If they were to defend the city, she would need the help of every guard. There was one question on her mind that she couldn't even guess at an answer. Why was it taking so long for the shadow creatures to appear? The only solution that she could justify in her head, was that the meteorite was required to open the way faster for the shadow creatures. No matter, she had to tell the guards what was about to happen.

"You there, I need your help, " Ayleen shouted a command to the nearest guard. As the guard turned to face her, she noticed it was the same Lieutenant that tried to arrest her yesterday. "Lieutenant, I need your help and as many men you command."

"Captain Ebella, I wasn't aware that you had been released from house arrest," the Lieutenant replied. "If the Queen has released you and dropped charges, then this storm is worse than I thought. What can I do to help?"

"I don't know how much time we have," Ayleen reported. "This is similar to the attack at the New Year's Eve celebration. We need to evacuate the city as soon as possible and then prepare for a long fight. We will be unable to harm our attackers. We just need to fend them off until the spell that brought them here wears off."

"Understood, Captain. I will rally every guard under my command and will spread the word to the other lieutenants," the Lieutenant responded, then he ran to the guardhouse.

As soon as the Lieutenant left, Ayleen began to see orbs of darkness falling from the sky. She knew what was to come next. She grabbed a bow and arrows from the guardhouse. If she couldn't hurt the creatures, she would try her hardest to distract them. Just like before, as the orbs fell to the ground, a creature of pure shadow appeared. Thankfully, as the creatures appeared, the guards were starting to evacuate the city.

Ayleen saw a group of civilians frozen in terror. While keeping an eye on the creatures, Ayleen hurried toward the group shooing them ahead of her to the edge of the city where one set of the city gates stood. The creatures began their attack seconds after she gave orders to the group of civilians. Just like before, the creatures were hunting the weakest elves they could find. Attacking one of the creatures with arrows, she managed to shift its attention towards herself.

Ayleen wanted to keep her distance. She ordered any guard she saw to attack the creatures to distract them and then run. While she fighting one of the creatures, her eye caught a glimpse of two children trying to run away but still surrounded by the shadow creatures. Ayleen had to find a way to get to the children.

"Soldiers, can you distract these creatures for me?" she ordered the closest guard. As soon as the guard nodded in agreement, she started to run to the children.

As she tried to reach the children, a cart dropped in front of her thrown by one of the creatures. There was no time to find an alternate route. She had to get over that cart! Climbing over the cart, she dropped to the ground on the other side. She could see the children being cornered by the shadow creatures. What seemed strange to Ayleen was that the creatures were not attacking the children yet. Something was stopping them from attacking. But what?

As she ran towards the children, she slid through between one of the creature's legs. It was then she realized that one of the children was the daughter of the huntress she had helped a few days ago. The two children cowered behind Ayleen as she prepared herself for battle. The guards yelled and threw things at the creatures in hopes of turning them. There was no way she would let these creatures hurt the children.

It was at that moment the creatures began to approach Ayleen. She knew a fight was about to begin. She would die before she let the creatures lay a finger on these children. In her mind, she wanted nothing more than for Terra to intervene or give her the strength to protect the city.

VIII

CHAPTER

S THE SHADOW creatures moved in to attack Ayleen and the children, the girl began to scream. The boy tried to calm the girl down. As Ayleen assessed the creatures surrounding her, she realized there was a gap in their formation. With this knowledge, she picked up the boy and the girl and ran in the direction of the gap. Fighting the creatures would prove fruitless. All that mattered was to get the children to safety. Seconds later, she arrived at a crossroads. One direction had a group of guards escorting civilians to safety while the other direction had a pack of creatures.

Ayleen ran towards the group of guards, hoping that they would be safer in a group. Without any way of harming these creatures, she needed to make sure that every citizen was evacuated. As she reached the group, she saw the girl's mother was in the group. As soon as she put down the children, they ran to the woman and gave her a big hug.

"Thank you, Captain Ebella," the huntress cried out as she embraced both children. "I'm so glad my little girl and nephew are all right. How can I ever repay you?"

"No need, ma'am, I'm just trying to get everyone out of the city," Ayleen replied.

Relief for Ayleen didn't last long. Creatures started to crawl out of the alleyways in front of the group blocking their path towards the edge of the city. There was nothing Ayleen could do to stop these creatures. Had Terra abandoned them? As she looked around, she realized that most of the group were children or young mothers. None of which deserved to die like this. One last time Ayleen said a prayer in her mind asking for the goddess' help.

The guards defending the group started to charge at the creatures trying to distract them. Unfortunately, there was no path for the rest of the group to make it to the city gates. One of the creatures came up beside the group without Ayleen's knowledge and grabbed one of the children, ripping his stomach open. The entire group was screaming! This was the last straw! She couldn't stand by and watch innocent people be slaughtered.

Suddenly, a golden light began to emanate from Ayleen's body. She looked down at her hands and saw that her skin had turned to pure gold. As if it was instinct, she raised her hand to the creature who had just killed the boy and a beam of golden light came out of her hand and destroyed the creature in one blow. The rest of the group stood in awe as they couldn't believe what they had witnessed.

"Come with me. I'll get you to safety," Ayleen commanded the group. She had no idea where the words or her newfound powers were coming from. It was like someone was working in tandem with her. As she continued forward, she blasted each creature in her way, destroying it.

As she and the group reached halfway to the gate, they entered a town square. It was the quickest way to the nearest gate. As they walked through, another group of creatures appeared on top of the buildings. This time the number of them was more significant than Ayleen had seen before. Even though she knew the number of creatures surrounding her was more than she had ever seen before, somewhere deep down, she knew she had the power to save everyone.

"We're surrounded! How are we going to survive this?" one of the women yelled out.

"Please, remain calm and stay together. If we stay calm, we can get through this," one of the guards said, raising his voice and trying to calm the crowd down.

The creatures charged at the group. Ayleen realized that there were more than she had seen just a few seconds earlier. Where were they all coming from?

Once again, she prayed to Terra to help her protect these people. The second she ended the prayer she began to levitate. The light from within Ayleen started to shine brighter. Clasping her hands in front of her, she then flung her arms wide, spreading golden light like a sound wave over the city. As soon any creature came in contact with the light, it quickly disintegrated. The moment this wave of energy was finished, Ayleen collapsed to the ground unconscious.

The black vortex surrounding Mobious vanished. He staggered slightly. He was not expecting his spell to end this quickly. He knew that someone or something had interrupted his magic, but how? Seeing through the eye of the storm, he remembered seeing a golden woman with waves of golden light pulsating from her. She must have been the one who interrupted his spell. Whoever it was, she needed to die!

"Jorrard, with me now!" Mobious shouted at the butler, storming out of the building, forgetting the Cube behind.

Jorrard knew something was very wrong but he didn't have enough nerve to question Mobious. The pair stormed to Mobious' study where the butler closed the door, locking it behind them. He wondered if he had secured the entrance to the restricted building but couldn't remember. He had to check once he was done here. He decided to keep this detail to himself to prevent Mobious from becoming any angrier.

Mobious frantically hunted for a book from the shelves in his study. He knew which book he wanted, but his rage fogged his memory. He took one book after another, flipped through it and threw it on the floor. When he found the book he was looking for, he moved to his desk and sat down. The book he had settled on was called "The Children of the Eight Gods." Mobious knew that most of the text was up for debate but knew that this was the only book in his library that described what he saw.

"Master Mobious?" asked a worried Jorrard, "I have never seen you act this way before. Is there something wrong? What can I do to help?"

"Have you forgotten the rule of not to speak until spoken to?" snapped Mobious. "But if you must know, during my spell, I witnessed someone with immense power that could prove dangerous. If this woman were to interfere, do you know what will happen? Everything I have worked for the past year will be for nothing. I won't be able to bring back Elnora and Tavia. There is no way I can allow that to happen."

"Understood, Master Mobious," the butler replied. "If I may, sir, what does it matter? You have the Cube of Destiny. If you use it, you can erase this person from existence. That is, if I understood your explanation of what the Cube can do."

"So, you were only half listening when I told you about the Cube." Mobious stood up and walked towards the butler. "I may have the Cube now, but all I can do is access its knowledge. I have to wait until the day after tomorrow when I meet the person who has sent me on this quest. He will show me how to use the Cube to the full extent. That gives me a day and a half. In that time, whoever that woman is, can find me and take the Cube back. I refuse to be beaten by a woman. Even if she may be a servant of the goddess."

Jorrard took a step back. He had never seen this much anger in his master's eyes. "Master, please relax. I have contacts. We can hide you until your acquaintance comes. I can hire as many mercenaries as needed. There is no need to worry. You have already won."

"I have already won, have I?" Mobious punched Jorrard in the jaw, knocking him to the floor. He knelt down and put his hand on the butler's throat and began to choke him. "If I have already won, why do I feel like I am in the most danger? Why do I feel that everything is about to be taken away? Don't I have a right to see my wife and daughter again? Answer me that, Jorrard!"

Jorrard couldn't answer. Mobious made sure of that. He had kept his hands on the butler's throat until all life was gone. Mobious stood up. He now felt better. Returning to his desk, he continued reading the book he had started. He was still worried about the woman he saw but had a feeling that he would find something in the book that would help him.

As he continued to read the book, he came to a section on demi-gods. He had heard of these beings before but doubted that this was possible. The idea of a god giving their children to a mortal sounded like something out of a children's story. While the book did not have a good description of how to identify a demi-god, it did say that these beings were immensely powerful and must not be underestimated. Mobious needed more information if he was to deal with a demi-god.

Once again, he left his chair to walk over to his bookcase. He was annoyed at himself for throwing books on the floor and making his study a mess. As he finished cleaning up the books, he decided to grab a few books that might help him in this research. He put the books on his desk, then he looked at the body of Jorrard. "Good help is so hard to find these days."

He would deal with Jorrard's body later. Right now, he had to find a way to combat this new threat. He knew that whatever she is, she would be as powerful or more powerful than he is. At first, the idea of someone more powerful than him made him angry, but as he thought about it, he realized it was a challenge. Like the Cube of Destiny's trials, this challenge would make him stronger. If he were to capture this woman, maybe he could study her and find a way to transfer her power to him. There had to be a way. Mobious smiled as he realized that this challenge might be an opportunity in disguise.

Ayleen awoke standing up. Her surroundings were unfamiliar to her. She was no longer in the city but in a field of flowers that looked normal with a profusion of colours. Wherever she was, it hadn't been changed by the meteorite.

Off in the distance, she saw a golden dining table with two chairs at either end of the table. She felt compelled to walk to the table. Once she reached the chair closest to her, she felt drawn to sit there. Every thought in her mind told her to investigate this place further. However, deep within her she knew that she was safe and sound.

As she looked across the table, she realized there was another female elf in the other chair. Unlike every other elf she had come across, this woman had pale skin and long golden blonde hair. As she stared at the woman, something about her facial features looked familiar. It took Ayleen a minute to realize that this woman resembled the description of the goddess Terra from the elven holy text. The woman was wearing a simple white dress.

"Greetings, Ayleen," the woman spoke gently. "I hope you're not too alarmed. I've been waiting for you to waken for some time. As much as I wanted to meet you, this means that Giana is in grave danger and I need your help to protect it."

"Where am I?" Ayleen questioned trying to raise her voice but realizing that the air around her only allowed her to be calm. "What happened to the people I was escorting, and who are you? None of this makes any sense."

"Surely you recognize your own goddess?" Terra replied. "You don't have to worry. I made sure everyone in the city is safe. I can only do so much. If I interfere any more, then I will be breaking the law of the gods. We can only interfere when there is no other option. We must allow mortals to decide their own fate. That is why we have children in the mortal realm such as yourself, my daughter."

"Daughter? My mother is Nanya Ebella," Ayleen said, confused. "What you are talking about is the concept of a demi-god. Lady Terra, I'm honoured that you think I am one of your daughters, but I'm just an average elf."

"Are you now?" Terra mused. "Then I'm sure that you have an explanation for how your skin and hair turned to gold? Or how you managed to shoot energy beams out of your hands? Or make a wave of golden energy that wiped out hordes of shadow creatures? I know this is a lot to take in, and I usually want my daughters to live their lives in peace, not knowing their true potential. However, there is a problem brewing that only you will be able to solve. I can't intervene anymore, Ayleen, I need your help."

As she listened to Terra's words, memories flashed through Ayleen's mind. She remembered gaining powers and saving the city from the creatures. Even though those events happened moments ago, they seemed like a distant memory. "Are you saying the powers I was granted was because I am your daughter? And by great danger, you mean Lindar Mobious, right?"

"Both of your assumptions are correct, to a point," Terra replied. "I have been watching the last few years; if Mobious continues on his journey, he will permanently open a portal for the armies of Val-Sharect to enter your realm at will. He has already let them in twice. Every time he brings the dark god's army to the mortal realm, he risks making that gateway permanent. This must not be allowed to happen. He does not realize it, but he is under the control of Val-Sharect. You must find a way to stop him."

"I understand, Lady Terra," Ayleen acknowledged.

"I have the utmost confidence in you, my daughter," Terra assured Ayleen. "I sense that you have another question for me. While I know what it is, I want to allow you to ask the question yourself."

Ayleen did have another question for the goddess, but she feared the answer. "Lady Terra, it seems like the elves are no longer a united people. Most of the purple-skinned elves believe that they are your chosen people and that the other elves don't matter. How can you allow this to happen?"

"That is unfortunate." Terra lowered her head. "It saddens me to see my children fight amongst themselves just because of their skin colour. As I said, I cannot interfere any more than I already have. The elves must learn to co-exist with each other. This is a challenge for them to overcome and grow stronger."

Ayleen thought that the goddess was all-powerful, that she could do anything she pleased. Why would Terra allow her people to fall apart? If this woman was indeed her spiritual mother, then why couldn't Ayleen understand her reasoning for not intervening? The elves looked up to her. They would change their behaviour if Terra said so. Surely this would be a time where the goddess should intervene.

"But surely you can do something about it," Ayleen asked. "What is the point in bringing the person who changed Giana to justice if the continent will still be divided? I just want all the elves to get along like they used to do. Is that too much to ask?"

"Sometimes, change is inevitable, Ayleen," Terra answered. "What you really want is a peaceful continent. I can assure you that peace will come. I have seen it. But let me remind you that peace doesn't always mean unity. Sometimes we need to go our separate ways. Now go, my child, and save Giana."

Ayleen's eyes grew heavy as they began to close. She knew the goddess was right. She could feel it deep inside her. She must save Giana. She must stop Mobious. If the elves could never be unified again, she would have to find a way to accept it. The goddess was counting on her and there was no way she would let down her mother, whether biological or spiritual. With all the knowledge that she had acquired in the last few minutes, she felt like she had the tools to bring the continent back to peaceful times. And yet, she was scared to see what the world would look like after she brought Mobious to justice.

Tyran watched as Mobious and Jorrard left the restricted building. Luckily for Tyran, Jorrard forgot to lock the door. The guards were nowhere in sight. He had to get back into that building. He had been given a break from the kitchen. There was little more Tyran could do until after dinner. He had listened to the conversation Mobious had with the head butler and continued to eavesdrop while they were in the room. However, looking through a window had its drawbacks. He could make out only part of their conversation. Now that the two men were gone, he could investigate the room.

As he entered the room, the first thing he noticed was a black substance on the floor that wasn't there when he investigated the room earlier in the morning. From what he could make out from the conversation that he had overheard, Mobious was casting a spell. He figured that this black substance was residue from the energy of the spell he had cast. His eyes shifted to the table at the back of the room where a golden cube now lay.

As he walked towards the Cube, he felt like someone was watching him. He looked around the room to see if anyone was there, but no one had followed him. He wondered if the feeling he had was coming from the Cube itself. He had no idea what was going on or if he should touch the Cube. But it was gold! Deciding to leave the room, he locked the door to make sure that no one would suspect that he was snooping around in the room. He was sure he had enough evidence against Mobious.

He decided to head back to the kitchen even though they didn't need him for another half hour. As he entered the kitchen, he heard heavy breathing coming from inside the kitchen. It sounded to Tyran as if someone was having a panic attack. He turned a corner to see Zalissa leaning over a counter trying to calm herself.

"Hey, Zalissa, is everything all right?" Tyran slowly walked up beside her.

Zalissa turned around and immediately hugged Tyran. "Tyran, it was awful! I was taking a walk outside after Lord Mobious came home and saw a giant black vortex coming out of the restricted building. I don't know what it was or why it was there, but I know there is something evil behind it. I'm worried that if I tell anyone other than you, they won't believe me."

"And why shouldn't I believe you, even though no one else would?" Tyran asked. "I do believe you, Zalissa. You can tell me anything at all. I won't judge you if that's what you are worried about. If you must know, I saw it, too."

Zalissa let go of Tyran and looked relieved. She took a few breaths to calm down. "For the past year, I have been seeing weird things happening around the estate. Whenever I try to talk about it to the other maids, they think I'm crazy."

"I'm here. You can talk to me anytime you want," Tyran assured her. "Over my life, I have seen some weird things happen to people I care about. It's a strange world out there. We all need a friend to talk to. I hope I can be that friend for you."

"Thank you, Tyran," replied Zalissa. "Maybe later we can get together and talk before bed. Right now, you need to clean up the supper dishes. I'll help so you can be done sooner. The day after tomorrow, the master has a visitor coming and has requested that a big meal be prepared. We will have no time for anything that day."

"Isn't that the job of the chef?" Tyran asked.

"Normally it would be," Zalissa answered. "Unfortunately, the cook will not be here until the afternoon that the meal needs to be served. He has a day and a half off and is visiting his family in town. Lord Mobious has requested a fish dish for the main course. We will need some fish brought up that morning, some Pearl Coast salmon from the cellar."

Tyran was shocked that anyone would store fish in the cellar. He knew that it would be spoiled. "Are you sure you don't want me to go to the market and buy fresh fish that morning?"

"There is no need for that," Zalissa assured him. "Lord Mobious has enchanted part of the cellar to be constantly frozen. Food has never gone bad here."

Tyran didn't argue with her. He knew that she was probably right, but he wanted to see for himself. He exited the manor to head to the entrance of the cellar. Sure enough, Zalissa was telling the truth. There was a room in the basement that was magically cold with a variety of meats and fish. After looking at the frozen selection, he left the cellar. Outside he peered at a small wooden house to the left of him. He knew that this was a play area for a young child.

"It is beautiful," Mobious said from behind Tyran. Tyran jumped and turned around to see his temporary employer. "My daughter used to play in that house every day from morning to night. I miss her dearly. Mister Dori, given that your brother recently died, do you think you would do anything to bring him back?"

"I would do anything to see my brother again, Master Mobious," Tyran begrudgingly answered. He did not know why Mobious was asking him this question. The only reason he could think of was that Mobious was missing his family. "It is normal to miss loved ones, but we all must accept that they are gone and move on with our lives."

Mobious nodded his head. "Very well, Mister Dori, please get back to your duties. Just a word of warning; I believe someone has been sneaking into my ritual room. If I find out that it was you, I guarantee no one will find your body. I have that kind of power. Good afternoon, Mister Dori."

Tyran's hair stood on end. He had to have been sloppy for Mobious to be suspicious. He just needed some time alone and then he could use the stone to contact Ayleen. Until then, he couldn't afford to mess up. He knew how smart Mobious was; and how dangerous.

A thought popped into Tyran's head. If Mobious were the person who summoned the shadow creatures, then would Ayleen have the skill to stop him? He had to work fast. He knew that Mobious had a visitor coming the day after tomorrow and felt that if Ayleen didn't come here before then, it would be too late.

Ayleen awoke to the sight of an unfamiliar room. She took a minute to examine where she was. To her right side, an orange-skinned elfin woman whom she recognized as the huntress from yesterday was preparing a stew over the fireplace. As her eyes wandered, she saw the daughter and nephew in the corner of the room. Seconds later, the door opened to reveal a tall and muscular blue-skinned male elf. He walked over to the huntress.

"Grileena, we can't stay here any longer," the blue-skinned elf quietly said. "There is a group of purple-skinned zealots who believe that the blue-and-orange-skinned elves are responsible for the shadow creatures' attack."

"We just can't leave now, Roderick. That woman saved my daughter and your son," Grileena argued. "We have to at least wait until she's up. That would be the polite thing to do. As soon as she is awake, and I can make sure that she can take care of herself, we can leave."

"Fine." Roderick conceded as he looked to Ayleen and realized she was up. "Grileena, your friend is awake. I will get the horses ready to leave town. We can't stay any longer; the purple skins are hunting us."

As Roderick left the room, Grileena rushed to Ayleen's side and started to examine her to make sure she was all right. Ayleen assured her that everything was fine. "Thank you for bringing me back to your home. I think I can stand on my own. I just want to know what happened. My memory is a tiny bit foggy. How did I get here?"

"You saved us all," Grileena commented. "When the shadow creatures attacked the group that we were in, you began to emit a bright golden light. Soon after, your hair, your skin, your eyes became solid gold. I have only heard about this in legend. Beams of light were coming out of your hands, killing each creature as the beams came in contact with it. You saved us all, Captain Ebella. Thank you!"

"So that wasn't a dream." Memories flooded Ayleen's mind as she remembered defeating the shadow creatures and having a meeting with the goddess Terra. She knew that her defeating the creatures was a real memory but wasn't sure her meeting with Terra was reality or a dream. As soon as she thought the memories of Terra were fading, a flood of new memories flowed through her mind. She knew these memories weren't her own. She had no idea what was happening to her. Even though she thought that her host might be unfamiliar with what was happening to her, it was worth a shot to ask. "Huntress, do you know what a demi-god is?"

"Yes, I do. My mother was a priestess," the huntress replied. "Please, Captain Ebella, you can call me Grileena. As for my knowledge of demi-gods, my mother used to tell me about these beings when Roderick and I were toddlers. They are avatars of the goddess, always a woman. They have the ability to summon up great power and do the will of the goddess. My mother told me that when a demi-god unlocks their power, they acquire the memories of all the demi-gods before them. I never thought they were real, until I saw how you saved us. I immediately took you back to my house to make sure you were unharmed. There were no other guards in our group since they had all fallen. I hope you don't mind what I did."

"No need to apologize, Grileena," Ayleen assured her. "You did what any reasonable person would do, and I thank you. Your brother was talking about leaving the city. How long was I out, and what is going on now?"

Before Grileena could answer Ayleen, her brother re-entered the room. Hearing the last part of the two women's conversation, he decided to answer for his sister. "Like I said earlier, the purple-skinned elves have become zealots and are now hurting elves like my sister and myself. If you don't mind, Captain Ebella, I would like to get my sister, my son, and my niece out of the city as soon as possible. I am glad that you are all right, and I want to thank you for saving my family, but we have to go."

"Sorry about my brother, Captain, he is just worried," Grileena apologized as her brother gathered the two children and took them outside. "To be honest, ever since I came back to town yesterday, I have been on edge. Seeing my neighbours being tossed out of their homes for no good reason gets to you. I know it is a matter of time before the same treatment extends to us."

"That is understandable, Grileena," Ayleen once again assured her. "You need to leave the city. If the purple-skinned elves think that the other elves are dangerous, your family is not safe here. I don't know what I can do, but I will try to talk to the Queen and figure out a way that you can come back to the city."

"I don't think we will ever come back here," commented Grileena. "The last couple of days has just been one tragedy after another. I have seen so much that I need to get away from here and start over."

Ayleen nodded. She understood what the elves of blue-and-orange skin had been through. No one deserved that much torment in one week or ever. "Even though we just met the day before yesterday, you have been the nicest friend I have ever met. I wish you well. I hope one day we will be able to see each other again without the worry of skin colour and creatures."

She and Ayleen exchanged farewells. Grileena told Ayleen that she could stay in the house for as long as she needed; and then she left. Ayleen was alone again. She knew she had to return to the castle to convince the Queen to let her arrest Mobious. She also had to prove that Princess Dariusa had put the Queen under some form of mind control. That would be harder.

The events of the past three days wore heavily on her. She kept remembering Terra's words "peace doesn't mean unity". More and more, she found herself agreeing with that statement. She did not have time to worry about the unity of the continent. Right now, she had a madman to catch. After a while, she left the home of her new friend wondering if her family would ever feel at home anywhere again.

In her chambers, Princess Dariusa fumed over her failure. How could she be so inept as to make a potion that only lasted one day? Her skills in alchemy were way more advanced than some apprentice. She had to think quickly. The Council of Dukes was meeting tonight at the castle. If she didn't provide the right kind of evidence to the council tonight, then her mother would still be in power. Even worse still, if her mother could prove that she was the one that had given her a potion that controlled her mind, she would be removed from the line of succession to the throne. While in deep thought, Dariusa realized that Duke Edwin Morgwyn was standing outside her door which she had accidentally left open.

"What do you want?" snarled Dariusa. "Can't you see I want to be alone? Our plans have failed."

"If I may come in, my love, I bring some news," Edwin asked, as Dariusa nodded in acceptance. Edwin entered the room, making sure that the door was closed behind him. "My love, the attack on the city has been thwarted. However, one bit of talk among the guards has me a bit worried. Apparently one woman alone wiped out all the shadow creatures. They described a female whose hair and skin turned pure gold; she was a purple-skinned elf originally. She was able to shoot energy out of her hands and finished off the remaining horde with a wave of golden light."

This sent Dariusa into a fit of rage and fear. She knew what Edwin had described, a demi-god! If the demi-god was currently alive, there was no way she could give birth to another one. There was only one demi-god allowed in the mortal realm at a time. She had to know who this woman was. "Did the guards say who this woman was?"

The Duke shifted uncomfortably where he stood. Dariusa knew that he knew the identity of the demi-god and waited until he answered her question. "My love, apparently the woman is Captain Ayleen Ebella of the Investigation Branch."

Dariusa was furious. How could a woman like her be the demi-god? She didn't agree that the purple-skinned elves were Terra's chosen! The idea that Terra would pick her was insulting! Why was a mere Captain chosen to be Terra's avatar and not her? Didn't she devote enough of her life to her goddess? She had to prove to Terra that she made a mistake by not choosing her or her future daughter. As she stood up, she went to the table where a pitcher of wine rested. She poured herself a glass and quickly drank it all. It would help her calm down.

"Do you know what this means, Edwin?" Dariusa asked while containing her anger and locking eyes with him. "What the guards saw was a demi-god. A being that Terra herself put on a mortal realm to enforce her views. If Ayleen Ebella is this demi-god, then it means she could dismantle everything I have worked for. She doesn't believe that the purple-skinned elves are Terra's chosen and the others are no better than dirt. This means Terra believes that as well. This is outrageous! I will prove to the goddess, Terra, that purple-skinned elves are the only beings worthy enough to worship her."

Duke Morgwyn moved closer to his fiancée and put a hand on her back. "Relax, I have a plan to deal with your mother and Captain Ebella."

"Really?" The Princess turned around surprised that Edwin would have a plan already. "I never thought I would hear you say you had come up with a plan to deal with my mother. I always thought that you were the loyal type and did whatever you were asked to."

"You brought me in this far. It wouldn't be wise to admit defeat now." Edwin looked into her eyes. "We should allow Captain Ebella to continue her investigation of Lindar Mobious. From what I hear, she has enough evidence to arrest him. While she is gone, allow the Council of Dukes to vote on whether to keep your mother in power or not. Later that night you bring her another potion. This time, however, it won't control her. It will kill her. Tomorrow morning you and I will make up a scenario where the Queen was so overcome with guilt for what she has done that she killed herself. Lastly, we will blame her guilt and her actions on Captain Ebella."

"That is not a bad idea, my love," the Princess said with admiration. "If everything goes according to plan, even if Ayleen is the demi-god, the purple-skinned elves will not be able to trust her. We can make them believe that she is only pretending to be the demi-god. I like your idea. By tomorrow night, I could be Queen of Giana and be able to bring order back to this realm. My only concern is, how are we going to deal with my mother's royal guard? They are extremely loyal and would protect her at any cost."

"You don't need to worry about that." The Duke smiled as he looked into the Princess' eyes. "In two hours, I arranged a meeting with another duke and a member of the guard that is high up in the ranks and is loyal to us. We will discuss how to deal with the royal guards in a manner that benefits your ascension."

"That is amazing, Edwin, you have thought of everything," Dariusa commented. Maybe he was smarter than she thought. Too smart. She would need to deal with him once she was done with him. "With you by my side, my ascension will be a sure thing. No one will be able to stop us. We will bring peace to the true children of Terra."

With that, the two lovers kissed. Dariusa knew with this plan, she would be able to bring an end to her mother's legacy. At first, Dariusa thought Edwin was a useful pawn and if he proved unfit to be her husband she would dispose of him. However, with the plan that he concocted she felt he was as dangerous as she was. As long as only a few purple-skinned elves knew that Ayleen was the true demi-god, they could be dealt with. Once she had a daughter, she would be able to convince her subjects that her daughter was the true demi-god. She would have complete control over the kingdom, if her subjects believed that she was the mother of a demi-god.

IX

CHAPTER

OBIOUS SAT ALONE in his study. Everything he wanted was so close, and yet the discovery of the demi-god defending the capital made him nervous. While he might be able to use this knowledge to his advantage, he knew that if he weren't careful, this would backfire. Beside him, the Cube of Destiny lay on the table. He couldn't wait any longer. He had to see Elnora and Tavia again. Even if it was only an illusion. It would satisfy him until he had the knowledge to bring them back from the grave.

Without turning to see the Cube, Mobious made a request. "Cube, can you please show me my wife and daughter?"

"Yes, I am able to show you this," the Cube replied. "But keep in mind, it is based upon your memory."

"Just show me what I want to see," Mobious stated. He did not have time to argue with an object. Luckily for him, the Cube had no further questions. Within seconds the room changed to the way it was before Elnora and Tavia died. It was only after the two died that Mobious decided to strip the room of anything that would remind him of them.

Mobious was now in the room that used to have toys, tables, comfortable chairs; while a small fire crackled in the fireplace.

"Lindar, dear, aren't you going to sit down. You've had a long day," Elnora said while reading a book. She was in her favourite rocking chair, keeping an eye on Tavia while she played with her dolls near the fireplace.

Mobious headed towards a chair across from his wife. This was one of his favourite pastimes. As he sat down, he realized that his blue-coloured skin was now as pale as it had been before the change. It took a minute for him to feel comfortable with this illusion. He knew in a day or two, this would be a reality. "I've missed you so much, Elnora. Soon our lives will be back to the way it was."

"Dear, what in Terra's name are you talking about?" His wife turned her head and gave him a puzzled look. "Did Queen Merri overwork you again? I swear, as much as I like her, she can be a real slave-driver. You need to relax. Tomorrow you have the day off. I was thinking we could go on a walk around the lake with Tavia."

"You don't need to worry about that, honey." Mobious smiled with genuine happiness for the first time in over a year. "I would love to take Tavia for a walk around the lake."

His daughter stood up and walked towards his chair with a doll in hand. "Daddy, look what Mommy bought me today. A new doll that looks just like me."

This was almost perfect. If the Cube could bring back his family, then days like this would be more frequent. He wanted nothing more than to spend his days with his wife and daughter. He longed to see his daughter grow up and become the great woman he knew she would be. He also understood that if he wanted this and wanted to keep this, he would have to fight for it. To him, mortals wanted nothing more than to take what they don't have. That's what he was doing. And why would anyone else be any different? But enough of that kind of thinking, right now, his focus was on his daughter, as it should be.

"That is amazing, Tavia," Mobious said lovingly as he leaned towards his daughter. "Have you given the doll a name yet? I thought that Mom and I agreed we wouldn't buy you a new doll for a little while."

"She reminded me that she had done well on her first magical test." Elnora sighed. "We can discuss the financial part of it later. Tavia, it is almost time for bed. Can you put your toys away?"

Without a word, the little girl nodded and started to walk back to her dolls. It reminded Mobious that this was just an illusion. His daughter would usually tear up when his wife told her to get ready for bed. "Cube, take me out of this illusion now!"

That second, the room returned to his study; cold, empty except for his desk and the bookcases. He didn't expect that the Cube would make a perfect illusion, but he wanted to feel like it was real. He missed the crying of his daughter, as annoyed as it sometimes made him; it was part of reality. "Cube, why did you show me a non-reality?"

"I calculated that this was what you wanted to see," the Cube replied in a monotone voice. "If you wish to view your family in the way you feel is correct, I would have to dig deeper for more memories. We chose to make our servant happy."

"Are you mocking me, Cube?" Mobious snapped. "Once I bring my family back, I will have the knowledge I require so that you will bow to me. Just you wait, I will be your master."

The Cube did not respond to Mobious' rant, nor did Mobious want a response. He continued to sit alone in the room for a little while longer. He had to fight off the tears that he knew were coming. When he was finally willing to leave the room, he decided to leave the Cube locked inside.

Normally he would have had a spell cast on this room to let him know if anyone entered without his knowledge. Usually he wouldn't make this kind of mistake but given how much was on his mind over the last week, something was bound to slip.

The next twenty-four hours would be the busiest time of his life. He had to prepare for his guest. Once his acquaintance showed him how to master the Cube, he would probably have to kill him. No one with that much knowledge shared it without using his student. Mobious refused to be anyone's pawn. And he had just the magic spell to catch a magical person.

Princess Dariusa and Duke Edwin Morgwyn sat patiently in one of the castle's meeting rooms. They were waiting for Duke Stefan Lakeseer and Colonel Fredryck Stonehawk. These two men were already followers of Dariusa's religious doctrine. The pair did not have to wait long until the other two arrived. As the Princess had expected, both men had the same purple skin and black hair that she and Edwin had. If the pair did not carry these features, there would be no way that the Princess would ever allow herself to work with them, or to be seen with them. Once the group introduced themselves to each other, they all sat down around a table.

"Princess Dariusa, I am honoured that you have allowed us to be part of your ascension." Duke Lakeseer started the conversation. "I am not sure if you are aware of this, but my family has been displeased with Queen Merri for a while and feel like your methods would fix the problems plaguing Giana. I am willing to do whatever it takes to facilitate your rise to power."

"Thank you, Duke Lakeseer," Dariusa said graciously. "As much as I love my mother, I feel that her way is outdated. We need new ideas. Giana is already in chaos because of that meteorite. It was a gift from Terra that she deliberately separated us by colour so that we would know who was chosen. We also have another problem. I assume you both have heard the rumours that the demi-god has appeared. She is a good friend of the Queen's and we must discredit her for my ascension to be a success."

"I will be able to handle that," Colonel Stonehawk stated. "Years ago, I was part of the Queen's intelligence branch. My job was to spread misinformation to the Queen's enemies. While yes, we haven't been at war in ages, I was involved in a few conflicts with rogue Dukes trying to separate from the kingdom. I was part of the reason why we never saw a successful uprising on the continent."

"I want to personally thank you, Colonel Stonehawk." Edwin inclined his head in the Colonel's direction. "It is partially because of you that I am the Duke of Thaldor. The previous Duke was a coward who didn't know how to take charge of his own domain. With you on our side, I have no worries that my fiancée will be the Queen by tomorrow."

Princess Dariusa was pleased with how well this meeting was going. There was no doubt in her mind that she could accomplish her plan. "Duke Lakeseer, do you think you can convince other members of the Council of Dukes to vote against my mother tonight? I have no doubt that most of the blue-and-orange-skinned Dukes are furious at my mother. My only concern is, would the purple-skinned dukes follow our lead?"

"The only two we should worry about is Duchess Forestseeker and Duchess Norin," commented Duke Lakeseer. " Duchess Forestseeker is loyal as a dog to her cousin. Like your own cousin, she would never vote against the Queen. However, since there are twelve members of the council, we only need ten of them to get the Queen out of power. With the number of people Queen Merri has displaced, we should have no problem convincing the Dukes who are still undecided. I predict that we will have a vote of ten to two."

Duke Morgwyn stood up and started circling the table. "I have no doubt you are correct, Duke Lakeseer. The problem we need to concern ourselves with right after the vote, is the two Duchesses that are guaranteed to vote to protect the Queen's power. Even though we may win the vote, they will provide their army's support to protect the Queen. We can't afford a civil war, even a small one, at this time. We have to deal with these two Duchesses quickly so that we can focus our military efforts on the invading shadow creatures' realm."

"You are absolutely right, Edwin," Dariusa commented. "If we are to successfully overthrow my mother, we need to prove to the people of Giana that I can combat the threat of the shadow creatures. The one thing that Captain Ebella has done for us is to provide evidence that Lindar Mobious is the culprit behind the attack on the New Year's Eve celebration and the attack on the city yesterday. Duke Morgwyn and I suggest that we allow Captain Ebella to stop this criminal and then we can discredit her later by preventing her from entering the city."

"That would be wise, Princess," Colonel Stonehawk agreed. "If I may suggest we could spin a tale saying that Captain Ebella was a co-conspirator with Lindar Mobious. We would have to wait until Captain Ebella has dealt with him. Then on her way back, we arrest her for conspiracy. If she runs, we can tell the citizens that she is indeed guilty of the crime. If she surrenders, I have enough experience that I could falsify evidence against her. Either way, the purple-skinned elves of the South will be convinced that she was part of the attack. There will be no reason for our citizens to believe that she is the demi-god."

"That is the best idea I have heard all day, Colonel," Dariusa complimented him. "That settles it. Tonight, we will overthrow my mother and deal with her supporters. Tomorrow I will be Queen. Then we will ride to meet Captain Ebella after she stops Lindar Mobious and either she will be our prisoner, or a criminal on the run. After that, I will make sure that the three of you are well compensated."

The three men agreed with their future Queen. They had a plan now. Soon the kingdom would belong to Dariusa. No one could stop her now; she knew she could kill anyone who tried. It was only a matter of time before everything fell into place. While her plan seemed like a sure thing, Dariusa didn't want to let her guard down. Any one of these men could betray her. She had to have a back-up plan in case of betrayal. The only person she didn't want to have killed was Edwin. He had proven himself to be the most loyal to her. She didn't care about the other Duke or the Colonel. However, if the time came where she had to eliminate Edwin, she wouldn't have a problem doing so.

As Ayleen walked back towards the castle, her mind started to wander. She realized she had memories from many different women. She accepted this was part of the process of her awakening. The question was how much of these memories were going to be helpful, and to what extent could she rely on them. One memory she acquired was that of a bounty hunter that could throw a dagger in a way that it would come back to her. She had to try to see if the memories would transfer over in skills.

She spotted a sign hanging from a rope. Even though she had to get back to the castle quickly, she felt that she needed to test her theory. She grabbed a knife from her boot, holding it by the tip of the blade. Without thinking, she threw the knife at the rope holding the sign. To her surprise, the knife headed back towards her after cutting the line, and she instinctively caught the blade by its hilt. This was incredible! Not only did she have the memories of all the past demi-gods, but she also carried their skills.

Now that she had her curiosity satisfied, she quickly walked towards the gate to the castle. Once there, she realized that there were only two guards stationed. Usually, this gate would have anywhere from eight to ten guards depending on the time and day. She figured that most of the guards were occupied with securing the city after the attack. The other option was that they already finished that job and continued to force out the blue-and-orange-skinned elves. She prayed that it wasn't the latter.

One of the guards spotted her approaching the gate. He obviously recognized who she was since his attitude was respectful. "Greetings, Captain, I am glad to see you are not injured. We were about to send a search party for you."

"There is no need for a search party since I am here," Ayleen commented as she looked at the insignia on both guards. Both were privates, which she expected. "Private, why are there only two of you guarding the gate?"

The two privates looked at each other. Ayleen could tell that something wasn't right. It was the other private that finally answered after a moment of silence. "After the creatures vanished, all the guards continued the Queen's order of expelling all the blue-and-orange-skinned elves from the city. An hour ago, Queen Merri reversed her order. However, that didn't stop the riots outside the city. All the purple-skinned elves are inside the castle walls for their protection. Everyone outside is demanding that the Queen step down."

"This can't be happening," Ayleen said as she shook her head in disbelief. "If the Queen has reversed her order, then why aren't the blue-and-orange-skinned elves returning to their homes?"

"They don't trust Her Majesty anymore, Captain," the first private replied. "They refuse to return home as long as Queen Merri sits on the throne. They don't feel safe here. If you ask me, it is hard to blame them. The Queen asked us to do something that we never thought we would ever have to do. We even had to detain fellow guards and throw them out of the city. I had to throw out my own wife and son!"

Ayleen still could not believe this was happening. This had to be the work of the Princess. "Can you two let me through the gate? I need to talk to the Queen."

The two guards opened the gate without question. As Ayleen walked through the gate, she saw purple-skinned elves camping within the castle grounds. She had no idea how many believed in what the Queen had done. She knew for sure though that all of them would put the blame on Queen Merri if she couldn't prove that Princess Dariusa was the one behind the order. There was a significant problem, she could either stop the Princess from tearing the continent apart or stop Mobious from killing all the population. There was no way she had time to fix both problems, and unfortunately, Mobious posed the biggest challenge.

As she headed towards the castle, she overheard whispers from the crowd. The whispers conveyed a feeling of shock that the Queen would make this order. Ayleen expected this type of conversation. What she didn't expect was the next topic she heard. Many in the crowd were spreading a rumour that the blue-and-orange-skinned elves had conspired with the Queen to be banished, to cast a bad reputation on the purple-skinned elves. Ayleen couldn't believe she was hearing such nonsense! If she had more time, she would find a way to put the rumour to bed. She knew that the people spreading this theory would have to be followers of the Princess' sect. She hoped that the Queen knew how to squelch the rumour and repair relations with the other elves.

Tyran sat in his quarters, contemplating his next move. He knew he had enough evidence for Ayleen. However, the last encounter with Mobious still was unsettling. As he thought about it, he realized that Mobious did not threaten him at all. There was just something about that man that Tyran couldn't place. Whenever the two were near each other, Tyran felt a dark presence watching him. Before he could contemplate any further, there was a knock on the door. He opened the door to see Zalissa in an outdoor jacket and holding a second jacket.

"Tyran, I was wondering if you would like to go on a walk with me?" Zalissa asked.

Tyran accepted her offer. Some fresh air would do him well. The pair exited the estate and headed towards the lake. It was the biggest lake in Giana. It was commonly known as the Goddess' Lake. Tyran had heard about this place from friends of his but had never seen it for himself. He wished he could have seen the lake before it was frozen over. The lake was almost as beautiful as the woman who asked him on this walk. He knew that he may never get to tell her that.

"Thank you for coming with me," Zalissa said. "I know that we agreed to talk later, but I had an hour off and found out that you also had the same hour off. So, I thought that this would be a great time to talk. I hope you don't mind."

"I don't mind at all. I needed some fresh air," Tyran assured her. "I've had a lot of things on my mind. Most of it I should have dealt with when I had the chance."

"I know what you mean," commented Zalissa. "My family calls me the Queen of Procrastination. It has been three months, and I still haven't visited my sister's grave. I guess I'm worried that once I see it, I will have to admit that she is really gone. Do you ever feel the same about your brother?"

"Unfortunately, I do," replied Tyran. "When my brother died, it took me awhile to accept the fact that he was gone. I only told Jorrard that my brother died on the night of the New Year's Eve celebration because I felt it was easier to deal with than the truth."

"I knew you told him at least one lie." Zalissa chuckled. "You're not the first servant to lie to that man. When I was first hired, I told him that I knew how to clean a chimney. Of course, I had no idea. I just lied to him to get this job. I was lucky enough that he transferred me to maid service before he caught on that I had no idea what to do. So... How did your brother die?"

Tyran stopped walking. He turned to the lake and took a deep breath. He wanted to share this information so that Zalissa would have no reason to not trust him. "My brother was a debt collector for a crime lord in the capital. One night he was sent to collect from someone who his boss thought would be a pushover. When he met the person, he wasn't alone. The guards found my brother; badly beaten. In his weakened state, he caught the plague in its early days when there was no help."

"I am so sorry, Tyran." Zalissa patted his hand. "I was told that my sister had symbols carved into her body as she took her own life. We both lost the people we cared about most. If you ever need to talk to me about it, I'm here to listen."

As Tyran listened to the words, he knew that her sister was one of Mobious' victims, and her soul was probably in one of the giant diamonds that lay in the restricted room. "You know what is funny? Out here with you, I feel like I don't need to worry. I can tell you anything. I don't know why I feel this way."

"I feel the same way, Tyran," Zalissa said as the two elves looked into each other's eyes. A second later, the two kissed. However, the moment they shared did not last. Another maid ran up to Zalissa and requested that she return to the manor. "I'm sorry, Tyran, maybe we could see each other later. I really have got to get back to work. You still have half an hour before you are due back. Please continue to enjoy the lake. I would love to have a house on this lake."

Tyran waved good-bye to her as she headed back to the kitchen. Two thoughts were in Tyran's mind. First off, he was angry at himself for allowing his feelings to surface while on the job. Zalissa did not deserve someone like him. She was too innocent. He had done so many terrible things in the past. What if she found out? Would she still feel the same way that she did now? The other thought he had was that he realized that this would be the perfect opportunity to contact Ayleen via the stone she gave him. Luckily for him, he always carried it in his pocket. He would only have one chance to call her. He headed into a thick group of trees to make sure no one would see him.

As Ayleen entered the castle, she was immediately met by a guard who told her that the Queen wished to see her. This was not surprising for her. Queen Merri had often confided in her whenever something went wrong. Unfortunately, while she would love to comfort her friend, she needed to get down to business. She was escorted to the same room where she often used to have private meetings with her friend, Merri. As the guard shut the door behind her, she sat down across from the Queen. She could tell that Merri was very upset at the current situation. Her eyes were red from crying. Ayleen waited for the Queen to speak first.

"Ayleen, what have I done?" Merri asked, not using the royal 'we'. Thankfully the two of them were in private, otherwise this type of speech would not be proper. "I let my own daughter bewitch me. I made an order demanding elves be kicked out of the city, just because of the colour of their skin! What kind of Queen am I to allow such a thing to happen?"

"Merri, it is not your fault. You were under a spell!" Ayleen tried to comfort her. "If you can provide evidence that your daughter did this to you, then the Council of Dukes will have no choice but to forgive you. It will take some time to repair relations with the blue-and-orange-skinned elves, but I have the utmost faith that you can reunify the continent."

"Thank you for your confidence, but it won't help me against the Council of Dukes," the Queen said ruefully. "I have no delusions that there is no easy way out of this. Out of the twelve Dukes, I only have two allies that will support me no matter what. They only need ten Dukes to overthrow me, and that is what will happen if I don't resign. I don't know what to do, Ayleen. Where did I go wrong as a mother? I know she drugged me, but I have no proof!"

"I'm going to be completely honest with you. I don't know." Ayleen shook her head in bewilderment. "We have another problem to deal with. You've seen it yourself. Lindar Mobious is behind the attacks. With his magical signature seen in the sky, it confirms that he is the only one who could be behind this. I must do something; otherwise, he will kill everyone in Giana. I wish I could stay here and help defend you, but I can't. If I'm able to apprehend Mobious and gather evidence that he was the one who caused the meteorite to crash into the sacred tree, it will disprove the Princess' lies that it was a gift from Terra and she will have doubt cast upon her. However, I can't do any of that without your permission to go after Mobious."

The Queen pondered this for a minute. She knew Ayleen was right. "You have my permission to go after Mobious. However, I want him alive if possible. We have rules for a reason. The only way to maintain justice is to follow the rules of the kingdom. If we don't follow the rules, we are no better than animals. I will stall Dariusa as long as possible."

Ayleen nodded in agreement. The Queen dismissed her. She wished that she could stay longer to protect her friend, but they both knew that Mobious was the more significant threat. As she headed back to her quarters to gather some items before the journey, she found that Princess Dariusa was waiting for her at the doorway of her room. This surprised Ayleen. She thought that the Princess had nothing more to say to her. Apparently, she was wrong.

"Captain Ebella, I assume you had a good conversation with my mother," Dariusa sneered. "Tonight will be interesting. The Council of Dukes will vote whether or not they still support my mother. Can I assume that you will be there to help defend our Queen or have you decided to track down the monster responsible for the attack on the citizens of Giana?"

"Princess Dariusa, as Captain of Investigation, you know it's my job to apprehend Lindar Mobious. You've seen the evidence for yourself," Ayleen replied as politely as she could. She knew Dariusa was already aware. "But I can assure you when I have Mobious in custody I will return to the castle and make sure that nothing has happened to your mother. I'm certain that you will do everything in your power to convince the Council of your mother's innocence."

"I will be eagerly awaiting your return, Captain." Dariusa smiled. "I would just like to warn you. It's essential for mother's case that you bring him back alive. A confession is needed. I have confidence in my ability to protect my mother, but in the case that my mother is forced to resign I will take her place. I will do everything in my power to make sure my vision of Giana will be fulfilled. I hope you remember that."

Ayleen was very aware of the veiled threat from Dariusa. However, any action against the Princess at this moment would make her an enemy of the purple-skinned elves. "Well, it was lovely chatting with you, your Highness. But if you don't mind, I need to enter my quarters to prepare for my journey to Mobious' estate. I will see you as soon as I have Mobious in custody."

The only response from the Princess was a smile. She left without saying another word. Ayleen had to be careful. She knew that Dariusa was planning to take over the throne. She only hoped that Dariusa wouldn't be as ruthless as she feared. She prayed to Terra that Merri would be safe. It still felt weird praying to her goddess now that she knew Terra was her spiritual mother. It saddened Ayleen to have to leave the capital when there was so much at stake. One thing was clear, Mobious would pay for everything he had done to this kingdom, even if that meant giving up her own life.

Entering her quarters, Ayleen took a deep sigh of relief. As much as she wanted to deal with Princess Dariusa at that moment, she had too much on her plate. She would only be in this room for a couple of minutes then she would head to Mobious' estate; even though she hadn't heard from Tyran. She hoped he was all right. As she began to collect her things for the journey, she noticed that her mother's journal was open. She didn't remember leaving it open. In fact, she remembered putting the diary away in her desk. She scanned the room to make sure that nothing had been stolen. Nothing seemed to be out of place.

She intended to close the journal and put it back in her desk where it belonged. However, as she looked at what page was open, she became more confused. She thought she had read the journal so many times before that she had memorized every entry. Strangely she did not recall ever having seen this entry before. She had planned to leave within an hour. If she spent five minutes reading this entry, then it wouldn't delay her much. She sat down and began to read.

5922 of the Third Gods, 13th Month, 7th Day

Ayleen, if you are reading this, then you have discovered who you really are. I put a spell on this page of my journal so that if your powers never awakened, then you would live a normal life. Before you were born, I had visions of our goddess telling me about your life and asking permission to allow her to make you her avatar. I, of course, said yes, but I didn't realize at what cost. From the moment I accepted, I had a vision of every event regarding you up to and including

my own death. I will do everything in my power to make sure I don't die tomorrow, but if it's the goddess' will that I die, I am unable to change my fate. I know you will blame yourself. Please don't. I tried to change the future so that I could be alive for you when you needed me most. In the end, I don't think I can change anything. For that, I am truly sorry. Your loving mother,
Nanya Ebella

As Ayleen put the journal down in shock, tears welled up in her eyes. Her mother knew that she was a demi-god. As she thought back on the life she had with her mother, she realized that her mother's training was preparing her to fulfill her destiny. That's why she had insisted on training Ayleen herself. At that moment, Ayleen did not know what to feel. Should she be angry at her mother for keeping this from her or should she be honoured that Terra had chosen her? If her mother hadn't started training her so young, maybe she'd still be alive. Before she could think on the matter any further, she heard a voice coming from her bag. As she rummaged through her bag, she realized it was coming from the communications stone. She grabbed the rock and replied.

"Tyran, I hear you. Are you all right? What have you managed to find?" she asked.

"First off, sorry for the late report. While I was with Mobious, I didn't feel comfortable using this device," Tyran replied. "I managed to get enough evidence to connect Mobious to the attack on the New Year's Eve celebration, and the thirteen murders that included Bear. It's not good, Ayleen, he is using demonic magic. I thought that was impossible, since all of the demonic cults were banned. I haven't heard of any demonic cult activities since I was a teenager."

"Are you sure that it's demonic magic?" Ayleen asked. "As far as I know, all masters of that kind of magic were quietly executed. At that time the Queen did not want to provoke any of the cult supporters. If Mobious is indeed using demonic magic, then we need to be careful. There is no telling what he can do. How did you find out about this?"

There was a moment of silence before Tyran responded. "I had to break into a restricted area. It was my only option. I was getting nothing otherwise. In the room, I found thirteen giant glowing diamonds in a circle. In the back of the room, Mobious had a book. As I flipped through the pages, I realized that it provided, in great detail, how to do what we saw at the New Year's Eve celebration. It can only be demonic magic. No other form of magic would allow for that kind of occurrence. I just have no idea where Mobious would get thirteen giant diamonds."

"Don't worry about that. I have it covered." Ayleen remembered the three elves she met near the sacred tree. "I'm already preparing to make the journey to Mobious' estate. I should be there in two days. Keep your head low until I get there."

"No good," Tyran told Ayleen. "He's on to me. Can you use a portal to Valberg? It's far enough away that you can be here in the morning, but not close enough for him to know you have arrived. I have to go. I can't talk any more. I'll see you tomorrow morning. I promise that you will have a way into this place."

With that, the stone went silent. She knew that she could no longer contact Tyran. She just hoped that he would be able to keep himself safe until she arrived. As she left her quarters, she headed to where her horse was stabled. She would not bring her carriage with her, without it she was less likely to be seen. This was the final part of her journey. She needed to stop Mobious or die trying. She prayed that Terra would be with her so that she would have the strength to do what must be done.

CHAPTER

UEEN MERRI SAT alone in her chamber. The last few days had been hard on her. In a few hours, she would have to go in front of the Council of Dukes. While they could not force her out of the throne, they could take away their army's support. With how many dukes were unhappy with her, there was no possible way that she could defend her territory if the dukes decided to wage war against her. She would have to fight with all her might to keep order.

She couldn't be seen looking unkempt. For the past few hours, she had been crying. She didn't know what else to do. Everything was either waiting on the Council's decision, or someone finding evidence against her daughter. The latter would now be nearly impossible. The investigation team she assigned to investigate Dariusa had all but been disbanded. Most of the group were blue or orange-skinned elves; they were expelled from the city. The purple ones sided with Dariusa.

Merri heard a knock on her door. She knew it was her daughter. She had asked Dariusa to come to her quarters in hopes that she could convince her daughter to stop her plans. Queen Merri opened her door and greeted her daughter. She then guided Dariusa to a set of chairs in the corner of the room. She knew that she had to be firm with her daughter and not fall for any of her tricks.

"How are you feeling, mother?" Dariusa asked. "I have been trying to find out who was the one who bewitched you, but I haven't been able to find any evidence."

"Enough of your games, Dariusa!" cried out Merri. "I know it was you who gave me the potion; the morning you announced your engagement. I know from my investigation branch that you have been planning to usurp the throne. I don't know why you would do this, but it ends now!"

"That is the most ridiculous thing I ever heard." Dariusa laughed. "Mother, I am doing what is best for Giana. I always have. I would never try to take the throne from you. I recommend you don't bring this theory up in front of the Council. They will not believe you either. You need to focus on the truth. An unknown criminal poisoned you which resulted in you making an order that you would never have done otherwise. Anything else is a waste of the Council's time."

Merri couldn't believe what her daughter was saying. Even though she confronted Dariusa with her lies, she wouldn't admit to any wrongdoing. With tears in her eyes, Merri once again tried to reason with her daughter. "Dariusa, please. I know there is a good person inside of you! Giana is falling apart as we speak! If you admit what you have done, I will pardon you! I need you now, more than ever! I want my daughter back!"

"That would be a good offer, Mother, if any of your accusations were true." Dariusa hung onto her lies firmly. "As I said, if you decide to continue this line of thinking through the Council's meeting, they will have no choice but to withdraw their armies. I have a strategy to defend you tonight. I would appreciate it if you allow me to use it. I do not want to make an enemy out of you, but I will if you continue with this nonsense."

"Leave. Now, Dariusa," the Queen demanded. "As of now, you are no longer my daughter. I will not call you or treat you as such. You are a vile and sick woman. I hope Terra is disappointed in you and when the time comes for you to be judged I know that you will be thrown into the Frozen Pit of Damnation. May you stay there for all eternity!"

Dariusa stood up and headed for the door. She was about to open it when she decided to reply to her mother. "I am sorry that you are unable to see the truth, Your Majesty. The world is changing, and you need to adapt to it. You're nothing but a scared child unwilling to do what must be done to survive. You are not for Giana; you are only for yourself. How I was ever raised by a mother like you, I will never understand. Good-bye, Your Majesty, tonight you will lose your throne."

As Dariusa left, she slammed the door. Merri vibrated in her seat with rage. So much for stalling. There was no way she could allow that woman to win. One thing was true. Dariusa was no longer her daughter. Tonight, her opponent shared her blood, but that didn't mean they were family. She needed to reunite Giana in any way possible. As long as the continent was divided, there would be chaos. She could foresee countless civil wars happening because of Dariusa. She headed to the make-up table in another part of her chambers. She would have to look presentable, and as the Queen, she should be. Tonight, she would take back her kingdom. Tonight, Dariusa's reign of terror would end.

Ayleen needed a portal to the crossroads South of Valberg. She didn't want Mobious sensing her arrival. She also knew that the area where the estate lay was now covered in snow. This would be the third time in her life that she had seen snow. She hated snow with every fibre of her being. The first time she encountered snow was while she was still a rookie. One of her early investigations had her looking for a suspect in the mountains. At that time, she shadowed two other investigators. They managed to find their suspect, but while the three of them were chasing the bad guys, Ayleen tripped and fell down a snow-covered slope forcing the others to leave her behind. It was one of the biggest embarrassments she experienced in her career. The last time she saw snow was only a few days ago, after the celebration. She looked towards the Northeast of the continent and thought, the sooner I get this over with, the better.

As soon as she arrived at the crossroads and the portal closed behind her, she encountered a camp of elves. She could tell that the camp was made recently. Most likely the result of the mass eviction of blue-and-orange-skinned elves from the South. She wanted to make it to her destination before the inn was closed for the night. At the camp, she saw blue-and-orange-skinned elves trying to set up tents and make a fire. Some of them had a few belongings from their homes, but most of them only carried the clothes that they had on. They didn't notice Ayleen at first. When they did, a blue-skinned elf was the first to address her.

"Whoa, we don't want any trouble." The blue-skinned man held up his hands. "As far as we knew this was not royal territory."

"Don't worry. I am not here to cause any trouble," Ayleen stated. "I was on my way to a location up the road and saw your camp and wondered if you needed any help."

"We don't need anything from you, you hateful purple-skinned elf!" shouted an orange-skinned woman. The blue-skinned man that was talking to Ayleen tried to calm the woman down. Ayleen knew that these people had every right to be angry. She contemplated just leaving them and carrying on to her destination.

"I'm terribly sorry for that, miss," the blue-skinned man continued. "My mother has always been short-tempered, and given the situation that we've been put in, she has been distraught."

The orange-skinned woman was escorted away by two young men. Ayleen felt terrible for the whole group. Just when she thought it was best to go, the blue-skinned man made a gesture to ask for a private conversation. She had to take this opportunity. Even though she knew what was going on, it was not a good reason to not to help if she could. She got off her horse and followed the man behind a snow-covered bush.

"Again, I am sorry about my mother," the blue-skinned man apologized. "I saw your badge as you came up. You're from the Investigation Branch of the Guard, aren't you? My name is Carth, and I used to be part of the Investigation Branch as well."

"I thought you looked familiar, although I don't think we ever worked on a case together." Ayleen now recognized the man. "I am Captain Ebella. All I wanted was to make sure that your group was all right. I was one of the few members of the guard who refused to carry out the Queen's orders. I can't say much, but what I can say is it was not the Queen's fault that the blue-and-orange-skinned elves were kicked out of the South."

"Let me guess. It's the Princess' fault we are in this predicament." Carth said, to Ayleen's shock. "Before I was forced out of my position, I was in a group that was investigating Princess Dariusa. The Queen asked us to investigate her daughter to see if the religious sect posed a threat to Giana. It was supposed to be one of the most secretive investigations in the kingdom. However, we could not make a report before we were exiled due to our skin colour and then the attack on the capital happened. We just needed another day or two, and then we would have the evidence that we needed to prevent all of this. Or fix it."

"I'm not surprised that Queen Merri would keep me in the dark about the investigation," commented Ayleen. "If I were part of the investigation, it might have been considered a conflict of interest or bias. I'm just surprised that Princess Dariusa would be so bold as to make the Queen kick out such a massive group of people."

"The change gave her an opportunity," Carth replied. "My team found evidence that Princess Dariusa was trying to convert people to her version of Terra's religion. Once she became Queen, she planned to make the capital city the centre for her version of the religion and remove everyone who disagreed. By our estimate, if the change hadn't happened on New Year's Eve, then we would have had a year or two before she made her move on the Crown. That would have been enough time to prove to everyone the monster that she really is."

"Then you've been investigating her for some time? Thank you for that information, Carth," Ayleen said. "While I would love to deal with Dariusa personally, I am on my way to apprehend the person responsible for all this chaos. If I can get back to the capital before Dariusa can do anything to Queen Merri, I hope I can find the evidence that your team has gathered and present it to the Council of Dukes. Hopefully, that will fix this mess."

"See that you do," warned Carth. "I appreciate you trying to bring the man responsible for the change to the land to justice. However, as long as Princess Dariusa is free, then everyone who does not have purple skin is in danger. We should still have allies in the Investigation Branch who will help us in this quest. When you return to Terra, find Captain Bridge. He was my superior and had purple skin."

The elves agreed on this. When Ayleen returned to the capital city, she would find the evidence that Carth's team had gathered. She only hoped that during her absence, Princess Dariusa would not cause too much damage to the political system. She bid farewell to Carth. The amount of time she had lost was worth it. If she got back on her horse right now, she might still reach her destination by closing time. There was no more time to stop for any reason. She needed to get to the inn so that she could have a decent night's rest. She needed to be fresh and alert to arrest Mobious tomorrow morning. That was her hope, to arrest him, but she knew that he would not go down without a fight. Terra help me, she thought.

Mobious waited in his library with the window open. He expected two individuals, one after the other. A raven flew into the library. This was the first individual he was expecting. It wasn't any normal raven. It was a magical beast that he constructed with his limited knowledge of druidic magic. He intended for the bird to fly around his estate and report back to him if anything was off. He did not want the demi-god sneaking up on him. It was the bird that spoke first.

"Master Mobious, I am here to report." The bird settled onto Mobious' arm. "I followed Tyran and Zalissa to the lake. When she left, Tyran contacted someone magically. Tyran is working with someone called Ayleen. She will be here tomorrow morning to attempt to arrest you."

So, Ayleen was investigating him. Just as he expected. But perhaps he had a spy in his workforce. Then an idea clicked in his mind. He remembered the golden woman inside his vision when he attacked the capital. He realized that Ayleen and that golden woman must be the same person. Knowing this was the truth, he smiled. If Ayleen was coming here, he could capture her and begin his studies on the demi-god.

"Do you need anything else, Master?" squawked the raven.

"I don't need anything until tomorrow morning," Mobious said with a wave of his hand as the raven vanished. "This is great news. Tomorrow I will have everything I want. First, I will capture Ayleen, then I will meet my acquaintance, and then I will finally see my family again."

A knock at the door told Mobious that his second guest had arrived. This invitation was necessary. Right after he killed Jorrard, he realized that he needed a replacement butler. He usually wouldn't ask it of a woman, but he needed a temporary butler for the dinner tomorrow night. He called to her to enter. How fortunate he had chosen Zalissa, everything was falling in place.

"Master Mobious, you called for me?" Zalissa asked timidly.

"Yes, I did. I appreciate you being on time." Mobious smiled. "I have a predicament. I have a guest tomorrow night, and Jorrard is nowhere to be seen. Usually, I would ask another servant to fill his shoes, but since it is a dinner party, I thought you would be the best option. Tomorrow night you will temporarily be my butler."

"Thank you, Master Mobious." Zalissa curtsied. "If I may ask, Master, should we search for Jorrard?"

"You don't need to worry about that," Mobious replied. "All you need to know is that he has abandoned his duties and I will be looking for his replacement."

With that, Zalissa nodded and curtsied again; Mobious dismissed her. The moment the maid left the room, he heard a voice from inside his desk. He opened the drawer and pulled out the Cube of Destiny. After he'd found out someone had entered his restricted building, he realized that he needed to keep the Cube close to him at all times. It was his ticket out of this nightmare. He was too close to winning.

"Lindar Mobious, I calculate that our time together is nearing its end," the Cube stated. "By this time tomorrow, I should be in a different location, possibly back at the monastery where you found me."

Mobious chuckled at the Cube's remark. "I believe you are wrong, Cube. At this time tomorrow, I will have a demi-god in captivity while waiting for the man who will spill all of your secrets. If you see any other possible future, then it is you that is mistaken."

"I'll keep a record of that," the Cube answered. "However, it will be in your best interest to listen to the advice I am about to give you. You are so close to the thing that you wish to accomplish. It would be foolish not to consider every possibility."

"Oh, believe me, I have," Mobious replied as he put the Cube back into the drawer. "As I said earlier, I refuse to listen to an inanimate object. You are nothing but a tool to be used by elves. Remember your place."

Mobious sat down and began to read a book on the desk. He had to calm his mind down in order to get a good night's rest tonight. Tomorrow would be a busy day. There was no room for errors. Ayleen would probably arrive here thinking that she had a surprise advantage. Oh, how wrong she would be. He would wait for her inside his estate, allowing her to believe she had the upper hand until he sprang his trap. No longer would he have to wait to deal with all his problems. Tomorrow would be the day he would finally get everything he deserved.

Queen Merri waited outside the Council's meeting room. She had already met with the Council and presented her case. As per Giana tradition, all parties in court had to offer their case alone before the Council without the eyes of the opposing sides. She sat nervously waiting for the time she would be called back into the Council's chambers. Out of all twelve Dukes, there were only two who she could feel assured would be on her side. The only positive thing she could think of, was that if any fewer than ten of the twelve Dukes voted to withdraw their armies, she could request an investigation which would stall her enemies. If ten Dukes withdrew their troops, then there would be no way she could stop Dariusa.

After a while the doors opened, and she was escorted into the chambers. It was one of the second largest rooms in the castle. The twelve Dukes and Duchesses sat at a horseshoe-shaped table; the Queen stood in the centre. The Duke overseeing the meeting was Duke Lakeseer. Queen Merri hated this man with every fibre of her being. He was rude and said everything that came to his mind; unfiltered. If he hadn't been born into the Lakeseer family, there would have been no way Queen Merri would have allowed him to oversee anything, let alone the Lakeseer territory.

"Now that everyone has spoken, we can make our judgment," the Duke said, addressing the Queen. "Queen Merri, you are accused of discriminating against elves with a different skin colour than yours, resulting in the exile of a third of the population of Terra. We acknowledge that you believe that you were under a spell. You accused your own daughter, Princess Dariusa, of bewitching you. I, for one, do not believe you. I think it's ridiculous for a grown woman to blame her own daughter for her actions. However, it is not solely up to me. It is up to a vote. Before the vote happens, would you like to say anything more in your defense?"

"Members of the Council," the Queen addressed the room. "As you know when we first gave our defense in the first part of this meeting over an hour ago, we provided evidence proving that our daughter planned to force out anyone who didn't subscribe to her version of Terra's words. We saw this play out yesterday when she bewitched us and ordered us to exile all elves that did not have purple skin. We know that shortly after the meteorite hit the Princess was preaching that the purple-skinned elves were the true children of Terra. And yet this Council refuses to believe that the Princess could act in such a way. We ask that you re-evaluate the evidence. Additional evidence has disappeared from my investigative team. Captain Bridge is missing."

"We have heard enough from the defense. Bring in the accuser," the Duke ordered.

To the surprise of no one, the accuser was Princess Dariusa herself. As Dariusa walked into the chambers, it took everything in Queen Merri's power not to react to the presence of her daughter. It would do nothing but hurt her case. However, the rage that had built up inside her body was so intense that she could feel herself shake. Princess Dariusa walked up and stood beside her. The Queen couldn't believe that the Council could possibly take Dariusa's word over hers, but it was becoming more likely that they would. Duke Lakeseer asked Princess Dariusa to state her closing argument.

"Ladies and Gentlemen of the Council," Princess Dariusa opened. "As you can see, Her Majesty is not mentally fit to be in her position anymore. This started when she opened an investigation into her own daughter. It was only today that I found out about this. She couldn't bear the thought of me becoming the next Queen. She never could. When the meteorite hit, she couldn't accept the fact it was a gift from Terra; that Terra is the only one who could change the elves on this scale. She instead saw the opportunity to first exile the non-purple elves and then slander me by accusing me of bewitching her. When I confronted her earlier today about this fact, she deflected and put the blame on me yet again. Never in the history of Giana has an heir to the throne put a spell on the ruling monarch. My mother is ill and needs to be relieved of her duties as soon as possible."

The Council of Dukes chatted amongst themselves until Duke Lakeseer banged his gavel to bring order to the room. "All right, everyone. We have had time to discuss this. As per tradition, we are to vote on whether we will withdraw our military support from the capital or stand with the Queen. Everyone's vote is independent, and anyone who is caught colluding with another Duke or Duchess will be punished to the full extent of the law."

One by one, the Council members revealed their vote. Duke Lakeseer was the last to reveal his vote. Ten out of twelve Dukes voted to withdraw their armies from the capital. It was enough votes to end Queen Merri's reign.

"The results are in." Duke Lakeseer began his final words. "Ten members of this Council have voted to withdraw their support from the kingdom. Merri of Terra, you are no longer the Queen in the eyes of this Council. You have twenty-four hours to exile yourself or you will be removed by force. Anyone who stands with you will be considered an enemy of Giana. I advise you to get a good night's rest. Tomorrow morning Princess Dariusa will be crowned as Giana's next Queen. This meeting is adjourned. All hail Queen Dariusa!"

Merri was shaking with rage; fighting back tears. As much as she had anticipated the results, nothing could prepare her for how she was feeling now. Her kingdom was gone. The guards came to escort her back to her chambers. Tonight would be the last night in her own bed. As the guards escorted her out of the room, she did not bother to look at Dariusa. She didn't care how her daughter felt after her victory. She didn't want to give her daughter the satisfaction of humiliating her more. Her only hope now was to exile herself and find the only one she could trust, Captain Ayleen Ebella. She just hoped that her daughter did not have any more tricks up her sleeve before she could escape the castle.

Ayleen arrived at the Queen's Lake Inn late in the evening. She knew that if she came any later, there would be no hope for her to get a room. As she expected, the inn was quiet. Most of the patrons were in their rooms. After she spoke to the innkeeper, she headed to the bar. She had time for one drink before heading to bed. With the way things had been going, she needed something to take the edge off. There was too much sadness going on.

She sat on a stool right at the bar. At the table behind her three blue-skinned elves were talking and being loud. She knew that these three men had likely had a bit too much to drink. This didn't bother her. If she believed that being that drunk would solve her problems, she would probably do it, too. The bartender was a short man who was going bald. She put down a silver coin and asked for a drink called a Hydra.

"That is going to be a lot more than a single silver coin, miss," the bartender growled.

"One silver coin should buy me a Hydra and cover the tip." Ayleen was shocked that the bartender would ask for more money. The drink she had ordered usually only cost three-quarters of a silver coin. "What is your price for a Hydra here?"

"For you, it's eight silver," sneered the bartender. "It's one silver for any blue or orange-skinned elves. But after what you lot did yesterday, I can't risk serving purple-skinned elves like you unless you want to pay a lot more."

Ayleen couldn't believe what she was hearing. The bartender must have known that if she was with that lot, intending trouble, she would not have come alone. No one in this building was in any danger just because of her skin colour. She decided to pay the man anyway. Any argument would only cause further trouble. As she got handed her drink, the three blue-skinned men from the table behind her approached her.

"Well, lookee here! A high and mighty purple elf," one of the men sarcastically said.

"You've got a lot of nerve showing your face here, especially after what your kind pulled." The second one threatened.

"Gentlemen, I'm having a drink," Ayleen stated not looking at the three patrons. "If you continue to bother me, I promise it won't end well for you. So, I suggest you go back to your table and sit down."

"Oh, look, this woman thinks she's tough. Who does she think she is, a guard?" the third one piped in.

"Even if she is a guard, she is far away from the Queen. I bet she abandoned her post to get a drink." The first man laughed. It took everything in her power not to react to the comment.

"How about we teach this purple elf a lesson because she obviously forgot her manners," the second elf said as he put a hand on Ayleen's shoulder.

As soon as the second man touched Ayleen's shoulder, she slammed her head into the man right behind her, hitting him in the jaw. She kicked the man to the left of her in the knee, forcing him to fall. As he fell to the floor, the other two men backed away from her stool. She turned around and got off her seat to see the uninjured man pull a knife out of his waistband. She quickly grabbed the man's wrist and forced his arm around to his back. He dropped the knife.

"I said this would not go well for you!" snarled Ayleen. "If you wish for this to continue, please, I have all night. I would suggest that you leave me alone and we all go to our rooms and rest for the night."

The three men nodded as the free man went to help his friend up off the floor. Ayleen let go of the man she was holding and watched carefully as the group left the bar and headed to their rooms. She sat back down to finish her drink. Then she realized that the bartender hadn't moved a muscle throughout the whole fight.

"With your lack of reaction, I assume this happens often?" Ayleen asked the bartender.

"More than I like to admit," answered the bartender. "Those three idiots often pick fights with my customers. The only reason why we haven't kicked them out is they pay the most money of any patron. Thank you for teaching them a lesson."

The bartender gave Ayleen back seven silver pieces. She knew whatever bad blood there was between her and the bartender, it was resolved now. "Thanks. I don't blame you for being worried. I have seen a lot of my kind say and do some hideous things. I can guarantee you won't have any trouble from me."

"I can see that now," the bartender acknowledged. "I apologize for my behaviour earlier. My daughter-in-law got out of The Capital safely with my grandchildren. However, my son wasn't as fortunate. He decided to fight the guards when they came to his home. He thought a couple of thugs had stolen a couple of guard's uniforms and were attacking his family. I only found this out an hour ago via a magical message from my daughter-in-law. They are walking here so it will take them a few days to arrive. Again, I am sorry."

"I am sorry about your son, sir," Ayleen said as she finished her drink.

The bartender nodded. After she finished her drink, she decided to give the bartender another silver piece as a bigger tip. He could easily have helped the thugs she fought off. He chose not to. Like her, he was broken and saddened at the events of the week. You couldn't fault him for not trusting her. If Ayleen had been in a slightly different location when the meteorite hit, she would have had a different skin colour. Would she feel the same way as the bartender if she had blue or orange skin? She did not know the answer to this or whether she should even ponder the question. Right now, she needed to go to bed and rest up. Tomorrow would be a long day. Tomorrow she would fix all of this. That was her hope at least.

Tyran couldn't fall asleep. His mind was too focused on tomorrow. He hoped that Ayleen would get here and everything after that would fall into place. He knew it wasn't going to be that easy. Mobious was a powerful wizard and knew many spells. Tyran knew that Mobious suspected he was a spy. He got out of bed and stood up for a stretch. Before he could get back into the bed, he heard a knock at the door. Who would bother him at this hour? At this time of night, everyone was expected to have turned in for the night. He opened the door to see Zalissa in her nightwear with her hair down.

"I hope you don't mind, Tyran, I couldn't sleep. Can I come in?" Zalissa asked quietly. Tyran motioned her to come in. Both elves sat on his bed. Before Tyran could say a word, Zalissa spoke again. "I have an awful feeling that something has happened to Jorrard. I haven't heard from him all day, and Lord Mobious told me that he abandoned his duties."

Tyran knew that this was a lie from Mobious. From the few times he interacted with Jorrard, he felt that Jorrard would never do this. However, he did not want to worry Zalissa. "I'm sure Jorrard has a good reason for leaving. He will probably be back in a day or two. He doesn't seem like the kind of person who would abandon their post."

"You are probably right," Zalissa agreed. "Ever since New Year's Eve, I have been on edge. I'm still getting used to the fact that the estate is covered in snow. This is coming from a woman who was raised in the mountains. None of this feels right, Tyran."

"I couldn't agree with you more." Tyran looked into her eyes. "I'm not exactly sure what is going on, but I have my theories. Whatever happens, I will make sure that I will do everything in my power to keep you safe."

"You care about me that much?" Zalissa asked.

"Yes, I do, Zalissa," Tyran answered. "I know it's been only a few days since we met, but I can't deny how I feel about you anymore. After tomorrow I'm yours. I would happily commit myself to you right here and right now, but there is something that I need to do tomorrow, and it will change both of our lives. I just don't want to see you get hurt so promise me, tomorrow you will not go near Lord Mobious unless you have to. Can you do that for me?"

"I can try to stay away from Lord Mobious until dinner," Zalissa said. "However, at the dinner, Lord Mobious is expecting me to be his temporary butler for the dinner party."

Tyran knew if Ayleen came in the morning, then Mobious would not be having that dinner party. He would either be in a cage or dead. One thing he did need to know was who Mobious' guests were. "Do you know who Lord Mobious is hosting tomorrow night?"

"I have no idea," Zalissa replied. "I wondered that myself. After I met with Lord Mobious, I asked around the estate to see if anyone had any idea. When that didn't work, I crept into Jorrard's office to see if he had any record of the mysterious guest. There was nothing, only that there was a guest tomorrow."

While Tyran wanted to know the identity of the mysterious guest for Ayleen's sake, it was the least important thing to worry about right now. "It doesn't matter right now. What matters is your safety. As long as you can stay away from Lord Mobious until dinner that will give me enough time."

"Enough time for what?" Zalissa asked. "I don't know what you are up to, but I trust you more than anyone else these days. I was thinking, after tomorrow would you accompany me back to Thaldor? I think it's about time I see my sister's grave."

"I would be more than happy to go anywhere with you," Tyran replied. "By this time tomorrow, I'm yours. There is no one else in this world I would rather be with than you. Please don't ask me more until then. I cannot tell you anything right now."

With that, the two lovers kissed. Tyran had had many lovers before Zalissa, even one that was close to becoming his wife. None of them made him feel the way he did about her. He just hoped that he would survive tomorrow so that he could enjoy the rest of his life with her. He also had a worry. Would she think differently if she were to discover that he was a spy? Would she feel like he had lied to her? Used her? He would need to lie to her until the job was done. There was no point in exposing himself when the job wasn't completed. While he knew it was part of his job, every time he withheld the truth from her, it hurt him more and more.

XI

CHAPTER

IN THE WEE hours of the morning, Dariusa couldn't sleep. She walked out of her bedroom where her fiancé was still sleeping and headed to the balcony that was part of her chambers. Her thoughts kept bothering her. Even though her mother would be exiled by the end of the day, she still had supporters. Dariusa could not allow her mother to form an alliance with her enemies. If this were to happen, a civil war would break out. She didn't realize that Edwin was slowly approaching behind her.

"I'm surprised that you couldn't sleep, Dariusa," the Duke murmured as he approached her. "What could possibly be bothering my Queen?"

"I should feel like I have won," Dariusa replied, not turning to face Edwin. "My mother still has allies. She still has Captain Ebella. If we allow her to be exiled, she will gather them and possibly try to overthrow me. I can't allow it to happen."

"I have an idea, my love," Edwin assured her. "Your mother cannot be exiled. She needs to be dealt with. Like I said before, I think we should make the Queen's death look like a suicide. That way, people will think that she was overcome with grief and couldn't handle losing her crown."

"That was before we forced her into exile," Dariusa snapped back. "If we kill her now, then it will look suspicious. Yes, we can make it look like a suicide, but neither one of us has that kind of skill."

As much as Princess Dariusa wanted to do away with her mother, Duke Lakeseer had made that more difficult by exiling her. If they were to kill the Queen now, it would be highly suspicious. She did not have confidence that they could make her death look like a suicide. However, it seemed like Edwin had an idea. Normally it would scare her, being in love with a man who came up with plots to kill people so quickly, but given the circumstances, she knew that her fiancé would be her most valuable ally. For now. She decided to hear him out.

"Don't you worry about that." Edwin smiled. "My family knows an assassin who is more than willing to assist with this problem. He should be arriving in an hour and a half. I took the liberty of inviting him here as a back-up plan. I will meet with him and discuss our situation. We should also talk about the blue-and-orange-skinned elves. They will be a threat in the future. With their numbers, they can overwhelm us and take over the kingdom. You don't want to be Giana's shortest reigning Queen, do you?"

"That I do not," Dariusa declared. "My first order after becoming Queen will be the invasion of the Northern part of the continent. They are not Terra's chosen. That means they are no better than animals. I will order my army to slaughter as many of them as they can. That will make two-thirds of the Council my enemies, but I have a plan for taking care of them before they become a problem."

"Please, do tell." The Duke was intrigued by this.

"Since you already have an assassin on the way, you provided me with a great opportunity." Dariusa turned to face her lover. "At my coronation, all twelve Dukes and Duchesses will be in attendance. First, we will spread a rumour that a resistance group is on the rise. Then when everyone has settled down and start to drink, we will give any nobility that has blue or orange skin poisoned wine. We will blame the tragedy on the new resistance group that we have made up. We will tell people they killed their own nobility due to their loyalty to the Crown. This will rally the troops and convince the purple-skinned elves to fight for me."

"That's the most wonderful plan I have ever heard," Edwin said admiringly. "Giana hasn't had a war in over a century. The history books have been boring as of late. A war of this magnitude will be talked about for ages and you, my love, will be the hero of it all. Imagine, if you will, I see a Giana where there are only purple-skinned elves who worship you long after you are dead. They will believe that you had vanquished the great evil of the blue-and-orange-skinned elves. Your name will be known until the end of time. I will be by your side doing whatever is necessary to turn you into a legend."

"I like the sound of that," she said, stepping forward to get closer to him. "With you, I can do anything that I want. Nothing will stop us from making Giana a utopia for purple-skinned elves. It will be my legacy. And I will bring peace and order to the continent. People of this world will know my name."

Dariusa kissed Edwin. Together they would make Giana a better place. Anyone who stood in their way would die. The will of Terra would be carried out. The blue-and-orange-skinned elves were nothing more than wild animals and were a threat that needed to be dealt with. The new Queen understood what needed to be done. It would cost many lives and bloodshed, but it didn't matter to her. As soon as she was crowned Queen, she would bring order to her kingdom no matter what the cost. With Duke Morgwyn willing to plan and carry out any dirty work the Princess needed to have done, she could almost see Giana becoming a paradise.

As Tyran awoke, he realized that something wasn't right. He had no clothes on, and there was a weight beside him. He opened his eyes and turned his head to see Zalissa's naked body beside him. He moved carefully as he left the bed. He didn't want to wake her. *Damn my weakness. I wanted to wait,* he thought. As he got dressed to go out and meet Ayleen, he heard rustling from his bed. Apparently, he wasn't as quiet as he thought.

"Do you have to get up this early?" a groggy Zalissa asked. "Last night was so pleasant I didn't want it to end."

"I have to go and meet a friend. I'll be back shortly." He leaned over to kiss her. "And besides, the sun is almost up. That means you should be going to your post soon."

It felt right. Being with Zalissa and waking up to seeing her every morning was what Tyran wanted more than anything. Hopefully, Ayleen wouldn't find out about this part of his undercover operation until after they took down Mobious. He knew that the mission was more important than his personal life. However, he couldn't deny his feelings any longer. He didn't want to lose the chance to be with Zalissa, and he knew that if he waited until after his investigation, he might not see her ever again.

Zalissa looked out of the window and instantly sprang out of bed. "I totally thought it was earlier than this. Why didn't you wake me up, Tyran?"

"I didn't want to disturb a beautiful sleeping angel." Tyran giggled. "Remember what I asked? Please don't go near Lord Mobious until the dinner party if you can."

"I will do my best," She replied as she hurriedly dressed.

Tyran left the estate to head to a small village twenty minutes away. The small town only had a dozen houses and each was owned by families of the estate staff. This was the first time he walked to the village. He could see it from the estate and had heard many tales from Zalissa about the place. None of them were particularly impressive. Everything that he had heard, you could say about any farmer. He met Ayleen on the edge of town closest to the estate. She was paying a farmhand to look after her horse until she returned.

"Good morning, Ayleen, hope you had a pleasant evening," Tyran greeted her.

"Once I finally got to my bed, I had a good evening," Ayleen replied as the two walked back to the estate. "Giana is falling apart. People don't trust others because of their skin colour now. It saddens me that the continent has dissolved into chaos like this. Princess Dariusa bewitched Queen Merri and made her throw out anyone from the Southern part of the continent who didn't have purple skin. I just don't know if I will be able to stop her in time."

"Please tell me you are not serious," Tyran begged, but the look on

Ayleen's face told him that she wasn't lying. "We have to stop this today. Whether we kill Mobious or arrest him, he must see justice now. This has gone on for too long."

"As soon as I am done here, I need to return to the capital as quickly as possible," Ayleen stated. "Last night the Council of Dukes were supposed to vote on whether or not they would support Queen Merri any longer. I know Queen Merri has two allies that are loyal to her no matter what, but I fear the other ten Dukes and Duchesses may have turned on her. Any new developments on your end?"

"I have two things to report, Captain," Tyran replied. "As I told you last time we spoke, Mobious has a guest tonight that seems to be very important. I am unable to find anything about this guest at all. Secondly, Mobious acquired a weird object. A golden cube with some strange symbols on it. I was going to try to pocket it, but I figured that Mobious would miss it and it would blow my cover."

"That cube sounds like something I read about in my studies, but I can't remember," a puzzled Ayleen commented. She was alarmed at this bit of information but couldn't figure out why. Every fibre of her being told her that this was going to be a problem. Could her new powers be responsible for her feeling this way? "Tyran, if that object poses a threat, I need you to take it away from Mobious by any means necessary."

Tyran agreed as the pair entered the estate through a back gate covered in overgrown bushes. Little did they know they were being watched by Mobious' raven. The wizard heard their conversations through the eyes and ears of his pet. This would not end well for Ayleen, he thought. Soon he will have his new test subject. As for Tyran, Mobious knew that his maid, Zalissa, had fallen in love with the orange-skinned elf. He had no problem using her against him. Everything was going according to plan. He left his library to meet the pair in the dining room where he would deal with them. There would be no way that Ayleen or anyone could stop him. After this day he would be the master of Giana.

Dariusa and Edwin waited patiently in the Princess' quarters. Edwin's guest was to arrive any minute. Dariusa had heard many things about this assassin from her fiancé. Apparently, he was known by only one name, Xelo. In Elvish, this meant "enveloping shadows" which was very appropriate. From what Edwin had told her about the man, he had killed many nobles and heads of the military without being seen.

More importantly, he also had killed the royal advisor from Dariusa's childhood. When she heard this news, she immediately liked the assassin. The royal advisor that was killed was hated by Dariusa and tolerated by Queen Merri. The only reason her mother kept that man on the job was due to his intelligence and efficiency.

Just when the pair thought that Xelo was going to stand them up, he stepped out of the shadows in the corner of the room. He was dressed all in black; only his eyes showed.

"I can see that your name suits you, Xelo," Dariusa greeted the assassin. "I assume Duke Morgwyn has filled you in on the situation. I would hate to go over any unnecessary details."

"I assure you I have done my research," the assassin replied under his mask. The only part of the man that the Princess could see was the skin around his eyes. She could tell that he had blue skin. "It seems to me that your mother needs to die via suicide. Luckily for you two, that is my specialty. The best way to kill people, and for no one to ask questions is to convince everyone that they killed themselves. People may say they investigate suicides, but they usually find evidence to confirm their hypothesis."

While Dariusa was angry inside that she was forced to work with someone of different skin colour, the opportunity she had here was too good to ignore. "My fiancé has told me a great many things about you, Xelo. I hope all the stories he told me are true. As much as I hate to admit it, I may need your services again after we have dealt with my mother. Will you help us?"

"If you want to kill her properly, then you will need this," Xelo said as he handed Dariusa a small stone. "If your mother, like any other Terra-worshipping noble, has a bowl of meditation stones somewhere in her room, put the stone in the bowl. I assume she has a dagger in her room? A scarf to strangle herself? The stone you have there is enchanted with a one-way communications spell. Through this, I will convince her she has lost all control of her situation and her thoughts. I will convince her it is her idea to kill herself. When I am done, the spell will dissipate from the stone and be indistinguishable from an ordinary stone. If anyone suspects, no one will know how it was done."

"I see. Just like the time you killed my second cousin for me." Edwin laughed. "I still remember the position we found him in. I sure hope my father paid you well for that."

"He did, your Grace," the assassin purred with a twinkle in his eyes. "Before I go to monitor the Queen's room, we must discuss the method of payment. Since I have never killed a Queen before, my price will be a thousand gold. Do we have an agreement?"

"I'll pay you four hundred gold now and six hundred after my coronation. Should you fail to complete the job before my coronation, use the four hundred to flee the country," Dariusa stated coldly.

Xelo nodded and declared, "I never fail." He once again disappeared.

She turned to Edwin with rage in her eyes. "You didn't tell me that he didn't have purple skin. I despise the idea of working with one of them!"

"How was I supposed to know, Dariusa?" Edwin snapped back. "He is a low-life scum bag. Do you know what New Year's Eve is to the criminal underworld? It's only the busy day of the year for them. Xelo was probably out doing a job for another Duke or crime lord. There was no way for me to know the colour he would be the day after. Last time I talked to him was three months before the New Year's Eve celebration. Worst comes to worst we can blame the blue-skinned elves for the death of your mother and justify our genocide of the lowlifes."

"I am sorry I got angry at you." Dariusa realized that Edwin was right for once. "I am so close to everything I ever wanted. I can't let anything get in the way of that."

"I promised you that I would do anything in my power to make your dreams a reality, didn't I?" Edwin walked closer to Dariusa and embraced her. "Tonight, we will have everything that we wanted. Yes, we will have a few small obstacles to deal with, but nothing will threaten your power any longer. You have won! I have set up the wine for the coronation. We will deal with the blue-and-orange-skinned Dukes then. You have nothing to worry about. I'll take care of everything."

Edwin was right. Dariusa only had a few more things to do before no one could stand in her way. She would have one last conversation with her mother. In the rare case that Xelo couldn't convince her mother to kill herself, Edwin had already ordered the assassin to finish the job anyway possible, preferably outside the castle gates.

It would be mere hours before Merri would die. After that everything would fall into place. She had already made sure that Lord Lindar Mobious would be taken care of. Ayleen didn't know it now, but she was a pawn of the would-be Queen. If Ayleen posed a problem for Dariusa, then she had a plan to discredit her. There would be no way that her plan could fail. There were too many contingencies, and she had too many allies.

With an arrow notched, Ayleen and Tyran searched the estate for Mobious. It was still early enough in the morning that most other servants were not in the hallways. Even though Ayleen saw no one around, she had a sinking feeling that they were being watched. She had to be prepared for anything that Mobious would throw at her. She knew that one misstep would cost her and Tyran their lives.

As the pair entered the dining room, they spotted Mobious at the end of a long table. She knew that he had seen them and entered the room without trying to be stealthy. When they did a quick visual check of the room, Tyran gasped in shock. Sitting beside Mobious was a blue-skinned maid that Ayleen figured Tyran knew. Even from this distance, Ayleen could tell the maid had been crying. Mobious began to clap as Ayleen aimed her bow at his head.

"Congratulations, Captain Ebella, it seems you figured out the mystery after all." Mobious continued to clap as he stood up. "Mister Dori, thank you for bringing the demi-god to me. Now if you don't mind, could you tie her up for me? I'm afraid if you don't, I may have to kill your girlfriend here. As much as I don't mind, I prefer not to kill women if I don't have to."

"Don't do anything he says, Tyran!" Zalissa cried out. Hearing this, Mobious backhanded her face.

"What is going on, Tyran?" Ayleen demanded as she backed away from Tyran.

Tyran had no idea what to do. On the one hand, he could do what Mobious asked and save the woman he loved. On the other hand, if Zalissa were to die, millions of elves would be protected from the shadow creatures. He had to make a choice. But the decision was made for him in a second. Ayleen let loose her arrow. It flew directly into Mobious, knocking him back. Tyran ran to where Zalissa sat and cut her loose. This seemed almost too easy.

"Thank you for saving my life," Zalissa cried as she clung to Tyran. "What is happening, Tyran? After I left your room this morning, Lord Mobious told me to come to the dining room. Then he told me that you were a spy and tied me up."

"It's all right now. I'll explain everything once we get out of here. I promise," Tyran replied, stroking her hair.

"As touching as this is, we have to make sure the job is done," Ayleen ordered as she looked for Mobious' body. There was a problem, though. Mobious' body was nowhere to be seen. She once again notched an arrow in her bow. "That was a decoy, Tyran, keep your guard up. He could be anywhere in the room."

As soon as the words left her mouth, a gust of wind knocked Tyran and Zalissa to a wall. As Ayleen looked to see what was going on, she felt a hand on her throat, lifting her up. Mobious reappeared in front of Ayleen with a cube in one hand and her neck in the other.

"Did you really think it was going to be that easy, Ayleen?" Mobious laughed. "I know you are smarter than this. I can't wait to begin my experiment on you, daughter of Terra."

Mobious threw Ayleen back, and she landed in a magical cage that appeared out of nowhere. Then he turned to the other two elves and with a flick of his wrist chains appeared around the lovers. Ayleen tried to summon her powers like she did before, but with all her might, she couldn't force them to emerge.

"Why are you doing this, Lindar?" Ayleen shouted out. "I know you were a good person once before. So, tell me why all the murders, why all the chaos, and why all the deception?"

Mobious could see Ayleen was struggling within the cage. This amused him. His test subject would prove useful to him. He liked his subjects with a bit of fight in them. "You don't have any idea what it is like losing everything you have in one day. I am so close to bringing back my wife and daughter. So what if people need to die? As long as I have what I care about, nothing else matters."

"You are wrong about something!" Ayleen shouted back. "I know what it's like to lose the person you love the most. I accidentally killed my own mother! Don't you think I would do anything to bring her back if I knew I could?"

"It's too late, Captain Ebella, I have what I want." Mobious smiled as Ayleen began to feel drowsy. "What you are now experiencing is a second spell I put on the cage. The first spell was to ensure that you couldn't break out or use any magical abilities. Luckily for me, you only used your demi-god power once before, so it was easy for me to configure a spell for your imprisonment. The next spell, and the spell you are currently experiencing, is a sleep spell that only I can wake you from. Don't worry. You will be woken up once I have experimented with your brain enough, so you are more co-operative. This cage will come in useful again later today for my second guest."

Ayleen had to stay awake. She had to break out of the cage. She had to save her friend. She couldn't do it. The spell was too powerful for her. Maybe if she had practiced using her abilities, she could get out of this predicament. How could she have fallen for such an obvious trap? She had training for this. She had to get free! With the sleep setting in, she lost her concentration. She couldn't fight it anymore. Her eyes became too heavy for her to keep open. She had to close them. When she did, she fell into a deep sleep.

Ayleen awoke to a constant stabbing pain in her forehead. It felt like someone was throwing tiny rocks at her head. When she opened her eyes, she realized she was no longer in Mobious' estate. She was in a void with black and green colours swirling all around her. As she looked around, she saw someone that she knew she had never met before but felt as if she had. He seemed to be sitting on part of the scenery.

The man she saw appeared to be reptilian ... and yet had hair on his head. His skin was scales and he appeared to have well-manicured claws. He had a long, striped tail that seemed out of place with what he was wearing. He wore trousers that had a crease down the vertical middle. His shirt was very white with material that overlapped stiffly at the top with sharp angles. There was a strip of coloured cloth that wrapped around his neck, under the overlapped shirt material, and was tied in a neat knot at the top with the tails hanging neatly down the centre. He had an overcoat that matched the material of his trousers but seemed somehow thicker and stiffer. The coat had pockets sewn on the outside. And shiny leather shoes! Very odd.

"About bloody time you woke up, Terra," the creature exclaimed. "This is the seventeenth time we have met and this time it took you the longest to awaken. I have other appointments, and I would like to get this done."

"Who are you? Where am I?" Ayleen asked the creature. Then she realized what he had called her. "My name is not Terra, it's Ayleen Ebella. Terra is my mother. This must be one of Mobious' tricks."

"You say that two out of three times we have met." The man stood up. "As for who I am, that is none of your business. All you need to know is I am the person they send when people with your type of abilities are about to screw up."

Ayleen could understand most of what this man was saying although he used language that she didn't understand. "You still didn't answer two of my questions. Where am I and why do you keep calling me Terra?"

"You will eventually learn why I call you Terra once you die." He chuckled. "I'm not allowed to give you those answers while you are still alive. I am just here to make sure you do your job and defeat Mobious for the sixth time. Trust me. I don't want to be here either. If we meet again and you need to beat Mobious for a seventh time, I'm really going to kick your butt."

"So, you are telling me I have done this before?" Ayleen asked in shock. She couldn't believe what she was hearing. None of this made sense. "What happens if I don't beat him the seventh time? You kick me in the butt? That doesn't make sense. How will that help?"

"That does not concern you, Terra," the creature stated. "All you need to know is that you are part of a much longer process. Even though your physical body may die, your soul has been fighting this war for countless millennia. I for one, am sick of you mortals always failing at the last minute. You do so well and then when it counts the most, you screw it all up."

"I what? What do you expect me to do?" she cried out. "I am currently locked in a magical cage that prevents me from using my powers. I am also under a sleep spell that only Mobious can awake me from. I'm kind of out of options here so if you have any suggestions that would be of great help."

"Are you really this stupid?" the man asked. "You are a demi-god, for crying out loud! That means you are the second most powerful being on the mortal realm! You have the power to break free from his chains. You can do whatever you want. Whether you arrest Mobious or kill him, I really don't care as long as the problem is dealt with. That is good enough for me."

It was then that Ayleen realized that everything this creature said was right. She closed her eyes and looked deep within herself. She could feel her power coming out. She could go back and save Giana. She had the ability to save her friends. She was a demi-god, and no one would be able to stop her. As her power emerged, she returned from whence she came.

"That's my girl!" the man said to himself as another man walked from behind him.

"I see that went as we expected. Good job, Gallon." Gallon turned to see his master coming out of the shadows. He was a tall man with long blonde hair and blue eyes who wore a white gown.

"Zurel, I keep telling you I have this under control," an annoyed Gallon exclaimed. "Why are you here? I don't need to be watched over every time I do one of these appointments."

"We can never be too careful. There is always a chance that one of these mortals chooses to give up," Zurel replied. "Besides, I keep telling you to dress and talk like the mortal pulled into this dimension. They won't understand if you keep acting and dressing like a twenty-first-century businessman from the planet Earth."

"This is the only thing that looks good on me," Gallon complained. "Besides, I wouldn't have to do this job if you hadn't signed that deal behind the Cabal's back. I am still mad at you for that, but I keep doing this job because I respect you."

"You know I signed the deal before I cast out my emotions," Zurel explained once again to his employee. "Enough of this talk. We need to prepare for the next guest."

Gallon had nothing more to say. There was no point in arguing with someone who did not have any emotions. He knew that there were benefits for Zurel not having feelings anymore, but he couldn't bring himself to do the same to his own. One day this conflict would be over, and everything would go back to normal, or at least he hoped it would.

Merri sat on her bed, contemplating her next move. She knew she had to go into exile, but she had no idea where she would go and hadn't left the castle in years. She was afraid. She had to find Ayleen, that was definite. She could start looking for her around Mobious' estate. The only problem was that she was the most hated person in Giana right now. There would be nowhere on the continent she would be safe.

As she dressed herself for the day, she knew she would not be wearing a dress. She put on an old horse-riding outfit that she hadn't worn in decades. She hoped she would remember how to ride a horse; it had been so long since she had needed to. The moment she finished dressing herself, she heard a knock on the door.

While she knew who it was and didn't want to talk to her, by Giana's law any exiled person had a right to speak to the Queen, if they requested it. Dariusa entered the room and motioned for Merri to sit down. Merri decided to decline the invitation and continued to stand with her back to Dariusa while finishing packing. Merri was done with Dariusa's games. There would be no way that she would allow this woman to walk all over her anymore. She didn't see the Queen-to-be place a stone in her religious rock bowl.

"We think this will be the last time we will talk, Merri." Dariusa sat down and poured herself a drink. "We would offer you a drink, but we doubt you will accept it. This is all your own fault. You wouldn't accept that you had delusions, and to learn that you ordered an investigation of your own daughter only proves that you are not mentally fit to rule. We tried to help you."

"What do you want, Dariusa?" Merri asked with only venom in her voice and turned slowly to face her. "You have done enough to discredit me, ruin my reputation and my life. I don't want any more of your games. I just want the truth, but I doubt you're even capable of telling the truth. Let me pack and leave. You won."

"It's 'Your Majesty' to you now," snapped back Dariusa. "We will forgive you this once. Merri, what we want is for Giana to have a proper ruler, one who won't hesitate to do what is needed and one that can accept responsibility for what she has done. You failed at both. It is our understanding that the Book of Terra says that this entire world is meant for us. That means we must expand our borders and the only way we can successfully do that is to kill everyone that stands in our way. You were never able to do that."

"I stand in your way. Does that mean you are going to kill me?" asked the former Queen.

"No. Not yet." Dariusa half lied. "We will allow you to leave the capital city, unharmed. But if you start an uprising against our rule, then we have no choice but to eliminate you as a threat. We came here to encourage you to go find yourself a quiet life and stay out of Giana's politics. Whether or not you will do what we suggest, we have no idea. But be assured that we have many contingency plans just in case you don't, and we would not like to use them."

"The moment I find Captain Ebella, I am going to stop you." Merri got right into Dariusa's face. "There is nothing you can do that will prevent me from stopping the monster you have become. It may take days or even decades, but I will not die until I remove you from the throne and expose you for the witch you are."

Dariusa backhanded Merri so hard she lost her balance and fell. "You know that no one is allowed to get that close to royalty without permission. You have four hours to leave the castle. You will not overthrow us. We have come too far to fail. If you are still in the castle after the four hours, we will have the guards kill you on sight. Good-bye."

"I'll be gone in two!" As Dariusa left the room, Merri started to cry. There was no holding back her emotions anymore. The woman her daughter had become was nothing more than a tyrant and religious fanatic. How did she go so wrong? How did she raise a monster? As soon as she got up off the floor, she started to hear a voice.

"You have really messed up, Merri, haven't you?" The voice came out of nowhere, soft and silken. "This is all your fault. You raised her to be this way. You couldn't prevent her from doing terrible things. But you can end this all quite easily."

"Who's there? Where are you? Show yourself!" Merri demanded as she pulled out a dagger from her dresser and looked around the room.

"Ah, you already have the dagger in hand," the voice purred. "But there are many ways you can solve this problem. I noticed that you have alchemy supplies in the room. You could always make a poison for yourself. Or you could go to the other room to get some scarves to hang yourself with. No matter what you choose, you can escape this nightmare and go see Terra face to face and plead with her to intervene."

She felt an immense pain in her head. She had no idea what was going on. She dropped to the floor again with the amount of pain she was in. "Whoever you are, stop!"

"I'm trying to help you. I told you the only solution," the voice said calmly. "This will only end with your own death. There is nothing to be ashamed of. To stop the pain, just end your life. Is that so hard to understand? Terra waits for you. You know she is the only one that can save your people."

Every time she even thought about disobeying the voice, the pain got worse. Maybe it was right. Perhaps all she needed was to end it all. She picked herself up and grabbed the knife off the floor and examined it. She never realized how beautiful knives can be.

As she thought this, she had to fight her own mind. There was no way she was going to allow this voice to tell her what to do. Then she remembered how to make a poison that would taste good and go with a bit of wine and cheese. She couldn't believe she was even thinking about poison, but it felt so right.

As she turned around, she noticed curtain ropes hanging by the large windows. She had ordered the hanging of many criminals. She often wondered how much pain they were in when they died. She turned her gaze back to her bed and realized that her thoughts were her enemy. The pain started to get worse again. She had to get away from here, away from the voice.

XII

CHAPTER

DARIUSA WAITED UNTIL the time she was meant to step out of the room and face the crowd. In less than an hour, she would be Queen of Giana. The ceremony would be starting in a few minutes. Everything was going according to her plan. She wore a beautiful ball gown. Her fiancé arrived at the precise time she expected him. Like her, he was dressed in the fanciest of his clothing. The day was going as perfect as she had planned.

"We assume everything we discussed has been prepared," the soon-to-be Queen asked her groom-to-be.

"Xelo has taken care of the wine," replied Edwin. "As far as I can tell, no one has caught on to what we are doing. Before I pay off Xelo, should I instruct him to give Duke Lakeseer and Colonel Stonehawk wine one or wine two?"

"Give them wine two," confirmed Dariusa. "We don't want any loose ends. While they have been a great help to our cause, we don't trust them to keep their mouths shut. That clears out most of the Council. We don't think we need a new one. We, including you, can do just fine without any more interference."

Edwin nodded as the sound of horns filled the air. It was the signal that the coronation ceremony had started and Dariusa could step out and face her subjects. As she stepped through the archway that separated the inside of the castle from the courtyard, she could see that all twelve Dukes and Duchesses were in attendance.

There were many other nobles there as well. Most of them she hated because the colour of their skin was not purple, but she would be dealing with them soon. Both a High Priestess and an Archdruid were waiting for her at the end of the purple carpet. There were two pledges that she would be required to take before becoming Queen. As soon as she made her way to a pedestal, the ceremony officially began.

"Dariusa of Terra," began the High Priestess. "The Book of Terra explains what it means to be a child of the goddess. You are required to uphold any law that Terra herself has communicated to the temple. You are to enforce any laws that have come before your rule unless you change them and provide a solid reason why. You are to treat every elf with the respect that he or she deserves. Finally, you are required to think of Giana first and yourself second. Do you vow to honour these tenets?"

"It is our duty to obey these tenets," she lied as she watched the wine being passed through the crowd. Now that the High Priestess was done it was the Archdruid's turn to present the second vow.

"Dariusa of Terra," the Archdruid started. "The Book of Terra explains that Giana is a gift. The means it should be treated with respect. As Queen of this great land, you are responsible for the safety of its people, the safety of its animals, and the safety of its nature. You will treat all three of these aspects with the same respect. No one of these three should be treated greater than the other. If the Council of Dukes find that you have disobeyed this tenet, they will have the power to vote you out. Do you honour these tenets?"

"It is our duty to obey these tenets," she once again lied. "Sacred Terra, this we vow: We will take care of the land that you risked your life to protect. We will not refuse to help any elf that is in need. We are all descendants of the elves that came from the blossoms of our sacred tree. We are all equal, no matter what life we choose to live or what we have done. We will love one another like you have loved us. Finally, don't let hatred divide us. Let us act as one. So mote it be."

In the back corner of the courtyard, she saw Xelo giving her the signal that everything was set up. In a few moments, the next part of her plan would begin.

"By the power of the Temple of Terra," the High Priestess began.

"By the power of the Circle of Druids," continued the Archdruid.

"We crown you Queen Dariusa the First of Terra." the High Priestess and the Archdruid spoke as one completing the ceremony.

It was now time for Queen Dariusa to make a speech. Both the High Priestess and Archdruid stepped to one side, allowing for a full view of the Queen. "Our beloved subjects, we thank you for coming to this momentous occasion. Giana has suffered too much over the last couple of weeks. We hoped that our mother would be the one to guide us to a new prosperity, but sadly she chose to act for herself. We promise you that we will do better. However, while this is a time of celebration, we cannot let our guard down. In a while, we will explain to you the new danger that has emerged. Now is not the time for that explanation. Right now, we would like to make a toast to Giana's prosperity."

The crowd in unison said, "To Giana's prosperity," and drank their wine. Within seconds every noble who had blue or orange skin along with Duke Lakeseer and Colonel Stonehawk started to convulse. Panic spread throughout the crowd as the surviving nobles threw their cups on the ground in case their wine was poisoned as well. Inside Dariusa head, she smiled but she couldn't show anything but concern on her face to keep up her ruse.

"Will everyone please remain calm," she addressed the crowd, and the group began to listen. "We hoped this wouldn't happen, but there were rumours that it would, and we were unable to stop it. For that, we are truly sorry. The people responsible for this tragedy are known as Terra's Guardians. It is a group of blue-and-orange-skinned elves led by a former member of the guard. Her name is Captain Ayleen Ebella. There is no telling how many of the orange-and-blue-skinned elves are part of this group. From all reports, it could be all of them. As our first declaration as Queen of Giana, we command that the army of the Queen invade the territories of the Northwest and Northeast to hunt down these assassins!"

The crowd whispered among themselves for a minute. Then one by one all the remaining purple nobles and the only remaining Duke and Duchess pledged their armies to the new Queen. It had gone better than expected. Everything was lining up perfectly.

By the morning after tomorrow, her army would be marching out of the capital. One half to the Northeast and one half to the Northwest. Any people in the armies' path would be slaughtered or taken prisoner. Little did Dariusa know her actions now would have effects that would be felt for hundreds of years. Although maybe that is what she wanted.

With Ayleen out of commission, Tyran had no other option but to talk to Mobious and convince him to spare Zalissa's life. Both of them were still chained to the wall. Moments after Ayleen collapsed, Mobious started to summon a black vortex. Tyran had only seen this type of magic once before but had no idea what the effects would be this time. Tyran could not look at the vortex. Every time he tried, images of indescribable beasts flashed through his mind. He saw these beasts eating himself and everyone that he cared about. When the vortex was stable Mobious turned to face Tyran. In one hand black energy pulsed from it and in the other he still held the mysterious cube.

"I'm impressed, Mr. Dori," complimented Mobious. "It was only recently that I fully realized what your purpose here was. It takes a lot of nerve to lie to me. However, it is obvious you know my crimes, and because of that I can't allow you, Ayleen, or your lover to leave here alive."

"You can do anything to me, Mad Wizard of Thaldor!" Tyran yelled. He looked over to Zalissa to see a shocked look on her face. Calling Mobious by the name that was given to the serial killer who had murdered thirteen elves prior to the New Year's celebration was a shock. "Just don't hurt Zalissa! She is innocent in all of this! Ayleen and I are the ones you want!"

"Mobious, you bastard!" Zalissa cried out. "You killed her. You told me that everything would be fine, and we would find the one responsible for her death. You killed my sister!"

Mobious turned and walked closer to her, putting a hand to her cheek. "Zalissa, my dear, your sister's death was the only way I could make Giana a better place. After today there will be no more murders and no more tears. With the power I have in my hand, I can make a world where everyone is happy, and I can bring back the people I had to kill."

"I don't believe a word you say!" shouted the maid. "You can rot in the ground, barred from Terra's presence, for all I care! May your soul be frozen for all eternity!"

"Let her go, Mobious!" commanded Tyran.

"You know I can't do that," replied Mobious as he turned to look at Tyran. "You don't have to worry about me hurting anyone. After today none of you will remember this event. With the Cube of Destiny, I can control reality and shape it to my will. Tomorrow you will be calling me Emperor Mobious, and I will have my family back and everything I ever ..."

Suddenly, all three elves saw a golden light come from Ayleen's cage. As Mobious turned to look at the light, the cage flew apart. As the dust settled Mobious saw the golden woman he had seen from his vision during his attack on the capital. She only vaguely resembled Ayleen.

"This ends now, Mobious!" shouted Terra's Avatar as a golden beam of energy came out of her hand hitting Mobious, lifting him and flinging him to the side. Without Mobious' concentration, the magical chains that held Tyran and Zalissa disappeared. Mobious also dropped the cube as he was flung across the room.

Soon after Mobious hit the floor he stood up and started throwing fireballs in hopes of hitting Ayleen, but they just bounced off her golden aura. Not realizing he had dropped the cube, he headed inside the vortex where he knew he could amplify his power to destroy them all.

A ripple of golden energy pulsed out of Ayleen, causing Mobious' vortex to dissipate, temporarily preventing him from casting any more spells. As Ayleen walked closer to Mobious, Tyran noticed the cube and picked it up. To Mobious' horror, the cube disappeared from Tyran's hand and he collapsed. Before he could scream in rage, Mobious felt a sharp pain pierce through his heart. He spun around to see Zalissa; her dagger had plunged into his heart. He had thought her insignificant, but she had slipped behind him. Damn her. Damn them all. Elnora,

Tavia ... I'll be with you soon, he thought. Mobious collapsed to the floor.

"I guess I'm not the hero I thought I was," he muttered as his life faded. These were the final words of Lord Lindar Mobious, Advisor to the Queen of Giana, the Mad Wizard of Thaldor.

Ayleen put a hand on Zalissa's shoulder as the golden aura faded, returning her back to her purple skin. "As much as I didn't want this result, there was no other option."

"That bastard deserved every bad thing that could come to him," Zalissa snarled as she turned to walk to Tyran, who was sitting up looking bewildered. Before she could get far, Mobious' body started to dissolve into dust while Ayleen's amulet began to glow. Ayleen didn't seem to notice because she was focused on Tyran. The dust drifted towards Ayleen and seemed to be absorbed into the amulet. "What in Terra's name is that and why did it absorb Mobious?"

"What? This? This is just a cheap amulet that I bought at the New Year's Eve celebration," Ayleen answered not realizing what had just occurred. "What do you mean absorb? We don't have time for this, we need to get out of here now. Tyran, what did you do with that cube?"

"What in Terra's name are you talking about?" Tyran asked in total confusion. "The last thing I remember is that I was magically chained to the wall and you were glowing! What is going on here, Ayleen?"

Ayleen knew that whatever that cube was, it had wiped away Tyran's memories. However, that was the least of her worries. They had to get back to the capital and she had no idea if she could find a portal wizard. It was two days to the Tree by horse. They had to save the Queen. She could explain everything to Tyran on the way there, but right now, she had to move and quickly.

One of Giana's problems was solved. Another one needed her attention. One thing kept bothering her. Why did Zalissa ask about her amulet at such a weird time? It was just an ordinary amulet that was sold to her by a kind gentleman. And why did the body of Mobious disappear?

The journey back to the capital did not go as Ayleen expected. Instead of two elves making the journey, there was a third elf accompanying them. She also didn't expect to have to explain the battle she had with Mobious to Tyran. He still had no memory of the object that Mobious was holding or the fact that he told her that Mobious had it in the first place. Whatever that strange object was, Ayleen knew that it was powerful. She had heard stories from her mother about an artifact called the Cube of Destiny. According to her mother, the cube could see the past and all possible futures. Her mother also told her that the cube was guarded by a group of monks at a monastery in the Northeast of Giana. If Mobious did have that cube, she prayed to Terra that the monks were all right. She would have to go to the monastery and make sure as soon as Queen Merri was safe.

They were about a three-hour ride from the centre of the continent when they had to stop. A large group of blue-and-orange-skinned elves were gathered blocking the path that the trio needed. Ayleen could see thousands of elves with weapons preparing for something. Ayleen had a sinking feeling that something significant was about to happen. She got off her horse and asked her two companions to stay there for a moment. She began to wander the crowd in search of a leader. It did not take long; she saw a group of elves surrounding a portable table. There were three of them. One middle-aged blue-skinned elf that was covered in armour, with an aide by his side, and one orange-skinned elf in leather armour. The blue-skinned elf was an elderly gentleman who Ayleen knew as Colonel Tracker. The other blue-skinned elf was around her age. She found this elf very attractive but quickly pulled her mind back to the job at hand.

"We don't have enough men, Walot!" Colonel Tracker raised his voice as he slammed down his fist on the table. "If we march with this number, her forces are going to slaughter us all. We need an army twice as big as this."

"We don't have time, Xev!" Walot shouted back. "The Queen's forces will be here by nightfall! As much as I want to ensure victory, we just don't have time. You know me. I would never ask you to go through with this if we didn't have to, but we have no other option. Your son is a great tactician. I wonder if he has anything to say. I think we should give the floor to Nyles."

"Thank you for your confidence in me, Walot, but the Colonel is correct, we don't have the manpower," commented Nyles as he quickly looked over to see Ayleen standing in the crowd. His heart skipped a beat. "However, a Druid told me of a vision he had this morning. He said that a purple-skinned elf would come to our aid and guide us to a temporary salvation."

"Nyles, don't be ridiculous. This is no time for ..." Walot tried to argue back as Nyles pointed his finger to Ayleen. The three men turned to look where he was pointing and stood in silence, unsure whether they should believe the prophecy the Druid gave as Ayleen sauntered over to them.

"Greetings, gentlemen, I am Captain Ebella." Ayleen saluted the Colonel and walked closer to the three men determined to find out what was going on. "I overheard you talking about the Queen sending armies to this area. That doesn't sound like Queen Merri at all. Am I correct in assuming that Princess Dariusa is now Queen? If so, what happened to Merri?"

The three men turned back to the table and lowered their heads before Colonel Tracker answered her. "Captain, we have received word that Dariusa became Queen after her mother was exiled and subsequently committed suicide. Her first act as Queen was to declare war on all non-purple elves. Our spies have discovered that she told her armies there is a group of rebels made up of blue-and-orange-skinned elves and that they assassinated two thirds of the nobility at the Queen's coronation; most of them blue-and-orange-skinned."

"Merri would never commit suicide! I knew Dariusa was a monster! I didn't think she would act this quickly or kill her own mother!" Ayleen gulped, brushed away a tear and moved to the table to see the group's battle plan. "If I'm reading this correctly, then your scouts have seen that Dariusa is sending most of her army to the sacred tree where they will break off in two groups. If you would allow me, I will join you in meeting the army at the Tree. Hopefully, Dariusa knows me well enough that she will listen to reason. But I doubt it. We will need an escape plan should thing go badly."

"That is good enough for me," Walot replied. "I know there is no way we can win a battle against the Queen's forces. However, if it means we save as many lives as we can, I'm willing to listen to the Captain, no matter what colour she is. I don't know why, but I feel I can trust her."

"So do I," Nyles added with a hint of a smile. "I believe she is the one that saved the day at the last shadow creature attack in the capital; the one they called the Demi-god of Terra. Colonel, I know you plan on having a great victory and showing the Queen that she can't push us around, but in all honesty, the closest thing we will get is a peace treaty or a retreat. And neither of those can happen without Captain Ebella's help."

Colonel Tracker took a deep breath and thought it over for a minute. He knew his son was right. "All right, you two have made your point. Captain Ebella, will you ride with us into battle?"

While she didn't want to fight against elves she knew and worked with, it looked like she would have no choice. She hoped that the battle would end in a peace agreement, but she was prepared to fight to the death to protect these innocent people. Terra guide me! She had a feeling that the next couple days would be the most critical in Giana's history. She prayed to Terra that she would have the knowledge to walk out of this situation with the best possible outcome.

Tyran observed the crowd. No one had to say a word. He knew they were preparing for war. The question was, who was their enemy? Until Ayleen returned from scouting the situation, he could not be a hundred percent sure what was going on. He had a few ideas though he hoped that none of them were right. He overheard a group of elves talking about how the Queen was sending two armies to the North of Giana. From what Ayleen told him the Queen's daughter, Princess Dariusa, had been trying to take over the throne for some time.

Before Tyran could ponder any further, Zalissa grabbed his shirt to get his attention. He could tell by the look on her face that she had something serious to talk to him about. He turned and gave the woman his complete attention. "What's wrong? I have never seen you this worried before."

"Tyran, you once told me that you would follow me wherever I went,"

Zalissa reminded him. "Given what we overheard in this crowd, this nightmare isn't going to end any time soon. While I would love to take you to my home village, I know you will hate yourself if you weren't able to help these innocent people. I also couldn't live with myself if I ignored their cries for help. I know I can't fight, but I want to help any way I can. But I will only stay here if you are beside me."

"You know people are going to die, right?" Tyran asked to make sure that she knew what she was getting herself into. "If even half of what this crowd is talking about is true, we could be facing a bloodbath. If you are sure about this, then I need you to stay out of the fight and help the wounded. I don't know what I would do if anything should happen to you."

"I understand, Tyran," Zalissa assured him. "After we are done fighting, whenever that is, I would like to keep my promise and show you my hometown. I would like to start a family with you."

"Now might be the best time for this." Tyran pulled a ring out from his pocket that he had stolen from Mobious' estate. "This may be a bit backwards since we already spent a night together. Zalissa Cholwell, will you marry me? I can't imagine a life without you. I know it has been such a short time, but I know I can't live without you."

Zalissa started to tear up a bit. This was everything she could ever dream of. "Tyran Dori, I would be honoured to be your wife. Yes, I will marry you. Just where did you get that ring?"

"How about we worry about that later?" Tyran replied sheepishly as the two elves kissed. He wanted this kiss to last forever, but Ayleen interrupted them.

"Excuse me, while this is lovely, we have some business to attend to," Ayleen snapped to break up the two lovers. She walked closer to them to make sure they were paying attention. "I wish I had good news, but there is none. The Queen is sending an army to the North to kill as many blue-and-orange-skinned elves as she can. Merri is not the Queen anymore; Dariusa is. We only have two hours before they get to the Tree. We are planning to fight them in that field, so we have to move quickly. I need both of you to help out."

"I hoped this wouldn't be the case, Ayleen." Tyran clenched his fist, realizing that everything he had heard in the last little while was true. "I will do anything you ask me to, Captain. Just say the word."

"I don't know if I can be much help, but I want to join," Zalissa stated. "I have a bit of first aid training, and I can cook. I will be able to take care of any soldiers that need to retreat."

"I appreciate that. Both of you will be of great help," Ayleen assured them. "I'm not planning on defeating Dariusa. I'm only hoping for a retreat. My goal is to keep as many elves alive as I can. Tyran, I need you to scout out the area and find out what route will be easiest for our retreat. We want to go as far North as possible. Normally I would do the job myself, but I can't while I'm on a battlefield. Zalissa, I need you to make sure all the supplies in this area are ready for transportation. The more supplies we have, the better our retreat will be."

"I will start scouting the area right away." Tyran began to leave the camp to find the best escape route to the north. He took a couple of the younger recruits with him.

"And I will begin preparing the supplies for transport." Zalissa headed for the direction of the crowd to see what supplies they had and what could be done to transport them.

Tyran did not want to spend his life as a soldier, but he would if he had to. He loved Giana with all his heart. He would die for this beautiful continent. His only concern was that this may have been the last time he would see Zalissa. As long as she was safe, he was willing to die to protect the people he loved. Before the meteorite hit, he was a thief and a con man. After the change, he was a spy. Now he was a soldier and scout. He had something to fight for; he had someone to fight for. He would do everything in his power to make sure that she would be safe. That was all that mattered to him. Everything else, even his own life, would come second.

Two armies met on the field where the sacred tree stood. The army from the South was fifteen thousand strong while the combined army from the North was just over five thousand. The Queen's army was the most well-equipped; each soldier wore a full set of plate. They had bows along with a shield and a short sword. Ayleen's army had some that were in full plate, but most of them only wore what they could find in a short time. Ayleen knew this army could not defeat the Queen's army, nor was it the plan. Ayleen and Nyles rode their horses to the sacred tree where Queen Dariusa and Duke Morgwyn sat waiting on their horses.

"Ah, the former Captain of Investigation arrives," The Queen called out as Ayleen drew closer to the Tree. "We figured you would be the one who would lead an army against us. We assume this means Lord Mobious is dead. Another name to the list of your murders. We have already given your cause a name, Terra's Guardians. Every purple-skinned elf is on our side waiting to kill every last one of the blue-and-orange-skinned elves on our command. We will give you one opportunity to surrender yourself, and we may spare some lives."

Ayleen knew that Dariusa was lying. She had to choose her words carefully and not fall into one of her many traps. "I have just come to negotiate for the safety of the people of the North. Dariusa, I do not want a war, but if you continue on this course of genocide, I will be your most dangerous enemy. I am told your mother committed suicide. We both know that is a lie. I will leave you alone and in return all I ask is that you leave the North alone."

Both the Queen and her fiancé burst out laughing. "Ayleen that is the most pathetic thing we have heard all day. You honestly believe you can stand against us? What we want is a pure Giana. One with only purple-skinned elves just like Terra intended. Unless you are willing to help us kill your own army, there is nothing you can do for us. And you will refer to us as Your Majesty!"

"Then I guess I have no choice but to stop you." Ayleen and Nyles began to ride their horses back to their army when Ayleen had one last thing to say to the new Queen. "No matter what, I will stop you, and Terra will be with me. You are not a child of Terra, and you never will be."

The two parties rode back to their respective armies. Ayleen could see her troops held fear in their eyes. She couldn't blame them. No one here wanted to fight. They had no choice. They had to defend the North until their last breath. She decided to make a speech before the battle to rally the troops.

"My fellow elves," Ayleen shouted to make sure that the entire army could hear her. "Today we face our greatest enemy. … hatred. Unfortunately, our enemy's numbers are too great for a victory. That does not mean we won't have a victory in the future. We are not aiming to defeat the Queen today. Our goal is to distract her army long enough so that our families can retreat, and we can fight another day. We will charge in and convince the enemy that we are willing to fight to the death. When I give the signal, we retreat north, and I will set the forest behind us on fire, with Terra's help. I know that may sound like a crime against Terra, but we have no choice. This is the only way we can survive the day. Watch for an explosion to the North. Head in that direction and join up with Tyran. Are you with me?"

Ayleen's army gave her a cheer, but she knew that they were skeptical of her plan, and Ayleen had to be honest with herself, so was she. Would Terra's power come when she called? Across the field, the Queen was preparing her own troops for the battle ahead. She was so close to completing her goal of making Giana a paradise for the purple-skinned elves. All she needed to do was to defeat this army. She knew that her men didn't need any words of encouragement, but she gave it to them anyway.

"Soldiers of Giana, listen to your Queen," she started her speech. "When the meteorite hit on the night of New Year's Eve, Terra told us who was loyal and who was a heretic. She showed us by way of changing the colour of everyone's skin. She chose her followers to have purple skin. You are Terra's chosen people. The blue-and-orange-skinned elves don't understand how superior we are to them. They don't respect you like they should. Today we are going to teach them a lesson they will never forget. We are going to show them that we are the masters and we should be listened to above all else. Are you ready to fight with us and show them the errors of their ways?"

The Queen's army cheered loudly as the Queen commanded a portion of them to charge at the enemy. The other army started to advance seconds after the Queen's army began their advancement. The two armies met with blade in hand fighting each other. Most of Ayleen's army had to fight two to one. Quickly Ayleen's army began to fall, but it wasn't time for the retreat. Ayleen needed that signal.

She did not have to wait long. An explosion in the Northern forest signalled what she was waiting for. She burst into golden light, rising into the air. The Queen's army froze in awe and Ayleen's troops ran for the trees. Ayleen drifted back to the treeline as the Queen's army receded, unsure of what to do in the presence of the Demi-god of Terra. Ayleen's aura caused the trees to burst into flames, blocking the army from following. The Queen screamed in rage as her plans fell apart. It was going to take some time to convince her army that this was only a trick and that Ayleen was not the Demi-god. She needed to have a daughter right away.

"My love, should we go around the fires and follow them?" Edwin asked. "It will take a while, but I'm sure our army can catch up to the heretics."

"No need for that, Edwin," the Queen answered coldly. "Let them think they have succeeded today. It is best to kill prey when it is off guard. We know where to find them. Once they realize that there is no hope for them, they will have no choice but to surrender. They will think that surrendering will mean that we will spare their families. That is when we will kill them all."

The Queen smiled. She knew that Ayleen was playing the long game. She didn't mind playing that game as well. No matter what, she would complete her goal of bringing Giana to a paradise of purple-skinned elves. She did not care how long it took. Ayleen's tactic of escaping while the forest burned behind them was genius and respectable. She would allow her to win this battle. It was the war she intended to win.

The army of the North gathered late that evening. While they had retreated to fight for another day, it came at a grave cost. This morning they had over five thousand men, now they had just over three thousand. Today did not feel like a victory. Ayleen sat alone, contemplating her next move. She knew that Giana would no longer be unified. She had many questions. These questions consisted of how could she bring peace to Giana and would Terra continue to help their cause? As she sat there, she gazed into a campfire, hoping that the fire would provide answers. She did not notice that Tyran sat down beside her. She only saw him when he began to talk.

"What do we do now, Ayleen?" Tyran asked with the most confusion in his voice that Ayleen had ever heard.

"We have to keep fighting," Ayleen answered while still looking into the fire. "What the Queen is doing is wrong. As elves, we can't sit back and let her treat the elves of the North like this. Before the battle, I managed to have a few words with the Queen. I fear the worst. She is insane. She also spread the lie that I'm the leader of a resistance group called Terra's Guardians. No matter what I do, I will be a criminal in the South for the rest of my life."

"You just gave me an idea!" Tyran exclaimed. "By giving our group a name, which means the Queen is afraid of us, she has spread that fear to the rest of the citizens of the South. And I hear you did your glowy thing again. We can use that to our advantage. We can gather elves who will fight with us and spread the word that Terra's Guardians are here to save any and all elves. Every day we will make the Queen fear us more and more. And when she is afraid of us enough, she will make a mistake, and that is when we will take back Giana."

"That is genius, Tyran," Ayleen cried out with hope as she stood up. "With this plan, every day we will be one step closer. One day we can reclaim the city of Terra and put in a ruler that will treat everyone fairly. I will bring this to the attention of ..."

She was interrupted by the sounds of a loud argument between the Colonel and Walot. This was no time for infighting. As Ayleen and Tyran rushed to where the voices were coming from, she could see a group of orange-skinned elves with Colonel Xev Tracker arguing with a group of blue-skinned elves led by Walot. Each side looked as if they were ready to kill each other. In the middle, Nyles was there pleading with both parties to see reason.

"Father, Walot, listen to yourselves. This is no time to argue." Nyles' pleas fell on deaf ears.

"It's Xev's fault that we lost nearly two thousand men!" Walot yelled. "If he didn't have so much blind faith in visions, then we wouldn't be in this mess! This is why you shouldn't ever be the commanding officer of your own children!"

"My son is a loyal soldier, Walot!" Xev yelled back. "You knew that there would be casualties! You were all for following Captain Ebella! It was your own men that did not follow the plan! If your men followed orders, more of us would be alive!"

"So, it's my fault that my men didn't do exactly what was said? They're not all soldiers like your men!" Walot was aghast at that accusation. "Maybe I should take my orange-skinned brethren and leave you to deal with the Queen by yourself!"

"Fine by me, you gutless slime!" Xev fired back as both parties walked in opposite directions.

"Father, Walot, please gather your senses," Nyles called after them. Once again Nyles' cries fell on deaf ears. It was then that he saw Ayleen and Tyran watching the whole thing. "Well, I guess that ends the resistance movement, and the Queen will slaughter us all."

"Not at all, Nyles," Ayleen commented as she watched as a few dozen elves gathered around them. "We don't need your father or Walot. We can start a small group here and now to resist the Queen. If we grow our forces every day, then one day we will have enough strength to confront the Queen. She will only defeat us once we have given up. I'm starting a new group called Terra's Guardians, and I would love if you would join us. We need to recruit any one of any colour that believes we are one people."

Without another word, Nyles reached out and shook Ayleen's hand. Every elf around them pledged their loyalty to Ayleen and Terra's Guardians. Today was the start of something great. Today marked the beginning of the people of Giana refusing to bow down to a Queen that viewed the blue-and-orange-skinned elves as second-class citizens.

In the coming years, the blue-and-orange-skinned elves would make their own governments separately. Many times, Ayleen would try to convince the leaders of both kingdoms to join the fight against the South. Every time the representatives of these two nations gather together, the meeting would end in an argument with both sides refusing to work together. It was then that Ayleen remembered the words of the goddess, "Peace does not mean unity." With those words in mind, she only recruited elves that were willing to work together. As much as she wanted for all three elven races to get along, they just couldn't because together they fall.

EPILOGUE

6012 of the third Gods, first month, fourth day.

IT HAS BEEN ten years since I started this journey. Ten years since Giana fell apart. I write this now so that history will not be forgotten. I have only been able to use Terra's powers in extreme situations, three times since the fight against the shadow demons at the capital ten years ago.

After the battle at the Sacred Tree, Queen Dariusa renewed her crusade against the Ice and Fire (formerly known as blue-and-orange-skinned) elves. I tried to save as many as I could, but I couldn't be everywhere at once. There are now half as many of them as there were ten years ago; many of them enslaved. The sacred Tree has withered.

My spies have told me that over the last ten years, the Queen has been unable to produce a daughter. Despite three different husbands, all of which committed suicide, she only gained five sons, four of which died shortly after they were born. Her fifth son was the only one to survive. She is currently looking for a fourth husband, but no one seems to want the job. Terra appears to have prevented the Queen's plan to convince Giana that she is the mother a Demi-god.

I have gathered a group of freedom fighters to help defend our people. We are called Terra's Guardians. We fight where we are needed most. We call the purple-skinned elves Shadow elves now. A few Shadow elves that spoke against the Queen fled her wrath and have joined our ranks. Captain Bridge was among them. The information he brought us about his investigation into Dariusa has been helpful.

Both the Ice and Fire elves have started working together more often. Their territory was pushed north by the Shadow elves, but day by day they are reclaiming their lands.

Most people have forgotten Mobious; he was a prominent figure in history. Some people remember that he was the one that caused our change and the attacks by the demons, but most elves have been led to believe Dariusa's version that Terra made the change. I don't know how I feel about this. I think people should remember what caused this change, but that's a discussion for another day.

It's not all bad news. Tyran married Zalissa, and they have three children. I made Tyran my lieutenant. After the death of Mobious, he proved more helpful to Terra's Guardians than I could ever imagine. His skills at acquiring information are essential to the cause. He's already talking about having his oldest son join the Guardians, but Zalissa and I are trying to convince him to wait until his son is an adult. His boys have orange skin and dark blue hair whereas his daughter has blue skin and red hair. It's been interesting seeing the mixed colours as the Fire and Ice elves often intermarry. I dream of a day when colour doesn't matter.

As for me, while I have been busy defending the people, Nyles and I grew closer as he fought by my side. Seven years ago, we married. Now we have a five-year-old daughter named Merri. I named her after my best friend to honour her memory and her sacrifice. Her pale purple skin looks beautiful with the white hair that she inherited from her father. There are moments where I see a resemblance to our former Queen. I miss her namesake every day. It saddens me to have to fight against her daughter.

The job is unending. There is so much work to be done. There are still elves in danger; elves in captivity or enslaved. There are moments that I want to cry, but I can't. I must stay strong. Many that we rescue speak of atrocities which some do not survive. These people need to be stopped. It is the duty of Terra's Guardians to bring peace back to Giana. We will not stop until every elf is treated the same. We will not stop until no one is being tortured. We will free every slave that the Shadow elves have. This is my purpose. It may take longer than my life, but it will be done; I swear it.

My name is Ayleen Ebella. I will not rest until every elf is treated with respect and the people causing these atrocities are brought to justice.

The quiet of the cave calmed him. He was waiting. The man in red knew this was the time when he expected an object to appear. Any minute now. When the Cube of Destiny appeared, a smile crept over his face. This was the moment he had been waiting for.

"Ah, the first one arrives. It should be safe here. This cave is only accessible in one timeline."

The man in red opened a portal to a desert landscape. Windy. He changed his appearance to a bird-like creature with a humanoid face. Wings sprouted from his back, but he knew he could not use them to fly; gliding was a possibility. Feathers erupted on the back of his head, replacing his hair. Talons grew on his fingers and toes.

As he stepped through the portal he said, "I really hate this heat. I hope I can get this done quickly. Gods and Goddesses. I hate this place Already."

Our journey continues in "United They Rise".

ABOUT THE AUTHOR

Born in Vancouver, BC, Matthew Croutch had an interest in story-telling from a very young age. However, due to being born with Cerebral Palsy, he had trouble with motor and speech skills. It wasn't until eighteen years, after he moved to Calgary, Alberta, that he completed his first novel with scribing assistance from his mother and grandmother.

Matthew has always been a fan of science fiction and fantasy novels, movies and video games. He always dreamed of making his own role-playing video game but upon going to university for his IT degree, he realized that video game design was beyond his capabilities due to the lack of fine motor skills. He then chose to focus on his English degree at Athabasca University; taking various courses in creative writing.

Made in United States
North Haven, CT
12 December 2023

45568235R10140